THE BLACK ISLE

POLICE SCOTLAND
BOOK 12

ED JAMES

1

'This place is amazing.' Keith looks round at me, grinning like a child, his hair blowing in the wind cutting across the oil rig platform. 'There's enough here for, like, ten shows.' He winks, hauls open the door, then sticks his head inside. 'Hello?' He waits a few seconds, shrugs and slips through.

I don't follow him immediately. A fresh blast of ice-cold rain hits my face, with it a salty taste and tangy smell, and it tears the paper out of my grip, sending it flying across the platform and out into the Cromarty Firth. I train the camera on the open water, getting that perfect line of golden sun hitting the waves where it breaks the clouds in the distance, aiming right towards us. In the distance, the Black Isle looms up out of the grey, lush and green. Like something from a King Arthur story. Beyond the Moray Firth, the land rises up to meet the Cairngorms, just about visible on the horizon.

Being up this high is the perfect vantage point. Not that there is anyone about. The whole platform is dead, all signs of occupancy removed, save the living quarters Keith is peering inside. I keep the camera focused on the clouds, just as the sun slips behind.

'Hot shit.' Keith slips through the door to the living quarters and his voice is muffled by the wood. 'There's at least...' And he's gone, more noise than signal, just a tone.

I hit the stop button on the camera but leave my head-mounted GoPro running. Never know what you might catch —always good for a swift cut, or that bit of point-of-view veracity as we give our viewers a cheap thrill. I open the door and peer inside.

And I feel the metal on my neck. A faint smell of machine oil. Shit. It's a gun.

'Stay still.' Slight accent—foreign, eastern European or Russian. The weak metallic scent of his aftershave washes over me.

'Okay, okay!' I slowly raise my hands. 'Take it easy, pal.' I start to swivel round. 'We'll leave and—'

'Shut. Up.' He presses the gun close, digging into my skin now. 'I—said—don't—move.' He punctuates the final word with a jab, making my skull rattle and my eyes lose focus.

Think fast here.

'Who are you?'

'You think you're in a position to ask that?' I see the muzzle of the gun wave at the door Keith went through, now shut again. 'Are you alone?'

I hope Keith heard enough of this to find a way back to safety. 'Of course. Who else in their right mind would come here?'

Something cracks my spine and knocks the breath out of

my lungs. I stumble forward, gasping for air, and my knees thump off the steel floor.

'This is the last time I'll ask you, and I expect the truth.' The gun rasps the skin on my neck—that exact spot where the spine connects to the brain. The brain stem or something. Seen so many YouTube documentaries on it, the perfect place to kill someone. This guy's a pro. I'm buggered. 'Are. You. Alone?'

'I am, I swear!'

'I heard you speak to someone.'

'I was on the phone.' I wave north-ish towards Invergordon and its phone masts. 'Got some reception up here.' I'm reaching, hoping to hell that he buys it. 'I was speaking to the guy who brought me on the boat. He left, but he was just checking in. I had the phone on speaker. Said he'll be back in two hours. But I lost reception.'

'Then we have two hours to get you away, my friend. But I don't believe you.' He grabs my arm and snatches at my phone. 'Who is—'

I dig my elbow into his gut and he groans. I wrestle free of his grip and hurl my mobile at the open sea. But it drops a few metres shy of the edge.

Shit.

Then the phone starts sliding in the wind towards the water.

'No!' He lurches after it, but it's gone, slipping off into the deep. He turns to face me, training the gun on me. His face is riddled with scars, a diagonal knife wound cutting from the top of his right ear through his lips to his neck. Hardcore. 'Stupid.' He pushes me, then frogmarches me over to the closed door.

And all I can do is go along with it, his arm locked around my shoulder, the gun back in its place against my neck.

'Open it.'

I reach out with my left foot—he doesn't give me much choice—and nudge the door, pushing hard against the wind. A long corridor, with countless doors peeling off in both directions. He pushes me forward again and we pass a large bedroom, two bunk beds. Metallic, stripped, bolted to the wall. Adult-sized, though. The window is open a crack. No sign of Keith. My captor pushes me again and we keep walking.

Halfway down the corridor he grabs my arms to stop me. 'Stay there.' He walks into a room that's identical except for the window being half open and rattling in the gusty breeze. He checks everything with military precision, just like my bloody brother searching my flat for dope. And I get another good look at my captor. A big lump. Bald and muscular, and kitted out in professional hiking gear. Outdoor wear. He stares right at me, a proper soldier's glare. Definitely ex-military.

I flash him the smile that gets me in places like this. 'Look, pal, I'm sure we can work—'

'Listen to me.' He steps forward, pinning me against the wall. 'You are not supposed to be here. As much as I would like to kill you, I have a much better plan. We are going to have so much fun.'

2

DC Craig Hunter sat back in the driver's seat, gripping the steering wheel. He checked the pedals for the five millionth time, depressing the clutch and tapping the accelerator to get a nice grunt from the engine. Then he jabbed the brake. All fine. All working.

A bus trundled along the quiet street, glowing in the misty darkness, and pulled up a hundred metres away. A man hopped off at the stop, his breath clouding the air, and he looked around, over both shoulders, then set off towards Hunter.

'Is that him?' DI Sharon McNeill leaned between the seats. She tucked her dark hair behind her ear, but her cold expression never wavered. 'Chantal?'

'Not sure, Shaz.' DS Chantal Jain leaned forward in the passenger seat, squinting. Hunter had to look round to focus on his girlfriend, her arms folded, T-shirt sleeves showing off toned coffee skin. 'Could be, but...'

McNeill tutted, then let out a slow sigh. 'Craig, can you confirm that's your suspect, please?'

Hunter kept his gaze on the figure walking towards them and tried to compare the man against his memory. 'Struggling here, ma'am. It's too foggy.'

'Bloody hell.' McNeill slumped against the back seat. The white glow lit up her scowl as she checked her mobile, her thin lips twisting into a sneer. Then she was back between them, holding out her phone. 'Is this him or not?'

Hunter compared the on-screen shot of Derek Farrell with the approaching figure passing between streetlights like a wraith, his breath hanging there. Same heavy coat, same business suit, same shiny designer glasses. But still, this was Edinburgh, most office drones dressed like that in winter. 'Still too far to tell, ma'am.'

'Christ's sake.' McNeill passed the phone to Chantal. 'Come on, is it him or not?'

Hunter twisted round and gave McNeill a stern look, the kind he'd deliver to captives back in his army days, the kind that'd have them quaking in their boots. The kind that bounced right off her. 'Are you trying to pin this on us?'

McNeill evaded his hard man act with a flick of her pencilled eyebrows. 'I just want to—'

'It's him.' Chantal pointed at the figure, lit up by another streetlight. 'It's Farrell.'

'Finally. Come on, then.' McNeill slid over the back seat and opened the street-side door. 'Stay here, Craig. And call it in, okay?'

'Ma'am.' Hunter put his police radio to his mouth as they both got out. 'Hunter to all units. Target spotted. Serial Alpha are go. Over.'

Chantal walked lockstep with McNeill, looking like a pair of Instagram-perfect friends, all shiny hair and giggles as they flitted between the streetlights. Under-dressed for the cold Edinburgh Friday night, saving that precious few quid on the cloakroom.

The radio clicked. 'Serial Bravo receiving. Over.'

Hunter sat back, slumping low to watch the scene play out. He tapped the pedals again. All three still worked perfectly. He engaged the clutch and checked that the gearbox hadn't broken in the last five minutes. Still stuck going into fifth, but he wouldn't need anything above third.

Ahead, the second unmarked Volvo SUV pulled up just past the bus stop. Blink and you'd miss it, but another two officers slipped out of the back, leaving some other poor fool in the same situation as Hunter. Watching, waiting, the exhaust pumping out needless fumes in case he needed to shoot off in pursuit. McNeill could take Farrell down just with a glare.

Their suspect stopped and got out his phone. He swung around, talking into it. Laughing. Joking.

Scumbag.

Drug dealer. Rapist.

Hunter wanted to shoot off, slam the car into him. Pin the bastard to the wall of the converted bond warehouse. Reverse. Then drive into him again. And again and again.

But he just checked the pedals once more, then the handbrake, then the gearbox, all the time watching Chantal and McNeill home in on the prick.

Farrell wasn't playing their game, though. Didn't make friendly eye contact with McNeill or Chantal, wasn't letting their lost tourist act play out as planned.

Metres separated them now. McNeill tried to wave him down. She looked so obvious to Hunter.

Farrell turned to face her, still listening to his phone call, but gave a slight nod, his lips moving, saying, 'What's up?' Something like that. Even out of earshot, Hunter could hear his Dublin brogue.

McNeill got in front of Farrell, asking something else.

The other cops homed in from behind, boxing him in.

Hunter put the car in first gear. Not time to go yet, but time to be ready to move. He reached into the middle console and got out another piece of gum. The mint hit his mouth like a slap in the face. He tried to keep focus.

Way too hot in the car. Chantal always liked the heating at 'Lanzarote in August' level, whereas that kind of heat brought back unwanted memories to Hunter. Reykjavik in November was his preference. He wound the window down and rested his arm on the door. Anyone watching him would take him for a bored dad waiting for his over-sugared kids. Hopefully.

Idiot—it was freezing out there, nobody would make that mistake.

He started winding the window back up.

A rumble came from behind, and he caught another approaching 36 bus in the wing mirror.

Shite. Hunter tapped the horn and McNeill glanced round, but quickly went back to talking. He spoke into the radio: 'This is DC Hunter. Bus encroaching on acquisition site. Do not engage. Repeat, do not engage. Over.'

'Received, over.'

But not by McNeill. She reached into her pocket and held out her warrant card.

Farrell jerked his head around, sussing out his options, then settled on one. He lurched forward, kicking McNeill in the knee, then pushed her into Chantal, both women collapsing in a heap, and he darted off, pounding the pavement towards Hunter. The other cops broke ranks and sprinted after him.

Hunter slipped off the handbrake and drove straight at Farrell, eating up the distance in seconds. Eyes bulging, Farrell noticed almost too late. But he jumped, skidding over the bonnet and landing on the road on all fours. Then he was off again, pushing away like an American football player —head low, thundering along Bonnington Road towards the bus stop and the crowd of gawpers getting off the 36.

Hunter was halfway through a three-pointer, bumping the pavement as he swerved round. He stuck it in first and shot off. The other two cops hammered along, keeping pace until he floored it.

Farrell ran in front of the bus. And stopped dead in his tracks.

And Hunter was going too fast. He hit the brakes, but the car slid on ice, out of control. The wheel locked, wouldn't shift. He pumped the brakes, but it seemed to speed up if anything. Heading right at Derek Farrell.

Then Hunter regained control. He swung the wheel to the left, fishtailing the rear towards the bus, still going to hit the man.

A figure darted out in front of the car, pushing Farrell away.

The car crunched into the bus and bounced back, the engine screaming. The cabin lights came on.

And Farrell was running up the side street, leaving a

woman on the pavement clutching her belly.

Hunter wrestled his seatbelt free and pawed at the billowing airbag until it wasn't in his face. His door wouldn't budge. He shifted over to the passenger side and clawed at the handle until it opened, then stumbled out into a run, his boots slapping the ground.

Farrell was way ahead, but looking back. Each step, the distance closed.

Hunter's lungs burned as he powered after the other man, narrowing the distance to inches by the corner. He threw himself into a rugby tackle and caught Farrell's arm. A scream tore out as they landed, something soft squishing under Hunter's knee.

'Get off me!' Farrell was all elbows and fists. 'Get off me!'

Hunter jerked Farrell's hand up his back and got a squeal. A really, really satisfying squeal. 'Derek Douglas Farrell, I'm arresting you for the rape of Jennifer Harris.' He snapped a cuff on, too tight. 'You do not have to say anything, but it may harm your defence if you do not mention when questioned something which you later rely on in court.' Then the other cuff, way too tight, but no sound from Farrell. 'Anything you do say may be given in evidence.' He sucked in a deep breath and hauled Farrell to his feet. 'Do you understand?'

Farrell hung his head low, staring at his feet. No emotion on his face.

Hunter jerked him again. 'Do you understand?'

'Course I understand. Wasn't me, though.'

'That's for a judge and jury to decide.' Hunter grabbed Farrell by the sleeve and led him back to the chaos.

The bus stood in the middle of the road, a giant obelisk

blocking the traffic. Bonnington Road was a rat run between central Edinburgh and Leith, and traffic was piling up in both directions.

McNeill stood next to the bus, mouth hanging open, shaking her head at the battered pool Volvo sticking out of the wreck. She looked over at Hunter, eyes full of fire and fury. Then she clocked Farrell and the glare softened, but not much. She walked right up to Hunter.

He took a deep breath, knowing he'd pay a price for the carnage, but collaring a serial rapist who'd been on the run for months and months was a huge tick in the plus column.

The two cops from the other car finally showed up, as usual after all the fun was over. Big Jim stood back, hands splayed like he was fighting Bruce Lee. Kate grabbed Farrell's jacket. 'Come on, then.' She looked down at his wrists. 'Christ, are you trying to stop the circulation in his hands?' She got out her key and stepped behind him.

Farrell snapped his forehead forward into McNeill's nose. She stumbled back against the bus and thumped to the ground.

He swung out with his left hand, the flailing cuffs slicing through Big Jim's ninja posture and sending him flying against the wall. Kate went down on top of him. Farrell's elbow lashed backwards and cracked into Hunter's eye socket. Pain exploded through his head. All he could do was try to keep a grip on him.

Metal flashed as Farrell swung the cuffs, cracking the steel off Hunter's teeth. He had to let go and dropped to his knees. A boot to the side pushed him over.

The sound of receding footsteps and everything went black.

3

McNeill's face was a mush of dried blood and bandages. Even sitting behind her desk looked like it hurt. 'This is a royal disaster.'

In the darkened room, Chantal was illuminated from behind by the full-blast lights from the open-plan office outside.

The glow made Hunter's eye sting again, all over the puffy flesh, so he looked back at McNeill in the darkness. 'I'm sorry, ma'am.' He touched the chair arm and lowered himself down. 'I take resp—'

'STAY STANDING!' McNeill's voice drilled into his skull. 'Get to your feet, Constable!'

But Hunter couldn't. All he wanted to do was lie down and sleep. Sitting would just about do. So he sat there, his eyes shutting, his head nodding.

Chantal grabbed his sleeve and tugged him back up. 'Shaz, he shouldn't be here. He's probably got concussion.'

'DS Jain, this was your operation.' McNeill narrowed her

eyes until they were tiny dots peering out behind the wreckage of her face. She reached onto her desk for a TV remote and jabbed the power button. A screen hanging from the wall lit up. 'Watch this.'

Hunter took one look at it and wanted to sit again. Even through the glue in front of his eyes, he could see Big Jim and Kate interviewing Megan Forsyth. Farrell's fourth victim. Twenty-four, short, her long hair cut to a severe bob. The dank interview room wasn't the place to learn that your rapist—your torturer—had escaped again. Megan stared at them, mouth hanging open, tears glistening in ultra-sharp HD, fearing for her life all over again.

'See what your failure does to people?' Sharon snapped the screen off. 'I knew that keeping you two separate was the smart move, but you insisted you could make this work.'

'Shaz, don't you—'

'It's DI McNeill.'

That shut Chantal up. She stood there, mouth hanging open. Her best friend became her boss in a snap.

McNeill pressed a tentative finger against her nose and grimaced. 'Derek Farrell has raped *five* women that we know of. And you let him go!' Her voice echoed round the room.

Hunter could swear the chattering outside stopped dead. He wanted to sit again, but he knew he shouldn't. But he was swaying. 'Ma'am, with all due respect, you were equally to—'

'DC Hunter, I suggest you keep your mouth shut.' McNeill's glare made him follow her instruction.

Chantal ignored it, though. 'Shaz, this is bollocks. We can—'

'DS Jain, I've warned you. Address me as DI McNeill.'

'If that's how you want to play it...' Chantal folded her

arms. 'DI McNeill, this is complete bollocks.' She paused. 'We can find Farrell. We've been following him for—'

'No.'

'No? What—'

'DS Jain, you've had six months to bring Derek Farrell to ground, during which time we received allegations of two additional rapes. I can't give you any more time.' McNeill opened her desk drawer and pulled out a document, the white paper glowing in the low light. 'This has happened one too many times. After the screw-up in Dunfermline and the incident in Portugal, we've now—'

'Come on!' Chantal was staring at the document like it was a sniper rifle. 'This is boll—'

'Effective Monday, you're both back in the Edinburgh MIT, reporting to DI Methven.'

Hunter collapsed into his chair again. 'Come on, ma'am.'

'This has been pending for a while. I've tried and tried to push back, but...' McNeill shook her head like a disappointed schoolteacher. 'I just can't do this anymore.' Her voice was shrill and thin. 'There is a significant staff shortfall after... well, what happened last year.' She slapped the documents on the table. 'They need bodies and I need people who can do their jobs. It's a win-win.'

Chantal stood there, hands quivering. 'Can I have a private word?'

Hunter looked up at her, frowning.

McNeill gave a tight nod. 'On you go, Craig.' Didn't even look at him.

Hunter used the chair's wooden arms to winch himself up to standing, then snatched the document with his name on it. 'Ma'am.' He walked out into the bright open-plan office.

At this time of night on a Friday, the place was usually dead, but tonight it was rammed full of cops nominally documenting the operational omnishambles, but actually wanting to listen in to the severe bollocking behind the boss's door.

He slumped in his chair and a deep groan escaped his body. The pile of case files was still the same height as it had been on day one. So little progress to show for two years of his life. Still, his drawer held only his box of notebooks, two pens and a blister pack of anti-PTSD meds that actually worked. Might need to up the dose after this shit show.

'Looks like you fought a bus and lost, Craigy boy.' Paul 'Elvis' Gordon perched on the edge of his desk, grinning like an idiot. His sideburns had been trimmed off at the bottom of his ears now and were thinned to a long strip, but he'd never shake that nickname. 'What happened?'

'What do you think happened?' Hunter reached for his leather messenger bag and tipped his crap in. A fresh wave of pain shot across his face, tearing into his skull.

'Sure you should be at work, mate?'

'Paramedics cleared me for duty. I'm not concussed.'

'Aye, bollocks you're not. I'd ask if you fancied a pint, but the state of you.' Elvis sniffed. 'There's a cracking new craft beer pub on Lothian Road I've been meaning to try.'

'Some other time.' Hunter looked back over at McNeill's office door. Raised voices muted by thick wood and safety glass. No sign that they were getting anywhere close to a resolution, but at least they weren't fighting. He folded his arms and tried to stop everything from swimming around. 'What brings you back here, anyway?'

'Usual shite, Craig.' Elvis cracked his knuckles. 'Methven lent me to Trouser Suit in there to do the old CCTV magic.'

'Trouser Suit?'

Elvis nodded at McNeill's office. 'That's what a few lads in the MIT call her.'

The door burst open and Chantal stormed out, her flat shoes thumping across the floor. She stopped by her desk and looked around. 'What?'

The rest of the Sexual Offences Unit went back to their documents.

'Wankers.' She grabbed her coat, then clicked her fingers at Hunter. 'Let's go.'

HUNTER SANK into the sofa and dabbed at his eye socket. The co-codamol was kicking in now, making everything nice and fuzzy. Could barely feel his face, barely feel his fingers. He took a sip of wine and savoured the taste, the only sensation that wasn't screaming misery. 'I've tried. He just isn't replying. Texts, calls, anything.'

'Your bloody brother...' Chantal stood by the cooker, stirring the pot. Smelled gorgeous, a gloopy red sauce bubbling away on the stovetop, tangy and sweet. She checked her watch again. 'What if we'd actually caught Farrell? We would've been in all night processing his arrest. And Murray would've been standing outside, calling you instead.'

'That'd serve him right.' Hunter reached over to the other side of the sofa. Bubble lay flat on her back, wedged between two cushions, her cream belly exposed, her eyes shut. One opened to a slit with a clear message—tickle my belly, sunshine, and it'll be the last thing you do.

Muffin was perched on the arm next to her, looking like a big blonde-ginger dafty, his flat tail swishing around.

Chantal tipped a pan of water into the sink and was engulfed in a cloud of steam, soon whizzed away by the extractor. 'I'm cooking veggie bloody pasta for your brother and he's not even bothered to turn up on time?'

'He's only an hour late.'

'Only...' She took a sip of wine and looked over at him. 'Christ, Craig, you really don't look good.'

'Well, I feel ten times worse than I look.'

Chantal took another slug of wine, the red almost matching her lipstick. 'The only good thing that's come out of this—the *only* good thing—is that Sharon got off worse than you.'

'You going to tell me what happened in there?'

She emptied her glass and splashed more in. 'She said I was to stay and fix this mess. I pointed out to her that it was her fault Farrell got away. Or Kate from Edinburgh letting his cuffs go. She didn't take it very well, so I told her I was done with her stupid team.' She took a long sip without looking at him. 'As of Monday, I'm reporting to Scott bloody Cullen.'

'Wait, he's a DI now?'

'That's the bit you're focusing on?'

'No, it's... It's a shock, that's all.'

She held up the bottle for Hunter, but he couldn't be arsed to move. 'Suit yourself.' She sank another couple of fingers of wine. 'Can you imagine what he'll be like as a DI? I mean, he's only Acting, but still... Sharon's my best friend and I've worked for her on and off for seven years. We've put bad people away, again and again, and in the SO unit, I've delivered for her. And this is how she treats me? All the years we worked together.' She aimed her glass at Muffin, now licking himself on the sofa arm like he was playing the cello, and some wine splashed onto the wooden floor. 'We even split up Muffin and his brother to re-home them.'

'You said Cullen's only an Acting DI, right?'

'Craig, get over it. Jesus.'

'No, I mean that, if he doesn't get it permanently, then maybe you'll get a turn.'

'Been there before. It didn't end well.'

Hunter sipped at his wine, slowly, so he didn't have to move to get a top-up any time soon. Still managed to spill some down his shirt. His mouth was numb, like he'd had a filling removed and the dentist had frozen his mouth. 'Look, come Monday morning, this'll all be a distant dream. You'll have DCI Methven moaning at you for—'

'Bloody Crystal bloody Methven...'

'And maybe Sharon will have apologised.'

'Far as I'm concerned, she can take her apology and ram it up her sorry arse.'

Hunter rested his glass on the coffee table and walked over into the kitchen. He wrapped an arm around Chantal and pulled her close. 'Come on. I'll text Murray and tell him to forget it, okay?' He kissed the top of her head. 'Serve that up and I'll pour some of that Châteauneuf-du-Pape he got us for Christmas. Then we can go out and get sufficiently drunk that we don't remember any of this.'

4

St Leonards police station basked in the harsh morning sun, three storeys of L-shaped brick misery lining the corner of the road. Or maybe J-shaped. Either way, it was exactly the same as it had been the last time Hunter worked there five years ago. Three stations crammed inside one, the best bits of Edinburgh's CID units merged into one dysfunctional team. Stale, tired, jaded. And way too busy. Or was that just Hunter?

He looked over to Chantal in the passenger seat. 'Still nothing?'

She shifted her focus from the make-up mirror to glance at her mobile. 'Nope.'

'Your message definitely sent?'

'Checked it seven times, Craig.' She clipped her bag shut and stuffed it in the glovebox. 'Have to say, I didn't expect this.' She shook her head. 'Years and years of friendship and *this* is how it ends?'

'She'll get over it. You'll see.'

'Maybe.' She gave a shrug. 'But I won't.'

Hunter opened his door and stepped out into the bitter morning, dark and buffeted by Edinburgh's famous wind. He looked across the car roof to Chantal, trying to psych himself up. 'You ready for this?'

'No, but since when has that stopped me?'

THEIR NEW OFFICE space was empty, just a loud voice booming out of an office to the side. DI Colin Methven shouting into a phone by the sounds of it. A laser printer spewed out pages and pages of some stupid report, the toner ozone smell mixing with burnt coffee from the filter machine.

Hunter found his desk. At least, the triangular name badge resting on top of the monitor read Craig Hunter, but someone had scored it out and written 'CUCK'. Charming. He picked it up and dropped it in the recycling. 'This place never changes.'

'You say that like it's a bad thing.' Chantal found her desk behind a row of filing cabinets. She held up a handwritten sign earmarking the area for 'The Dashing White Sergeants'. 'Really?'

'Think they'll be happy with a foxy brown sergeant?'

She actually laughed at that.

Hunter joined in, but the searing pain in his head stopped him. Made his eyes water.

'Craig?' Acting DI Scott Cullen struggled through the stairwell door, clutching two coffee cups. Idiot had clearly never heard of the concept of drinks holders. New dark-grey suit, though, bright orange tie, designer stubble. Every inch the detective sergeant pretending he was a detective inspector. He rested a cup on Hunter's new desk and held out a hand. Then his eyes bulged. 'Christ, what happened to you?'

'Should see the other guy.' Chantal strolled over to join him and did the old cheek kiss dance. 'I'd like to say it's nice seeing you, Scott, but I can't believe we're back dealing with this shite again.'

'This shite is my life.'

'Well, if it smells of shite and tastes like shite...'

Cullen sucked coffee through the lid. 'I'd have got you one, but Crystal didn't mention you were starting today.'

'Figures.' Chantal frowned over at the office, Methven's drone still booming out. 'Where is everyone?'

'That's not my story to tell.' Cullen tapped Hunter on the arm. 'Need a quick word, though.'

Hunter flicked his eyebrows at Chantal and got a grin. 'What about?'

'Well, when I heard we were getting new recruits, I was surprised it was you two. I thought you were doing well over there.' Cullen paused to take a drink. 'Sharon up to her old tricks again, eh?'

Chantal folded her arms. 'Something like that.'

'No easy way to say this, but I need to lay down the law about you two working together. It's not going to happen.'

'You say that like we—'

'Chantal, you need to remember that you report to me, okay? You and Craig can only be in the same room on the same case with my express permission.'

'You sound more and more like Methven every day.'

'Enough backchat. Please.' Cullen smiled at her. 'Now, do we have an understanding?'

'Fine.'

'Craig?' But Cullen kept his gaze on her.

'Who am I reporting to?'

Now Cullen looked over, but he struggled to maintain eye contact. 'DS Bain.'

'Oh for...' Hunter shook his head. 'Right.'

'Craig, know you've had your difficulties—'

'Aye, and you haven't?'

'Look, I can only play the cards I'm dealt.' Cullen gave a firm nod. 'Come on.' He led them over to the office.

DCI Colin Methven stood behind his desk, his ultra-marathon runner physique leaning forward like he was stretching. His wild eyebrows sprouted everywhere. A phone headset was clamped to his scalp and he was shouting down the line, like he didn't trust the copper wires to transmit his signal. 'We'll be up there as soon as I can manage, Carolyn. Please use DCs Gordon and Buxton as an advance party until I can get my A-team up the A90 to Perth.' He laughed. 'No, it was an accident. It's actually the M90 after the bridge, isn't it?' He pointed at them to sit at his table and chairs, laughing away.

Cullen sat facing away from Methven, shaking his head as he drank coffee.

'Okay, later.' Methven tore off his headset and tossed it on his desk. 'I swear, at least half this job is sending smoke signals up to their radar.'

Hunter stifled a laugh as he sat next to Chantal. Still got a good medium-sized kick in the shins.

'Thanks, Inspector.' Methven eased off his coffee lid and sipped at the milky froth, covering his top lip, and cast his gaze over his two new recruits. 'Thanks for coming in.' He wiped it clear. 'Normally we'd have a briefing where you could introduce yourselves to the wider team, who you probably already know, but I'm afraid that we've caught a case up in Perth. The Dundee MIT are swamped with a series of murders on the Angus coast, so we've been instructed by the high-heid yins to take this on with some uniform support to provide local colour. Hence my team being in a convoy up the M90.' He took another sip of coffee. 'Actually, some of them are on the train.'

Hunter looked over at Chantal, then Cullen. 'What's the case, sir?'

'One Alistair McCoull.' Methven tossed a set of crime scene photos onto his desk. The kind you didn't really want to look at for any longer than you had to. 'Shot six times, gangland-style. An execution, we believe. Something *very* out of the ordinary for Perth.'

Chantal nodded slowly. 'What do you want us to do, sir?'

'First, I need you to head home and get packed, Sergeant. Enough for a week. But,' Methven held up a finger as he slurped more coffee, 'I need to clear the air with you first.' He narrowed his eyes at her. 'I've had a word with DI McNeill vis-a-vis the Farrell case.'

Chantal's nostrils twitched, but she kept her peace.

'Just so we're abundantly clear, I will keep the pair of you separate. And I don't like liars.'

Chantal sat back, expression unreadable. 'Is that supposed to mean something, sir?'

'Just that I need you to be upfront about your relationship, okay?'

'Do you want me to list our favourite positions? I'm into the wheelbarrow, whereas Craig's all about Violet's Train Trip.'

'*Sergeant.*'

'Come on, sir.' Chantal rolled her eyes. 'Craig and I are banging each other's brains out and so long as he doesn't report to me, everything's cool. Right?'

Methven stared hard at her for a few seconds. 'I've spoken with DI McNeill and I know she wanted to keep you over there, sergeant, but you decided not to accept that offer? Well, as much as splitting you two up would be an apt punishment in her book, I have no choice. I'm desperate for resources and you're both excellent officers. But you will not be working together, am I clear? On this case, you'll be assigned very different roles and any discussions pertaining to it must occur in the presence of DI Cullen or myself. Am I clear?'

'Sure.'

Hunter nodded.

'Very well. Obey the rules and everything will be fan dabi dozi.' He finished his coffee and crumpled the cup as he stood. 'Now, please pack and I shall see you both up in Perth.'

'YOU PROBABLY SHOULDN'T HAVE SAID that.' Hunter crouched before opening the flat door. Just like every single time, Bubble charged at him. He grabbed her and picked her up into a cuddle, her purr strobing against his neck. 'Come here, you.' He took her through to the living room, keeping his eyes trained on Muffin as Chantal shut the flat door. 'Methven's hardly notorious for having a sense of humour.'

'Right.'

'And what the hell is "Violet's Train Trip"?'

'Never mind.' Chantal went through to the bedroom and started thumping around through there.

Hunter put Bubble down and joined her. Matching his-and-hers suitcases lay on the bed, padded black monstrosities with swivel wheels, big enough to fit both of them in. Not that it was either of their kink. 'You should maybe have —' His phone buzzed in his pocket, but he ignored it. The time for the joke had passed and he couldn't really remember what it was going to be. So he sat on the bed. 'You want to talk about it?'

She opened her underwear drawer and paused. 'Not really.'

'I think you should.'

Chantal grabbed a handful of knickers and stuffed them into her case. 'They're treating us like rows on a spreadsheet.' She stuffed in a pile of socks. 'We're people, Craig. We have feelings and career aspirations and...' She grabbed five blouses from her wardrobe, huffed out a breath, then folded them in one and stuffed them in her case.

More throbbing from Hunter's phone. He got it out and checked—a stack of email notifications. Great. He put it down and opened his underwear drawer. 'Oh pish.'

Chantal was comparing two pairs of trousers. 'What's up?'

'I've no clean pants.'

'Christ, Craig. I thought squaddies were supposed to be on top of this stuff?'

'I am. Was. But these meds... You know what they do.'

'Right, right.' She stared hard at him. 'We'll stop at Markies at the Gyle on the way.' She dumped both pairs of trousers in the case and jabbed a finger at him. 'But you're explaining to Crystal why we're late, okay?'

'Fine.' Hunter sat on the edge of the bed and got out his phone. He scanned through his inbox. PlayStation Store adverts, Kindle Daily Deal, his fitness app reminding him he hadn't worked out since Friday and at the top, an email from Murray Hunter.

Hunter let out a groan. The subject was 'Dead Man's Switch.'

What the hell? Heart thumping, he tapped it. Below was a ton of links, blue and underlined.

Craigy boy,
If I don't check in after a week, this email gets sent out automatically. You're receiving this because I've popped my clogs. Carked it. Left this mortal coil. Met my maker. I am an ex-Hunter.
I'm dead.
I have died.
They don't want this information to get out. Whoever they might be.
I'm either dead—in which case, avenge me—or I soon bloody will be—in which case, come get me.
I'm counting on you, bro. Send it all out. Screw them all hard in every orifice.
And remember Dalriada.

Peace and love,
Murray

5

Hunter jolted to his feet and read the message again. Tried taking it slow, but he just kept skimming the words.

It couldn't be right. Murray couldn't be dead. Could he?

But 'remember Dalriada'. The seaside pub in Portobello where Hunter bought Murray his first legal pint.

Assuming it was genuine, there could be any number of reasons it got triggered. Could've lost his phone and been ill somewhere abroad. Like three years ago in the Himalayas, when he was missing for two weeks and he'd just left his charger at his hotel before going on a massive hike, on his own. Or when there was no reception in Chile.

But in neither case was that message sent.

'What's up?' Chantal was holding a suit jacket over her case. 'You okay, Craig?'

Hunter didn't know. He passed her his phone and watched her read it, his fingers twitching. He couldn't escape the feeling that something really bad was going on.

Not that Murray wasn't one to joke, especially at his older brother's expense. But that message meant something happened last Monday, which explained him not showing up on Friday night. Explained the radio silence all weekend.

Chantal looked up at him, her forehead creasing. 'What the hell?'

'You know what a dead man's switch is, right?'

'Like when someone's wearing a bomb vest.' Chantal passed his phone back. 'They hold down the trigger all the time, so when the police shoot the wearer it releases and explodes.'

'Exactly. But this is like the bomb is an email.' Hunter checked the long list of hyperlinks. His mouth was dry and he had to swallow. 'He can't be dead, can he?'

Chantal nodded at the mobile. 'Christ's sake, Craig! Phone him!'

'Right.' Hunter hit dial and put it on speaker, his heart thudding in his temples.

Chantal glared at his mobile, like she could force Murray to answer the call. 'When did you last hear from him?'

'Couple of weeks ago. When we arranged dinner.'

'Nothing since?'

'Nope.'

It immediately hit voicemail.

Hunter ended the call and immediately redialled. Still nothing. He looked through the texts from Murray—nothing from his brother since two weeks earlier, just a few unanswered messages from Hunter, jokes and funny thoughts, the kind Murray would respond to maybe half the time. Same story with the emails, funny forwards and articles. But nothing in reply. Usually, that was fine and he wouldn't think twice about it. But with this message?

He dialled a Portobello number and listened to it ringing.

'Hello?' A woman's voice, out of breath. In the background, a washing machine rattled through its spin cycle.

'Mum, it's Craig.'

'What's up, son?'

'Just wondering if you'd heard from my idiot brother?' His voice was shaking.

'Murray? Not for a couple of weeks. He said he might pop in next week. Why?'

'Oh, no reason. He was supposed to come to dinner on Friday but didn't show up.'

'Sounds like your brother.'

'You... You had any emails from him?'

'He only texts me, son. Sorry. And my email is broken.'

'How can...' Hunter sighed, knowing not to argue with his mother. 'Well, if you speak to him, tell him I'm waiting for an apology.'

'Will do. Bye.'

Hunter clutched his phone, hoping it'd light up with a call from Murray any second now, and gripped his knees, still sitting on the bed. 'I need to go and see him. Murray's down in the Borders and Perth's completely the wrong direction. You head to Perth, I'll—'

'No, I want to come with you. It'll be just an extra hour, okay? I've booked a cat sitter. We'll go down, find him, read the riot act to him, then drive up to Perth.'

～

THE ROAD ahead blurred and Hunter struggled to keep his focus on it. He glanced over at Chantal behind the wheel, then back at Murray's email. None of the links gave any clue as to what happened to him, just a load of tinfoil-hat-wearing nonsense. Conspiracy theories, if they were even that fully formed. Confused ramblings. Paranoia.

Christ, Murray'd been getting further and further down the rabbit hole and Hunter hadn't noticed.

'You're muttering, Craig.' Chantal slowed as they entered a small town, then took the first right, heading up a hill. 'Something about tinfoil?'

'Sorry.' Hunter shut his sore eyes for a few seconds. 'You know those American nutters who think they can block the CIA's mind control rays with hats made of tinfoil? That's a tinfoil hat wearer.'

'Murray's one of them?'

'I mean, he doesn't literally wear one. It's a figure of speech. But they're not all American and it's not just the CIA. And it's not just tinfoil. Or hats.' Hunter stared down at the footwell, still smeared with dried mud from their Sunday hike up in the Pentlands. No time or inclination to clean it.

'You okay, Craig?'

'Not really.' Hunter looked over at her. The rugged land-scape rolled past, giant round hills covered in nothing but sheep and grass. Perfect hiking country. Dry-stone dykes marked out fields in arbitrary divisions, up and over the hill-tops. Stone cairns claimed three peaks, dual tracks linking them. 'Next right.'

Chantal started indicating way too early.

Through a thick wood, Hunter caught a glimpse of Murray's sprawling estate. An off-white house surrounded by four fields, two filled with trees. In the main one, a ragtag bunch of hens pecked the ground next to a stable. Murray's rooster, a big boy called Zlatan, darted across the grass to jump on one of them. A couple of seconds of wriggling and he jumped off again, strutting around.

Chantal ploughed on down the road. 'Still jealous of his house?'

'Hard not to be.'

'Guy might have all that money, but he's living alone.' Chantal took the corner way too fast and turned into Murray's drive, crunching over the pebbles. She killed the engine and the car rattled to a halt. A shiny old VW sat in the carport next to the two-storey garage. 'That his car?'

'Don't know. He changes it every six months.'

Chantal's phone rang and she sighed. 'Cullen.'

Hunter got out and walked over to the large modern house.

Someone inside. Cooking smells, fried eggs too. Movement in the bay window the other side of the front door.

Hunter's heart was thudding, but he felt a surge of relief. Murray was alive. Right?

He hit the doorbell, one of those fancy internet ones, and an ascending chime sounded inside.

Chantal joined Hunter by the door, cupping her hands and looking through the kitchen window. 'Cullen said we've got an hour to sort this out, then we've got to head to Perth, okay?'

The door clattered open.

'Murray, what the—'

'Craig?' A man peered out into the morning gloom, his

hair jet black despite his craggy face. Fooling nobody with that dye job. 'What the hell are you doing here?'

'*STOP!' A big, meaty hand blocks me getting inside. It's Daddy and he's looking angry. Blinking at me, like he sees two of me.*

Hunter tried to centre himself again, fighting against the flashback to his childhood. The PTSD, but his meds could only do so much. Felt like an army of snakes were crawling up Hunter's back. 'Looking for my brother.'

'Murray?'

Hunter narrowed his eyes. 'Have I got another one?'

'You tell me. Quite the lad back in the day, wasn't I?' He jolted round, head tilted to the side and aimed a grin at Chantal. 'Jock Hunter, pleased to meet you.' He held out his hand.

'Chantal Jain.' She shook it with a frown.

'I'm Craig's old man. Sure he's told you all about me.' Jock opened the door wide. 'Come on, let's get you a cup of tea.'

Hunter took one look at Chantal's frosty glare and followed his father inside.

Jock turned into the kitchen, a large room with lemon-yellow units on two walls and a giant kitchen table in the middle, surrounded by a sea of wooden flooring. He filled the kettle from the sink and stuck it on to boil. 'Back in a sec.' He slipped off towards the utility room.

Hunter grabbed his arm. 'I need you to—'

'And I need to drain the lizard, son.' Jock slipped out of his grasp and seconds later the bathroom fan started humming.

Chantal was over in the bay window, looking out across to the distant hills. 'You told me your dad was dead.'

'I wish he was.' Hunter looked through to the utility room to the source of the whistling and splashing. 'He left us when I was nine. Murray was six.' He let air slowly out of his nostrils. 'Kept slipping in and out of our lives, not really wanting anything to do with us until Murray got successful.'

The kettle rumbled to a boil.

'Still, you should've told me, Craig.'

Hunter walked over and started rooting around in the cupboard. He found some teabags in a copper tin and dropped them in the grey teapot, followed by the hot water. 'Sorry. I should've.' He clattered some mugs off a mug tree onto the countertop. 'I hate even thinking about him. Makes my flesh crawl.'

The toilet flushed and Jock came through, drying his hands on his trousers. 'What's up?'

'Well, for starters, I'm wondering what you're doing here.'

'Your brother asked me to look after his hens.' Jock opened the fridge, rammed with beer and ready meals. 'Let them out first thing, put them away last thing, keep foxy-foxy away from them, all that shite.'

Hunter poured the tea into three cups. 'Having a wee bit of accommodation difficulty?'

'In a manner of speaking.' Jock glanced at his son, then Chantal. 'How do you take it?'

She gave him a tight smile. 'Just milk.'

Jock splashed milk into two of the mugs and passed Hunter his tea. 'Are you his bidie-in?'

'We've been living together over a year.' Hunter blew on

the dark-brown surface of his tea. Nowhere near enough milk. He took a sip. Burning hot and weak as hell. 'So where is Murray?'

Jock walked over to the window and rested his cup on the sill. Staring out, head bowed. 'Up north somewhere, doing some new video thing.'

'When did he go?'

Jock took a sip and gasped. Just like he did every single time. 'At least a week, why?'

'You heard from him since?'

'Don't think so.'

'Not even to check the fox hasn't eaten his hens?' Hunter sighed. 'Look, has he sent you an email?'

'I don't know, do I? Not had the time to check. Had to take a hen to the vet this morning. Poor thing was ill. Didn't survive. I'll plant a tree over her later.'

'Murray cool with that?'

'Happens a lot, he reckons. Best to put them out of their misery as soon as you can, then bury them. Great fertiliser, apparently.'

Hunter got out his phone. 'I got this from him this morning.' He showed his father the message.

Jock took a glug of tea and grimaced. 'Ah, shite.' He sat at the head of the table and woke up a laptop that looked steam-powered. 'Let me see.' He finished his tea and rested the mug on the wood, frowning. 'That's bloody weird.'

Hunter looked over Jock's shoulder. His inbox was out of control, just like everything else in his life. 4,235 unread messages. But one was open and Jock was reading it. The subject was 'Dead Man's Switch'.

6

'Scott, mate, I'm sorry.' Hunter perched on the edge of the mushroom-coloured sofa, clutching his phone tight. 'But I'm worried about him.'

Cullen sighed down the line. 'Your bloody brother, eh?'

A clock ticked on the mantelpiece. Mum's old retirement thing, out of place in the spare minimalism of the rest of Murray's living room. She wasn't even dead and yet she'd given it to him.

'My bloody brother.' Hunter looked over at Chantal in the doorway, on a call too. 'My dad got the same message.'

'And your old boy... Is he still...?'

'A pisshead? Leopards never change their liver spots.' Hunter got up and started pacing the room. A male pheasant strutted on the front lawn. 'I forwarded the email to you. Dead man's switch.'

'And I'm looking at it now. Think he could be winding you up?'

'Doubt it.' Hunter's forehead twitched. 'He'd want to see our reactions.'

'See your point, but not sure I buy it. You been through any of this stuff?'

'Glanced at it. Looks bonkers conspiracy stuff.'

'Not the sort of shite he'd usually put on his YouTube channel?'

'That's all about urbexing, Scott.'

'Minor celebrity, eh? Must be making a decent bit of money.'

'Living like a king.' Hunter looked around the room, at the massive flat-panel TV, the minimal soundbar nestling in front of it, the stack of games consoles underneath. Such an empty life. 'He's made a packet from YouTube videos, him urbexing in various stupid places, and fair enough. I don't begrudge anyone their success. He's worked hard. But this conspiracy stuff, Scott... It's all lies. It isn't healthy.'

Sounded like Cullen was hitting a keyboard. 'I've checked the PNC and can't find him being reported missing. There's going to be a ton of John Does at hospitals and so on. I talked to Al Buchan about this, and it's now logged on the system. But there's a report of a MisPer by the name of Murray Hunter in the Highlands.'

'Seriously?'

'A PC David Robertson's been allocated the case. Based in Inverness. Technically, you're supporting him, so play nice. I've texted you his number.'

'That's it?'

'That's all we can do, Craig.'

'Right.' Hunter hauled himself to his feet. 'Thanks for nothing.'

'Come on, mate. My hands are tied. If he's dead and we've got a body, it's a completely different matter. But there could be any number of reasons behind this. Didn't he—'

'You mind if I take some time out?'

Cullen sighed. 'Look, I'm heading up to Perth as soon as Methven finishes speaking to every single senior officer in Police Scotland... Every phone call, you think "that's it, here we go", but no, there's another one and they want a different set of stats and I've got to pull them together for him. We should be investigating this murder, not—' He sighed again. 'Look, I wish I could help, but I'm up against it here.'

'I get that. But this is my brother, Scott. Just a couple of days.'

Cullen blew air down the line. 'Right. Today, then we'll see how it's looking. And I need Chantal in Perth. Deal?'

'Deal.'

'Call me at the end of the day. And keep it from Methven, okay?'

'Cool. Will do. Thanks. I appreciate it, mate.'

'Take care of yourself. And I hope you find him.'

'Cheers, Scott.' Hunter killed the call and opened Cullen's text, tapping on the number and putting the phone to his ear. 01463, meaning he was based in Inverness. Why the hell was Murray up there?

'Hi, you've reached PC David Robertson. I'm working night shift this week, so leave a message and I'll get back to you.'

Hunter waited for the beep. 'Hi, this is DC Craig Hunter, based out of Ba—' He had to catch himself. 'Out of the Edinburgh MIT. I'm looking into the disappearance of my brother, Murray Hunter. Just wondering if you could give me a call when you get a minute.' He left his number. 'Cheers.' He ended the call and pocketed his phone.

Chantal was sitting on the sofa, tossing her mobile in her hands. 'Well?'

'There's a MisPer up in the Highlands, matching Murray's name. Probably nothing, but you never know.' Hunter took a deep breath, just the faintest hint of nerves in there. 'Scott gave me the rest of the day, but I think I could string it out.' He held her hand. 'He wants you up in Perth ASAP.'

'And I want to help.'

'It's okay. I'm still clinging to this being my brother winding us up. You head off and I'll see what I can find here.'

'Sure?'

'Sure.'

'Listen, I'm worried what Murray's got himself into. And I'm sorry about not telling you about...' Hunter thumbed at the hallway, and the atonal whistling coming from the kitchen. 'About *him*.' That same skin-crawling sensation slithered over him. 'I'm not trying to keep anything from you, it's just... I cope by compartmentalising him. Sticking him in this little box in my head that I never, ever open.'

'Craig, you know you've got to stop bottling up your feelings, right? Your PTSD is under control because you've talked about stuff.'

'And the elephant sedatives I'm taking.' Hunter scratched at his neck. 'I'm sorry. You're right.'

'Is there another reason you've never mentioned him?'

Hunter nodded. 'My old man's always up to greasy shite, Chantal. Scams. Nothing major, nothing too illegal. He's a trained mechanic, so he could always get work wherever he roamed. But there was always a whiff of shonky about all of it. It's why I pretended to myself that he was dead. Helped me cope with the prospect of him actually being up to any really dodgy shite. Helped me become a cop.'

'And you left him off your application form?'

'Nah, must be he just never did anything bad enough to be caught.'

'I just wish you'd told me, that's all.' Chantal kissed his cheek and got up. 'Let me know if you find anything, okay?'

'Okay.'

She gave him one last look and walked into the hallway. 'Nice to meet you, Jock.' She left the house and her footsteps crunched over to her car. To their car.

Hunter got to his feet and stretched out. Chantal reversed out of the drive and spun off away from him, towards a murder case in Perth. He took a deep breath and headed through to face Jock, walking in to the smell of really, really nice coffee.

'Some left in the cafetière.' Jock was at the table, sipping from a giant Hearts FC mug, two piles of paper in front of him. 'That your bird heading off?'

Hunter helped himself to a cup, having to make do with a Scotland mug. Huge struggle to avoid throwing it on the old caveman. 'She's not—'

'She's not your bird?'

'No, she is. Just don't call her that. It's sexist.'

Jock grunted. Sounded like he said 'snowflake'. He slurped at his coffee. 'Right, so it's just you and me, then. She always that prickly?'

'Only to pricks. We're kind of going through some shite at work. You getting anywhere?'

'Hope your brother doesn't mind me printing off all this stuff.' Jock squinted at a sheet then put it in a pile. 'You always know where you are with paper.'

Hunter started looking through Jock's discarded pages. More of Murray's confused ramblings from the emails that Hunter had already looked at. Notes typed in bullet points, filled with comments to himself.

Six pages of "evidence" of a nuclear war between the Aztecs and the Romans in 350 AD, creating a Dark Ages which were two hundred years longer than otherwise known.

An article connecting vaccines with HIV.

Proof the Earth was flat.

If his intention was to get the truth out there, it'd be impossible to publish this lot without a shitload of work and, even then, what would it achieve? Besides, it was all complete bullshit.

Hunter looked over at Jock. Hard to believe he was in the same room as the old bastard. 'You found anything related to the Highlands?'

'The Highlands?' Jock was reading something. 'No. Why, should I?'

'No reason.'

'Be straight with me, Craig. Do you think something's happened to Murray?'

'Let's just say I'm sufficiently worried something has happened to him to be sitting here with you.'

Jock slurped at his coffee, oblivious to yet another barb. 'I've got two lovely laddies and that's how I'd like it to stay. But I've found the square root of bugger all here. This is all mad stuff. I mean, people believe that shite about vaccines?'

'Sadly. But you didn't pick up on the nuclear war between—'

'There's probably something in that, son.' Jock touched his pile. 'This one's all of his...' A frown. 'What do you call it again?'

'Urbexing. Means urban exploring.'

'That's it. Got some stuff about an old loony bin in the Borders. There's stuff about a place over near Fort William. And this is an old cinema in the Californian desert. Didn't know Joshua Tree was a town, just thought it was that Simple Minds album.'

'It's U2.'

'What? Of course it was Simple bloody Minds, Craig. You were a laddie when it came out.'

Hunter's head hurt too much to argue. 'Is he over there?' He knew he was clutching at straws, but anything to prove Murray wasn't in the Highlands...

'He wasn't flying, I remember that much. Kid's got one of them electrical cars now. Cost a bomb.'

'Okay, but where was he going?'

Jock clicked his fingers. 'The Highlands.'

It hit Hunter in the gut. 'I asked you if—'

'No, you asked if any of this shite related to the Highlands.'

Hunter took a sip of coffee to cover his anger. Full-bodied with a caramel finish. 'Do you know where in the Highlands?'

Jock frowned. 'Can't mind.'

'How the hell can you not remember where?'

'Craig, this isn't my fault. The boy's just disappeared in a puff of smoke.'

'No, he hasn't. He's gone somewhere and you were too pissed when he told you to remember where.'

'This isn't—'

'Let's just find him, okay?' Hunter drained his mug and picked up the bottom half of the pile of prints, the coffee taste still lingering. He started doing a fast sort. Junk. Conspiracy junk. Urbex junk. But all junk. Three urbex notes in a row. 'You know urban exploration is illegal, right? It's trespassing. He's lucky he's not had a visit from my colleagues. Especially as he's posting videos on the internet all the time.'

'Probably thinks you'll help him get off.'

'Like I've got any sway.' Hunter looked at the next page, entitled 'The Dangers of Urbexing'.

It read: 'The biggest danger to urbexers is running into other urban explorers. And I mean criminal types using the same places you're nosing around in for nefarious ends. These places are secluded, secret, hidden. Perfect for exploring, but—hoo boy—even better for stashing stuff. Drugs, guns, dead bodies. You name it.

'Where I'm going next, well, let's just say some past urbexers have suffered *underfortunate accidents*. You might think it's conspiracy bullshit but it might, equally, be some real murky stuff. Shady guys doing greasy shit. I'm going to find out what's happened. Then I'll publish it.

'And—holy moly—I don't want to end up like this guy.'

A YouTube video link.

'I'll be streaming some of our trip live, so keep an eye on it.

'Peace and love,

'Murray.'

Another YouTube link.

Hunter got out his phone. The email was still open. He found the same note among pieces on Antarctic civilisation and UFOs in the Andes, and clicked the first video link.

A dark room. The camera was low down, looking diagonally up at a man sitting on a chair. Bound and gagged, the grey material bloody. His left eye was swollen, like he'd been hit. Nose bent, but his lips were worse, puffy and twice the normal size. He was looking at someone the camera didn't pick up. 'Please, Admir. Stop.'

A fist lashed out and the man's head snapped back.

Then the video cut out.

Hunter's heart was fluttering in his chest. It could've been a fake video, the injuries all prosthetics. Staged by dickheads to get clicks from innocents.

But it could've been real. Admir sounded like a name. He typed it into Google and got millions of names. Looked like a common male name in Bosnia, Albania, and a few other places in that part of the world.

With a shaking hand, Hunter clicked on the second video and it started playing with a timestamp reading "1 week and 18 hours ago". Wind buffeted the microphone. A camera caught a steel-grey sky, then wheeled down to catch distant land then gloomy sea, foaming white and yellow. Then it rested on a concrete walkway. No idea where it was. Then a scream tore out, clear above the howling gale. A man's scream.

Murray?

Then the video stopped.

That was it?

Hunter stared at the video again, trying to discern

anything. Was it on a boat? Why would Murray urbex on a boat?

It didn't give him anything new, but it did put the fear of god into him.

Hunter went through the rest of the pile, barely focusing on anything that didn't mention the Highlands. What was Murray up to?

Wait. There. An Airbnb email. A booking confirmation for a cottage in the Highlands. He passed it over to Jock. 'You heard of Cromarty?'

'Town just north of Inverness, son. On the Black Isle. Course it's not actually an island.' Jock scowled at him. 'Christ, Craig. Me and your mother took the pair of you every summer until...' He trailed off. 'Your, eh, your grandfather grew up there. Your mother's old man.'

'Did Murray go there?'

'I've no idea.'

'Jesus Christ.' Hunter passed the page over. 'Does this ring any bells?'

Jock inspected it like it was a hefty gas bill he couldn't pay. 'I would've minded if he'd said Cromarty.' He frowned at it, then at Hunter. 'Think he's still there?'

Hunter pushed himself to standing. 'Only one way to find out.'

7

'Next episode should drop on Friday. Look forward to you joining us then.' The podcast's closing theme tune burst out of the speakers, all serious and political. Jock's ancient iPhone was connected up to the car stereo. One thing about Jock, despite the chaos in his private life, he was always on top of the political scene. Made sense he'd be switched on to podcasts, but the nonsense they'd been spouting made Hunter's blood boil.

Dark clouds loomed over the nearby hills, all covered in dark-green trees. Not yet into the Cairngorms where the bare mountainsides suck all life and hope out of you.

Another podcast image flashed on the car's display, a foaming pint of craft beer in a too-tall glass. Fake pub noise bled out of the speaker. Tinkling of glass, genial chatter, laughter.

'Welcome to the Crafty Butcher podcast with me, the King—'

'—and me, the Billy Boy.' A nasal whine, south Glasgow accent. 'Coming up this week, we've been sampling some Nuclear Winter, a lovely APA from a new Edinburgh brewery called Slam and Deeliant, but boy is it strong!' The voice was really familiar. 'And a lovely porter called Overlapping Centre Halves from our favourite South Yorkshire brewery, the Rich Blades.'

'And over in homebrew corner, I'll tell you how my experiment with mixing New World hops and some old-school ones from Kent has been going.' Christ, both voices were familiar.

Was the King... Elvis?

No, it couldn't be.

The image flashed to a photo of two men in a pub.

Hunter grabbed Jock's phone from the cradle and checked the screen. There they were, a photo of the pair of idiots—Elvis and DS Brian Bain, calling himself the Billy Boy. Doing a podcast about craft beer?

Hunter reached over and killed the sound.

Jock looked over, mouth wide open, taking his eyes off the A9 again. 'I was listening to— SHIIIITE!' He swerved back to their side of the single carriageway, narrowly missing clipping a navy Nissan.

Hunter shoved the paperwork back in the footwell and pointed to the right, at the sign for the House of Bruar. 'You need a break. Stop here.'

'I don't need a bloody break!'

'Tell that to the driver having palpitations back there.'

Jock let out a sigh, slowing as he slipped into the right-turn lane. A steady stream of traffic ploughed towards them, a bow wave of cars behind a slow-moving coach. 'Jesus, Mary and Joseph...'

'Just take your time.'

Of course he didn't. Jock fired across the front of a Jaguar SUV, narrowly missing adding them to the long list of fatalities on this stretch of the notorious road. 'There we go, safe and sound.' He wound through the corkscrew surrounding the beige building, a round tower and perpendicular extensions pretending they were way older than they actually were, then slammed into a disabled bay. He popped his blue badge on the dashboard.

Hunter picked it up. 'Where did you get that?'

Jock tapped his nose. 'If anyone asks, my name is Eric Hunter.'

'Uncle Eric gave you this? You know that's a crime, right?'

Jock let his seatbelt whiz up. 'He's not using it, not since his latest heart attack.'

Hunter let his seatbelt go and put a foot down on the tarmac. 'You're just using it 'cos you're too lazy to walk the extra hundred metres at Tesco for your yellow-item haul.'

'Wheesht.' And with that Jock got out. 'Lunch is on me, son. Soup and a roll.'

'We should just get a sandwich and drive.'

'I need to stretch out and take my eyes off the road.'

Hunter followed him at a distance, checking his messages. Still nothing from PC Robertson in Inverness, still nothing on any Admirs in the system. Just a text from Chantal: *Arrived in Perth. Love you.*

He replied: 'At House of Bruar. Haven't murdered him yet. And love you too.'

The ellipsis appeared on her side of the message chain. 'What the hell are you doing up there?'

'Long story. Short version. Murray might be in Highlands. Call you later. Love you x'

Over by the front door, Jock was chatting to a red-faced old guy wearing a tweed coat and garish crimson trousers. This section looked like a Victorian train station transplanted to the Perthshire countryside, ornate columns holding up a pitched glass roof over the walkway, the slate-roofed food hall behind it.

Jock thumbed at Hunter as he neared. 'No clean under-crackers, can you credit it?'

'All the same, that generation. Heids up their erses.' The old timer cackled, then slipped off with a slap on Jock's arm.

'Catch you later, my man.' Jock picked up a box of red grapes from the greengrocer stand. 'See the price on these, Craig?' He shook his head. 'Right, I smell Scotch broth. You get yourself some clobber, I'll get us some scran.'

HUNTER WALKED through the busy restaurant, scanning the rows for any sign of Jock. All those strange faces, checking you out as you passed, like being in the old Leith Walk station canteen. He found Jock at a table looking out across the car park, talking at a young couple who looked as bored as Hunter would be in their situation.

'Aye, here he is. Number one son.'

Hunter sat, dumping his bag at his feet and smiling at the couple. 'Nice to meet you. Hope he hasn't killed you of boredom.'

'As if!' Laughing, Jock slid a bowl of soup over the table. 'Don't say I'm not good to you.'

Hunter tore off a chunk of bread and dunked it in the thick, glistening broth. 'Didn't realise how hungry I was.'

'You get yourself all clobbered up? Need to take out a second mortgage?' Jock laughed and elbowed the young guy next to him, hitting hard like he was going up for a corner with him in a late-eighties Old Firm match. ''Cos it's so bloody expensive here!'

A pair of polite nods from the couple. Their sportswear brands were all unfamiliar names, German by the looks of it. Not that something like them not speaking English could ever stop Jock's banter.

Hunter took another mouthful of bread and soup. Thick meaty taste and not too many teeth-like lumps of pearl barley.

Looked like Jock had barely touched his. Too busy talking shite to random strangers while his son was missing, presumed dead.

The young couple got up and gave equally polite smiles to Jock. 'Thank for hospital, sir.'

Jock's frown was brief. He doffed an imaginary cap. 'Slainte, my friend.' He picked up his teacup like it was a whisky and his gaze followed them through the café, though at the height and direction of her rear end. A sharp intake of breath and he was back on Hunter. 'I was going to say, you should just go commando.'

Hunter scowled at him. Mouth full of soup, so he couldn't reply. He set up another spoonful as he finished chewing, then blew on it. He caught his teeth on the metal.

Jock finished his coffee and looked enviously at Hunter's

giant teapot. 'Could do with another coffee.' Without asking, he poured tea into his cup, splashing a lot on the table. 'Not sure how we're supposed to share your brother's nonsense with the great unwashed if we can't even understand it.'

Hunter poured himself some tea, bracing himself for the onslaught of milk-based chat, but Jock was still chewing. He splashed the smallest amount of milk possible into his cup, hoping Jock didn't notice.

'Have you watched any of his videos?'

Hunter shook his head.

'Absolutely mystified why he's able to afford that house from *that*. Still, it's nice to see your brother finally being successful. Your mum must be proud.'

'Like you'd care.' Hunter put his spoon down on the bowl edge and held his father's look until he won. 'You saw his income statements in your printouts, though?'

'Eye-watering.' Jock refilled his cup, getting halfway before it ran out. 'Ah, Christ, there's hardly any left.'

'You'll be wanting to stop every five minutes with the amount you've had.'

'Bladder like a tureen.' Jock sank his tea and stared enviously at his son's so-far untouched cup, hardly any milk or not. 'He gets a lot of money, son. Every month. And just for videos?' He shook his head.

'It's a global world now. Huge audience in the States and Japan.' Hunter took a sip of tea. Stewed, undrinkable.

'What do you think's happened to him?'

Hunter finished his soup and pushed his bowl away, fighting against the image of the bloodied face getting punched. 'Until we find out, there's no point in speculating.'

'Fat lot of use you are.'

'Thought I was getting a sandwich too?'

'These'll do.' Jock held up a carrier bag. 'Heading up into the arse end of nowhere, so I want us to be prepared.'

8

The fading sun lit up the road spinning off into the distance, crawling all over the Black Isle, old beech trees lining the way on both sides. Lush, and not at all what Hunter expected, especially after the brutal scenery of the drive up. Some horses roamed in a big field on the right, two cheeky-looking ponies hanging around by the gate midway along. Four or five oil rigs dotted the Cromarty Firth, Hunter couldn't quite decide the number. This was as far north as he'd been in his life, and quite what they were doing there was anyone's guess.

'It's beautiful.'

For once, Jock didn't have anything to say. Just head down, white knuckles on the steering wheel, a man pushed on by a goal.

'You okay?'

'Bursting for a pish, son.' Jock's knee was jiggling, his foot resting on the clutch. 'Shouldn't have made me finish that second pot of tea.'

Downhill now, almost to the level of the firth, wild bushes climbing the easy hill across the road. Round another bend and a 'Welcome to Cromarty' sign whizzed past.

'Christ, it's almost up to my eyes, son.'

The town eased into view, mostly white houses. The peninsula snaked out into the middle of the river to meet yet another dead oil rig. On the far side, tall buildings climbed up, looking like a shipyard or something. In the Highlands.

Jock didn't slow much as they hit the '30' signs.

A beach appeared, the tide far out. And the first homes of Cromarty, bungalows and post-war ex-council houses, the kind you'd see anywhere north of Berwick or Gretna.

Jock took the left fork to follow the coast into the town, heading for the harbour. The Royal, a grand old Victorian hotel, sat on the right looking out to sea. The car had barely stopped before Jock shot out, flying through a door underneath the Belhaven Best sign.

Hunter got out on the pavement and stretched out, his spine cracking in a particularly satisfying way. A Porsche rumbled past, low-slung, one of those eighties ones that did about an inch to the gallon.

And the car started rolling.

Shite!

He dived back in and yanked at the handbrake, crunching as it snapped back on.

Bloody hell.

He grabbed his bag from the back seat and followed Jock inside the hotel.

No sign of him, but tuneless whistling came from a door at the side.

Panelled walls, dotted with old brewery mirrors. A long bar, with several pumps of real ale, still reeking of smoke, years after anyone could legally light up inside. Then again, with police cuts the way they were, who was to stop them up here?

Three drinkers sat along the bar, enjoying their own company. One of them read a paperback, but the others just stared into their beer, self-medicating. The first looked round at him, did the old up-and-down, then went back to his fizzing lager.

Jock reappeared, grinning from ear to ear as he did up his flies. 'That's got it.' He paced over to the bar and grinned at the bear of a barman. 'Two reservations, name of Hunter.'

The barman looked even older than Jock, his wild beard climbed up to just below his eyes. He reached below the bar for a clipboard. 'Hunter, eh?' He looked at Jock, then his son, then back, like they were an unlikely couple.

'Two rooms.'

'Ah. that explains it.' He rested the form on the scarred wood.

Jock signed the form and pushed it back, and got a pair of keys in return. 'Set us up a pint of the blonde, my good man. I'll be back in a flash.'

'We're here to find my brother, not get banjaxed.'

'I'm gasping, son.' Jock's eyes were wild like he really needed a drink. 'And I am actually shiting myself about what's happened to your brother. You go shit, shower, shag, shave, and back here. Let me deal with it in my own way, okay?' He smiled at the barman. 'Thanks.'

The barman reached for a glass.

'BEAUTIFUL PINT THAT, CRAIG. BEAUTIFUL.' Jock was powering along the pavement through Cromarty. 'Swear I could go another twenty.'

Going to be hard keeping the old rascal sober. The beer glass had been empty by the time Hunter returned to the bar. He followed a few paces behind, the dull ache in his skull returning with a vengeance. The kind of vengeance that you got from downing painkillers on an empty stomach.

He struggled to tell where Cromarty's centre was. It seemed to be a collection of fishing cottages with the occasional grand old mansion. An antiques shop with green signage sat opposite a café, both open, but no sign of a high street.

Jock stopped and sucked in the air. 'Beautiful.' He set off down a backstreet, if anything, faster than before. 'Just up ahead, son.'

This road turned out to be the main street. A Day-Glo turquoise café was still open. A few doors down was the Cromarty Arms, a red Tennent's T hanging above the door.

Hunter stopped. 'I've not come all this way to go to the bloody pub.'

'Keep your wig on.' Jock walked past the pub, then a wild garden overgrown with weeds already, before disappearing off down a side street which the stone wall marked 'Big Vennel', marching down towards the water.

Hunter had totally lost his bearings. Again.

Jock looked up from a sheet of paper. 'This is the place.' He slapped on the door and stepped back.

Looked like a fisherman's home, 'Vennel Cottage' stencilled in slate. Tall and narrow, and really old. 'This is Murray's Airbnb?'

Jock looked at Hunter like he was simple. 'Where did you think we were going?' He thumped the knocker this time. 'Well, there's clearly nobody in, so we need to—'

The door shot open and an obese man peered out, thin shoulders and face hidden by a neat beard, his colossal belly barely constrained by his T-shirt. 'Can I help you, buddy?' East Coast American accent.

'Police, sir.' Hunter stepped in front of his old man. 'Looking for a Murray Hunter. He in?'

'Randy?' A woman appeared, flame-haired and about a foot shorter. Hunter couldn't place her accent, though— could be English, could be American. 'Who is it?'

'Police, Dani.' Randy focused on Hunter. 'What's going on?'

'We believe a Murray Hunter was staying here.'

'Might've been.' Randy grabbed the inside door handle, looking ready to shut it in their faces. 'But he's not now. Sir, we're tourists. Over from Philly, renting this place while we explore my ancestors' homeland.'

'What's your full name, sir?'

'Randy Jablonski. But my grandpappy was a Mowat, came from round these parts.'

'De Monte Alto.' Jock nodded. 'First Sherriff of Cromarty when it became a royal burgh. Became the Mowats.'

'Well I never.'

'The boy here's mother was of that clan.'

Hunter glanced at Jock, giving a snort of frustration. 'You know where Mr Hunter might be?'

'Sorry, never heard of him.' Randy waved back up the

street towards the road with the pub on it. 'But the woman who manages this place lives just next to the Cromarty Arms. She might know.'

THE ADDRESS WAS a symmetrical two-storey villa, two gables jutting out either side, the doors and window surrounds painted dark green.

'Think they were at it?' Jock stepped under the similarly green porch and pressed the buzzer, leering in the evening gloom. 'Because if they were, the boy was punching above his considerable weight.'

Hunter sighed. 'Do you mind?'

'Got to lighten the mood somehow.' Jock pressed the buzzer again. 'Sure you should be pulling that police trick?'

'Worked, didn't it? Besides, I'm not exactly off duty. This is an official case.'

'Think that boy would've told anyone anything just to get back to pumping—'

'Hello?' A wizened old woman squinted out of the right half of the door. 'What you wanting?'

Hunter folded his arms, keeping his warrant card in his pocket this time. 'Do you own Vennel Cottage?'

'No.'

'You don't rent it out?'

'Aye.'

Hunter huffed out a sigh. Felt like he'd caught the habit off Scott Cullen, but he'd only seen him for ten minutes that morning. 'So, which is it?'

'I manage it for the owners. Gay couple. Live down in Glasgow.' She spat out the city name like it was a swearword.

Hunter smiled at her, the grin that he'd usually reserve for elderly witnesses. 'I'm looking for a Murray Hunter. I believe he rented that cottage last week?'

'That's right, aye. Him and a pal. Pair of them left it in a right state.'

'What do you mean by that?'

She sneered at him. 'Had to get a cleaner to tidy it up, came all the way over from Dingwall! That's twenty miles! Cost me a pretty penny that I'll never see again.'

Hunter glanced at Jock and caught a bit of worry. 'What kind of mess are we talking?'

'Well, like someone had a few too many sherries and decided to wreck the place. Real rock star stuff, the TV was the only thing not smashed. A shocking state of affairs.'

'You said there was a pair of them. Did they cause it?'

'Didn't catch the other guy's name.' She opened the door and stepped out, leaning in to whisper, 'Were they lovers?'

Jock started fizzing like the beer he'd downed at the hotel.

Hunter shot him a shut-up glare, then smiled at the old woman again. 'What makes you think that?'

'I just thought that, what with the owners being,' she whispered again, 'that way.' She cleared her throat. 'That there might be some sort of club I didn't know about? I dunno. But there was this Russian chap asking about them.'

'By name?'

'Well, not in so many words.'

'He was definitely Russian?'

'I think so. Big lump he was too.' She eyed Hunter. 'Even bigger than you.'

Jock frowned. 'I'm taller than him!'

'Aye, in your dreams.'

Hunter flashed a smile. 'Thanks for your time, ma'am.'

She nodded. 'Funniest thing, though, they left a load of stuff behind.'

9

A chandelier shone inside the antique shop, the twinkling lights crawling halfway across the dark pavement towards the damp road. Hunter couldn't see anyone inside, but the sign hadn't been flipped over to 'closed' yet.

Hunter opened the door and entered the shop, the bells tinkling. The place smelled of dust and oil. A vintage radio played, just about revealing some classical music among the crackling. And nobody about.

'*Lovers.*' Jock was still fizzing, hands stuffed in his pockets, face screwed tight. Seemed more interested in the accusations against his son than in finding him. 'What the *hell* did she mean by that?'

'Come on, Jock.' Hunter shook his head at him. 'It's not like Murray ever brought a girl home, was it? Oh, hang on. You were never around, were you?'

'Craig, me and your mother, we...' Jock picked up a small

framed map and sniffed at the price. 'You remember we got back together when you were in the army?'

'Just like you should remember me not coming back to Porty for my leave that year.'

'Right, aye. Well, Murray was at the university.' A twinkle sparked in Jock's eyes. 'He brought this lassie home once, though. Tidy piece, she was. Can't mind her name, though. Alison? Marion? Kim? I'd've smashed her back doors in, I tell you.'

'And yet you can't remember her name.'

Jock started leafing through a box full of mounted maps, ready for framing. 'Some nice things in here, son.'

A clatter came from behind a half-open door.

'Back in a sec.' Hunter left Jock to his maps and looked out on a large back yard where a garden should've been. Mossy flagstones covered in junk: a Victorian swing set; wicker patio furniture; an eighties briquette barbecue; four of those gas patio heaters that were supposed to be illegal now. Another clatter came from a door to the right.

Hunter eased his way through the junk.

Inside the door, a bald man in tweeds perched on a cream milking stool, just his red-trousered legs visible below his belly. Looked every inch the vulture, but one dressed to the nines. He was sifting through a cardboard box with one hand, scribbling in a brown leather notebook with the other. He looked up at Hunter and beamed. 'Good evening, sir. Let me know if you need anything.' English accent, like his parents had spent big on his education. And he went back to his box.

Hunter entered the room. The stink of acrid coffee. A sink sat underneath a window looking over the yard, the counter filled with coffee paraphernalia like the guy fancied himself as an upmarket barista. Bean grinder, filter machine, high-end espresso setup, and one of those press things Murray gave Hunter for his last birthday. He swallowed down the memory and cleared his throat. 'Mary Donaldson said she gave you a box of—'

'Ah, yes.' Mr Tweed tapped a shiny brogue off the battered cardboard. 'This very thing.' He pursed his lips. 'I mainly source my wares from house clearances, but I sometimes take left-behind goods from guesthouses and what have you. It's amazing how frequently people just up and leave.'

'You manage to sell it all?'

'Most of it I can't, no, so it goes to various reputable charities in Inverness. But there's usually *something* here that'll—' He stopped dead, frowning. 'What are you looking for, exactly?'

'My brother. Just want to check whether the stuff is his or not.'

'Sure, sure.' Mr Tweed winched himself up to standing, barely up to Hunter's chest. 'Well, by all means, have a look. Anything you don't want or need, I'm more than happy to dispose of.' He poured a cup of coffee into a mug adorned with 'My Other Car's A Bentley'. 'Now, I'll just be through in the shop.' And he swaggered off, like he was doing something morally defensible.

Hunter took his seat on the warm stool and peered into the box. Larger than he thought, the size to fit an old TV in before the days of lightweight flat panels. An Adidas sports bag looked like the best first place to check. He unzipped it —just clothes and toiletries, but they were packed in Murray

fashion, all neat and tidy, strapped into the various compart-
ments. Despite the general chaos in his life, he knew how to
travel. Shirts, trousers and towels all rolled rather than
folded, designer underwear tucked into a box, socks balled
up, all tips fresh from the latest Marie Kondo book. He set
the bag aside and dug into another, bigger, and filled with
enough pasta and tinned goods to get through the first few
weeks of the apocalypse. Nothing out of the ordinary.

Then Hunter spotted his brother's designer leather
satchel. Could even remember buying it for him, torn back
to the shop in Edinburgh's West End, one that shut down a
few years later. Hunter just wanted a birthday beer with his
brother but, flush with demob money, he'd promised
Murray anything in the shop. The leather was a bit worn and
creased now, showing that Murray appreciated it.

'*Lovers.*' Jock was standing by the open door, hands still
in his pockets, an expression like sour milk. 'The cheek of
the woman.'

Hunter went back to the satchel. 'I've found Murray's
stuff.'

'Right.' Jock went over to the coffee machine and helped
himself. 'Can you believe her?'

'What would be so wrong about him being gay?'

Jock didn't answer. Either he didn't have one, or didn't
want to consider his son's sexuality any further than his
outrage would allow.

Hunter popped the catch and opened the satchel. A
MacBook was tied up like a hostage, the power supply neatly
coiled up next to it. A couple of paperback books on the
Highlands padded it out, but no notebooks or anything that
could tell them what the hell Murray was up to here. He

liberated the laptop and flipped the lid, hit a few keys and yep, got a password screen. He huffed another sigh. 'Any idea what Murray's password could be?'

Jock slurped coffee. 'Like I'm privy to any of his deepest secrets.'

Hunter tried HIGHLANDER and got nothing. Then lower case, then a few of the combinations he'd try himself. 1 instead of I. 3 instead of E. Nothing worked. If only getting into a laptop was as easy as in the films. Maybe Cullen could get that Dundonian guy back in Edinburgh to have a look? What was his name? Charlie something...

'Anything else there?'

Hunter looked it all over again. 'Square root of bugger all.' He tossed the clothes bag over. 'Take this, I'll grab the rest.'

Jock looked inside the bag, shaking his head. 'I don't want to seem homophobic, Craig. It's just...' He put the bag over his shoulder, the strap pushing his man boobs apart. 'Are you keeping any secrets from me?'

'What?' Hunter snarled. Then caught himself—that'd just feed the old sod's paranoia. So he smiled. 'No. Nothing big, anyway.'

'It's the...' Jock sucked in a deep breath. 'I don't know, son.'

'You really expect me or Murray to trust you?'

'I just don't like people keeping secrets, that's all.'

'You're the expert.'

'What the hell's that supposed to mean?'

'Let's speak to him.' Hunter led Jock back through. The bag was heavy as hell.

'Excuse me, but where do you think you're going with

that?' The vulture shifted over to block the door, arms folded. 'That's my stuff!'

'Correction, that's my brother's stuff. I'm claiming it back.'

'Under whose authority?'

Hunter dropped his bag and flipped out his warrant card. 'Police Scotland.'

'You should've told me when you came in, you know?'

'And you shouldn't be trying to sell my brother's stuff.'

'I'm an honest businessman.'

'Selling dead men's laptops.'

'There's a chap down in Inverness who can factory reset those Apple thingies. Can be quite lucrative.' Tweed frowned. 'Dead?'

'That's my working assumption, aye.'

'You're a murder detective?'

Hunter gave him a truthful smile. 'I am. Based in Edinburgh.'

'Good heavens.'

Jock handed him back the mug. 'Thanks for the coffee.'

'I didn't say you could have any.'

'All the same, it's lovely stuff. Where do you get your beans?'

'*Jock.*' Hunter shot a warning look as he held out his mobile showing a photo. 'Do you recognise him?'

A frown twitched across his forehead. 'This is...?'

'My brother. Murray.'

'Good heavens. Well, he was here. Him and another chap. Spent a while looking at the maps. His friend was interested in the piano score. Didn't buy anything, but such is the nature of the business.'

'They say anything?'

'To each other, yes. Constant jokes and comments and remarks about my shop. But I'm used to that.'

'Listen to me, son.' Jock got in the vulture's face, towering over him. 'That's my boy's stuff you're hawking there.'

'Please, I'm just trying to earn a living here!'

'I should kick your arse for this.'

And Hunter saw it. The telltale signs of Jock being hangry, seen so many times as a small kid, then sporadically as a teenager, then never since. Low blood sugar plus discovery of a secret his son had been keeping from him could only ever equal a paternal explosion and smashed crockery, unless Hunter got some calories in him.

10

'This is good.' Jock chomped his ciabatta, the brie and bacon mixing into a mush in his open mouth. He took a sip of cola before he'd finished and swallowed down the unholy mixture. 'I hear that pizza place by the harbour is beautiful. Hard to get a table, mind. This'll be our tea, aye?'

'Right.' Hunter picked at his salad, down to the last chunk of marinated squash. Still wasn't that hungry. 'You feeling any better?'

'Not really.' Jock snapped a crisp and swallowed it down. 'It's just... Do you think you can come to me about anything?'

'Do you really want me to answer that?'

'What's that supposed to mean?'

'Well, you left us when we were kids. A few returns over the years. How the hell can we trust you after that?'

Jock frowned, his lips twitching like he was ready to start

smashing shit up, but he leaned over his plate instead. 'Woman at your five o'clock keeps looking at you.'

Hunter nodded, then ate his last bit of salad. Kept it calm, chewing away. Then loud: 'Where's the waitress? Could do with another cup of tea.' He looked left, right, then behind him.

The café had clearly been a pub at some point. A big bar ran the length of the room, but the hardwood was now painted baby blue, with bunting running along the top and into the corners.

And the woman sitting at the next table was peering over. Dark hair streaked with grey, hanging around a cherubic face. Jeans, green T-shirt, Doc Martens. She locked eyes with Hunter, then went back to her scone, slowly buttering the top half.

Hunter waved over at the waitress who was thumping the buttons on the till. She gave him a frustrated nod, but didn't shift, just kept hitting the cash register. So he looked back at Jock. 'She's definitely watching us.'

'Why, though?' Jock finished chewing. 'What's she after? Not another lassie after my bloody body.' He spoke like it was a constant battle.

'I think it's more likely that she's wondering who the strangers in her café are. It's not exactly tourist season.' Hunter stared at his plate, smeared with dark dressing, dotted with green oil. 'But we need to focus on the fact the trail's gone cold.' He looked up and locked eyes with Jock. 'But that isn't the end. First, we now know Murray was here in town. Second, we know he wasn't alone.' He held up a hand. 'Whether he's gay or not doesn't matter. Third, we don't know who he was with, but we know Murray and whoever he was with left in a hurry.'

'That's hardly a lot to go on.' Jock scoffed his last crisp. 'Anything else?'

Hunter finished his tea, now lukewarm but still drinkable, and stared into space. 'It was just Murray's stuff.'

'What?'

'That was just Murray's clothes, right?' Hunter nudged the bags on the floor with his foot. 'The food might be shared, but it's all Murray's clothes and laptop and stuff. Agreed?'

Jock reached down and had another look. 'Take your point, aye.' He sat back and ran a hand across his face. 'One thing about your brother is, he always wore the same clothes. Those hiking trousers, that brand of T-shirts. The plain ones. American something.'

'Glad you agree.' Hunter looked over at the waitress, still battering the till. Their observer had cleared off, leaving the bottom half of her scone and a fiver on the table. He caught the waitress's eye and raised his tea cup. Got a nod and roll of the eyes, then focused back on Jock. 'When Murray's mate or boyfriend or whoever he is left, he took his own stuff but Murray's ended up in that vulture's clutches.'

'That *prick*. Selling my boy's stuff. It's disgusting.'

'Let it go. We know Murray was here. That's something, right? We need to find whoever he was with.'

The waitress sloped over with a fresh pot of tea for Hunter. 'Need more milk?'

'Please, but I need to ask you something.' Hunter picked up his phone and showed her a photo of his brother, caught on a crisp Borders morning with blue skies and red hens swarming round him. 'You recognise this guy?'

The waitress's eyes darted over to the door, then back at him, all narrow. 'You police or something?'

'If I said no, you wouldn't believe me. Right?' Hunter reached into his coat pocket for his warrant card and showed it. 'It's a missing person's case, so if—'

'He came in for breakfast a couple of times.' Eyes back at the door. 'Seemed very focused, working on laptops.'

'Laptops plural?'

'Yeah, pair of them. Two laddies. Get a lot of writers in here. Order a coffee and nurse it for hours.' She walked off.

Jock slid his plate to the side. 'You think that'll give us anything?'

'Not sure.'

A jug of milk snapped onto the table in front of Hunter. The waitress picked up Jock's plate and frowned. 'I did see them in the pub too.'

HUNTER STEPPED through the door and sucked in every detail of the pub. Just after seven and pretty busy. A pair of old-timers sat at the bar, staring into their beer, just like in the hotel bar. Hunter couldn't tell if they were the same men. Next to them, two female office workers were trying to order. The nearest table had four women, mid-thirties, a bottle of white in a chiller between them. A red-haired woman in a suit gave Hunter the up-and-down, then went back to laughing. A man with short dark hair sat in the window, hammering his laptop's keyboard like it'd insulted him.

Jock sidled up to the bar, an alpha male in his natural habitat, grabbing the barman's full attention despite the strong competition. 'Pint of the Rogue Wave, cheers.' He turned to the side. 'Craig?'

Hunter followed him over and checked the pumps. He groaned as the barman poured Jock's order. 'Dad, that's a bit strong.'

'Saying I can't handle a five point seven percent IPA?'

More like Hunter couldn't handle him when he was shit-faced. 'It's not the strength of one pint, it's the strength over ten or twelve.'

'Take a hold of yourself, son. It's hardly Special Brew!'

Hunter held his gaze. 'Get me a Happy Chappy.'

'You heard the man.'

The barman gave the nod of a consummate professional, then poured from a separate tap as Jock's wreck-the-hoose juice settled.

Hunter eased his phone out of his pocket and showed it to the barman. 'You recognise this guy?'

The barman didn't take much of a look, just stayed focused on the beer. 'He was in with a mate. Last week.' He started topping up Jock's pint. 'Oh aye.' He slid the glass over and finally made eye contact. 'Got a bit ripped one night. Started upsetting the natives.'

Hope was surging in Hunter's gut. 'Which night?'

'Be a week past Sunday. I almost had to turf them out but they left before I started threatening them with physical violence as opposed to ocular.' As if to emphasise his point, he narrowed his eyes at them.

Sunday would fit the timeline for the dead man's switch.

One week would be this morning, assuming Murray had checked in a week ago.

'Who was he with?'

'A man. Medium height, soul patch.' He tickled just below his lips. 'Pair of them were off their faces on that ale I've just poured for your old man there.'

Hunter braced himself against the bar. 'Were they speaking to anyone?'

'Who weren't they speaking to?' The barman rolled his eyes. 'Chatted to everyone. Absolute pish, too. Drunken nonsense. Pair of clowns.' He passed Hunter his beer. 'That's a lovely ale, pal. Good choice.'

'Thanks.' Hunter took a sip. Tangy and hoppy. Perfect. 'You speak to them?'

'Weren't interested in anything I had to say, other than how much their round cost. Tried to suggest they lay off the strong stuff, but they wouldn't be told.'

'Speak to anyone who's in here just now?'

The barman didn't even look. 'Nope.'

Hunter handed over a tenner, not expecting any change. 'What about anybody not currently here?'

The barman went over to the till. 'That bloody idiot Fiona was chatting to them.'

'Who's Fiona?'

'Kid's bad news, not that she's a kid anymore.' The barman returned, his nostrils flaring, and passed over two shiny pound coins. 'No idea what they were talking about.'

'Thanks.' Hunter took his beer over to an empty table, one with a good view of the door and the quiet street outside. He sat and caught the woman looking at him again, then she went back to her pals, tossing her hair like she knew someone was watching her. 'Apple didn't fall too far from the tree, did it?'

'What's that supposed to mean?'

'My brother sure liked a drink.'

'Still does, hopefully.' Jock sucked down a sip, covering his top lip with foam. 'Oh, that's gorgeous.' He passed it to his son. 'Try it.'

'I'm fine.'

Jock held it in his face. 'Go on!'

The door opened and the woman from the café stepped in. She ran a hand through her hair, her gaze shooting round the room, finally settling on Hunter.

Hunter looked over at the barman and got a narrow-eyed nod. *Fiona.*

'You're barred! Get out!'

'Aye, I'm pissing off.' Fiona walked back out again.

Hunter pushed up to standing and set off. 'Stay here, Dad.'

11

Fiona was a hundred metres or so away, head low and walking with great purpose. She took a left down towards the shore.

Hunter braced himself against the bitter wind, laden with tangy sea rain. The houses he passed were mostly dark and quiet. Probably holiday homes, or commuters from Inverness who hadn't returned yet. The house on the corner glowed, a family crowded round a television like in some advert.

Along the curve of the coast, the promenade's lights swayed in the breeze. A squat wall separated the shingle beach from the road and its parked cars, the waves hissing over the pebbles. Across the firth, industry rumbled, bright lights and cranes arcing slowly.

No sign of Fiona.

Up ahead, someone passed under a streetlight.

Hunter sped up and followed on the opposite side, using

the parked cars as cover, but he soon lost Fiona as the street bent round. He came to a junction, the coast road merging with another that headed out of town, guided by a tall stone wall. The old brewery over the way was bright, the sounds of a ceilidh band inside—the solid thump of drums and bass accompanying a fiddle, clumping feet almost matching the rhythm. Another stone wall sat at the end of the street leading back to the heart of the town, opposite two old houses lurking in the darkness.

A short woman stood, talking to someone just out of sight. Hunter could make some words out over the music. 'You're a good lassie, Fiona Shearer. I'll see you later.' She walked towards Hunter, crossed over and headed into the old brewery, letting the clatter of the ceilidh out. Didn't look like she had her dancing trousers on, but then what was going on inside wasn't exactly dancing.

Up ahead, Fiona powered on, back towards the pub.

Hunter walked faster now, narrowing the gap with each long stride. The street was barely wide enough to park cars and still let others past, not that it had stopped the locals. Fiona slipped down a narrow vennel, a row of small fishing cottages cast in pitch black, not quite catching the light from the promenade.

And Hunter had lost her again.

Movement, over on the left, by a gate leading to a back garden and a shed piled high up the windows with junk. Hunter set off towards it, slow and cautious.

Something hard pressed in his back.

Knife? Gun? Either way, Hunter stopped, hands up.

A voice in his ear, 'What do you want?' Deep, but still definitely female.

'I'm a police officer, Fiona.'

The pressure on his back slackened off. 'How the hell do you know my name?'

'Check in my left pocket, you'll find my warrant card.' Hunter felt a hand slip inside his jacket, then caught another flash of reflected light. 'That do you?'

The knife went away with a sigh. 'Can't be too careful.' The hiss was now a gentle Highland lilt and a lot less deep. 'What do you want?'

Hunter turned slowly, his foot almost giving way, and he reached into his pocket for his phone. 'Looking for someone.' He eased it out and unlocked it, then showed Fiona the photo of his brother.

She narrowed her eyes. 'Why do you think I'd recognise him?'

'Heard you were speaking to him in the pub.'

Fiona looked around, eyes darting about like they were in Waverley station at rush hour and she couldn't find his platform. 'Can't do this here.' She set off across the road. 'Come on.'

THE BAY WINDOW looked onto the lane, now lit up from stray light. Fiona drew the curtains and let it return to darkness. 'Coffee or tea?'

Hunter stayed standing. 'Tea's fine.'

Fiona shifted over to the tiny kitchen area, a dark alcove lined with units on three sides. The kettle hissed to the boil and she tipped water into a tired-looking grey teapot, which had probably been white at some point.

Hunter walked over to the window and leaned against the wall. 'Fiona Shearer, right? Like the footballer?'

'Duncan or Alan? Take your pick.'

'Who's Duncan Shearer?'

'Played for Aberdeen in the nineties.' Fiona's eyes glazed over. 'It's a fairly common Highland name, though.'

'What were you talking to my brother about?'

'Not sure I should be talking to you, bud.'

'You want me to take you down to Inverness? Put you in a room, maybe get a lawyer in? You want to play that dance? Waste your time and mine?'

'You're the one coming into a single woman's flat.' Fiona stared at him, long and hard. 'Who knows what happened in here?'

'I'm recording this.' Hunter held out his phone again. 'You just threatened a police officer.'

'Shite.' She didn't even look like she was going to go for it. 'I'm thinking that if this was above board, you'd have already arrested me when I stuck a knife in your back.'

'This is above board. Got a missing persons case on the go, allocated to some guy in Inverness who won't return my calls. But the way you're acting makes me think you know something about what happened to him. Maybe you're involved.'

Fiona reached into a countertop beer fridge for a squished carton of milk and sniffed it. 'Look, I saw them in the pub. Pair of them were hammered. Get that fairly often in there, people heading up here for a weekend jolly.' She poured tea into two battered mugs. 'You take milk or sugar?'

'Just milk, thanks.'

A splash and Fiona walked over to hand him the mug. World's Best Dad. 'Slainte.'

'Slainte.' Hunter held up the mug. One look round the tired room, the tired life, and he didn't want to press her on the mug's story. 'So, you were in the pub?'

'Right.' Fiona slouched back over to the kettle and her own tea. Her own territory. 'I was chatting to an old pal in there when that boy on your phone ordered a beer, you know how it is.' She paused, like Hunter's knowledge of buying alcohol in a pub was in any way important.

'I know.' Hunter blew on the tea, knocking the scum and breaking it into much smaller dots. No way was he drinking that. 'The ancient art of small talk, right?'

'Damn right.' Fiona drank some tea. 'Anyway, this boy, whatever his name is, started saying how he's up on a fishing trip.'

Murray, fishing? But Hunter played along with it, resting his mug on a stack of bills on the windowsill. Outside, a car trundled down the lane, headlights picking out the rough path.

'I'm a fisherman by trade. Fisherwoman. Been working on the water since I was yay high.' Fiona held out her hand. 'You have no idea how hard it is being a lassie on those boats.'

'As hard as being a laddie?'

She smiled at that. 'Based in Fraserburgh the last ten years. Tell you, nothing like driving round the north coast on a freezing Sunday evening as you know you're going to spend two weeks out at sea. Decent money, too. Not like the rigs, but decent.' She stared into space. 'Least it was. Not had any work for a while, though.' She shook her head.

'So what do you do for money now?'

'I've got my old man's boat. He raised me on his own after Mum died. Took me sailing all the time. Silly old bugger called it *Dignity*, like in that Deacon Blue song. Can you believe it?'

'I can believe most things about fathers, aye.'

Fiona laughed. 'Not that it's the season, but I take tourists out along the Cromarty Firth. Maybe up to Dornoch for the seals. Or maybe further out, whale watching. Or fishing, like these hipsters who were in the boozer.' She took another glug of tea. 'The ones you're so interested in.'

'You get their names?'

Fiona shrugged. 'This guy I was chatting to at the bar was called Murray, I remember that.'

'Murray's my brother.'

'Shite, bud. I'm sorry.'

'You catch his mate's name?'

'Nope.'

'What did he look like?'

'Average height. Muscles. Good looking, except he had one of those beard things under his mouth.'

'A soul patch.'

'Right. Didn't really speak to him.' Fiona finished her tea and poured a fresh cup, like she was buying time to either weave a sufficient lie, or to figure out which bits to leave out. 'They were looking for someone to take them out. Fishing, they said.'

'And did you?'

'I was too busy. Taking this pair of Yanks out, this big guy and his wife. They'd set it up months ago, paid in advance.

And I mean, overpaid in advance. Wanted to see the dolphins. Good money in that. Took them out, Monday morning, first thing. Decent weather, got a few sightings and a whale too.'

'Anyone take Murray up on his offer?'

Fiona tipped in the last of her milk and chucked the carton in the bin. 'Like I told you, I didn't take them. They were a bit cagey about the details. Didn't seem like too far out, though. But I passed them to my mate Shug. Sat on the happy bus to Fraserburgh together. They kept him on a few months longer than me, but they still booted him. Less internet-savvy than me, so he's got to take what he can get from punters in pubs.'

'You know if Shug took them out?'

'No idea.'

'Shug got a surname?'

'Mowat.'

Hunter almost grinned. 'De Monte Alto, right?'

'Take your word for it. Millions of them round here, though. Well, hundreds.' A coy smile flashed across her lips. 'Some old Mowat must've put it about a fair amount.'

Hunter started to see a path through this. Murray and his mystery friend looking for a charter. 'You any idea where Shug might be?'

'That's the thing.' She held up her phone. 'Okay, so I was messaging him on WhatsApp the other day. He told me he was abroad. Been there for a month.'

'But?'

'Well, I saw him last Sunday night when your brother was in. That's why I've been in there asking people until

Dougie the barman went radge at me on Friday.' Tears glistened in her eyes. 'I'm worried some bampot's nicked his phone, pretending he's fine when really he's dead.'

One missing person had become three.

12

The Cromarty Arms was even busier and felt like a much earlier age, when people used to spend their evenings in the pub, rather than destroy a box of cheap supermarket lager in one sitting.

Jock had a table over in the corner, three empty beer glasses with varying degrees of decaying foam on the insides, talking at the American couple they'd clearly interrupted earlier. The big guy got up and walked over to the bar, rubbing his thick beard but grinning like he was having the time of his life.

Fiona leaned on the bar, keeping her voice low as Hunter joined her. 'That's the Americans.'

The barman slapped his beer towel over his shoulder. 'Told you, Fi, you shouldn't be in here.'

'Dougie, I'm sorry for getting into that state. Bar me if you like, but I'm just worried about Shug, that's all.'

Dougie the barman slowly licked his lips, then caught

sight of the American. 'Same again, son?' He got a nod and started pouring.

'Dougie, I've not seen or heard from him since a week past Sunday.'

'Well, I've not seen him since, either.'

'And you don't think that's weird?'

Dougie jabbed a finger at her. 'Doesn't excuse what you did.'

Hunter got between them. 'What did she do?'

Fiona ran a hand across her face. Didn't answer. Or couldn't.

'She started a fight on Friday night. I had to end it.' Dougie passed three pints of beer to the American. 'I'll add it to the tab, son.' He returned his focus on Hunter. 'Got herself a bit rat-arsed, thought it'd be a good idea to punch Wee Ally, and his name's ironic. Guy's six five.'

'He was *lying*.'

'*Fiona*.' Hunter raised his hands, trying to defuse the situation and steer it where he wanted it to go. 'Who's Ally?'

Fiona looked over. 'Ally shares the *Pride of Cromarty* with Shug Mowat. Said Shug hadn't been here in ages, but I saw him with my own eyes with your brother. So what am I supposed to think, eh?'

'Can I speak to Ally?'

'McCoull lives down in the lowlands. Just up here at the weekend. Got a cottage. Shug gets more than his half-share of value out of that boat, I tell you.'

Dougie looked up with a frown. '*Again?*'

'Aye, another three.' Jock clapped Hunter on the back, almost hard enough to wind him. 'Tell you, my boy, these Americans don't know how to drink!'

Hunter took him to the side. 'Have you forgotten why we're here?' He stared at him, hard, like Jock used to before he cleared off, or on one of his infrequent returns when he wanted to instil some discipline in his unruly boys. 'This isn't a stag weekend. We're looking for my brother. Your son.'

'You found him?'

Hunter had to look away.

'Thought not.' Jock stared at the barman. 'Lovely ale that.'

'Right.' Dougie looked up from the beer, forehead creased. 'Listen, I might've heard Shug talking to these hipster boys. Like she says, they were in a week past Sunday. Talking about osprey.'

Jock scowled. 'They were looking for a bird?'

'Get a lot of them round here, as it happens.' Dougie rested the beer on the counter. 'The Osprey Alpha is an oil rig sitting off Invergordon, four of them waiting for decommissioning.'

Hunter groaned. All those files, all those videos. Not a boat. 'Stupid bastards were urbexing in an oil rig.' He nodded at Jock. 'Any of the documents a match for that?'

Jock frowned. 'Well, there were a couple, aye.'

'Then that's as good a place as any to start.'

Jock grabbed Fiona by the arm, tight. 'Can you take us out there?'

'At nine o'clock at night?' She laughed. 'In this weather?'

'I meant tomorrow.'

Fiona tugged at her hair. 'Two hundred quid and I'll take you anywhere.'

'You cheeky cow.'

'Who do you think you're talking to?'

'Hey, hey, calm down.' Dougie jabbed a finger at Fiona. 'Remember that you're waaaaay past your last warning.'

'Keep the heid. I'm not the one calling people cows.' Fiona stared at Hunter. 'Two hundred and I'll *think* about taking you out.'

Jock shrugged. 'First thing.'

'Aye, nae danger, bud. Got an appointment with the mechanic at ten. Motor's on the blink, hence me needing two hundred quid ASAP. If you can sub us a hundred now, I'll—'

'We're not just going up an oil rig.'

'Craig, we need to—'

'No!' Hunter glowered at Jock. 'I need to call this in and get approval. I'll find who owns this rig, then we can get up there. Okay?' He patted Fiona on the arm. 'You got a card?'

'Not as such.' She took a beermat and scribbled a number on it with a stubby bookie's pen. 'Here you are.'

'Thanks.' Hunter pocketed it and pointed at Jock's glass. 'Make that the last one.'

'Right, Dad.' Jock bellowed with laughter. 'Where you off to?'

'Got to speak to the boss.' Hunter slipped out into the pissing rain and called Cullen. Voicemail.

Great.

13

The hotel breakfast room looked across the bay, the first rays of the breaking dawn hitting the firth. A nice clear morning, the view stretching to some distant hills and to the thick grey cloud rolling in from the North Sea. If it still was the North Sea up here. Even down in the Borders where Murray lived, they didn't have the scale of the mountains up here. So many trees.

If it wasn't for the fact he was searching for his potentially dead brother, Hunter could consider moving up here. Away from Edinburgh and its drugs and crime and people.

Hunter checked his phone. Still nothing from Chantal or Cullen, just a missed call probably about 'an accident that wasn't your fault'. He hit dial and it went to Chantal's voicemail again. He tried Cullen this time. Same result.

He had a voicemail of his own, though, so he checked it.

'Hunter? Davie Robertson. No progress on the case, but call me back, cheers.'

Hunter hit dial, his heart thudding. Voicemail again.

Bloody hell. 'Hi, David, it's Craig Hunter. Please give me a call.'

Hunter blew on his porridge but it was still too hot to eat. No idea what it'd been cooked on—a volcano?

A small boat slipped across the water, puffing up foam in its wake.

He popped open his supplements case and swore. Just vitamin pills. He'd left his PTSD meds behind in their rush to leave Edinburgh. He needed to find a pharmacy and pray they'd let him get some. Either way, missing for a day should be fine. Shouldn't it?

His phone rang. Chantal. 'Hey, have you been avoiding me?'

She huffed out a long and weary sigh. 'Just finishing up for the night.'

'It's half six?'

She yawned. 'Aye.'

'You solve it?'

'Hardly. Got a couple of suspects. Methven wanted me and Scott to interview them and...' Another long yawn. 'Neither's our killer.'

'You sound like you need your bed.'

'I need our bed, Craig. With you in it.'

Even with all the shite going on, he couldn't help but grin. 'I miss you too.'

'Well, if you were here, you'd be able to share this hell. We've got nothing. *Nothing.* Guy was shot six times and nobody saw a thing. Nobody's talking. And the guy was just an ex-insurance man, retired to do some fishing and potter around in his garden. It's bizarre, and you know Brian Bain, right?'

'Not in the biblical sense, but he's my new sergeant.'

'Shite, aye. Well, he's running around shouting about Albanian gangs. Some deep insurance fraud or something.'

'And let me guess, he's got no evidence for that?'

'Right.' She laughed. 'How's your hunt going?'

'Hard to say. I mean, I'm an experienced detective but... We've got a thin thread and I don't want to tug it too hard in case we snap it.' Hunter tried his porridge again. Goldilocks temperature. 'And Jock's getting on my tits. His son being missing plays second fiddle to getting shit-faced.'

'Oh, Craig.'

'I swear, he's turning this into a stag weekend. After that trip to Portugal, that's the last thing I need.' Another mouthful of porridge. Too salty, but decent enough. 'So, what's Bain been up to?'

'He's off the leash here. He made a neighbour cry in an interview. Nasty little man.' Another sigh, mixing with a yawn. 'I mean, it's hard enough to sympathise with Scott Cullen, but he's managing Bain and me.'

'Tough gig.'

'Speaking of which.' Muffled voices in the background.

Hunter took another spoonful of porridge.

'Craig.' Cullen's dulcet tones, sounding as tired as Chantal, his voice that bit slower and deeper, the consonants sliding together even more. 'How's it going, mate?'

'Well...' Hunter took another spoonful of porridge, giving himself time to think it through. 'The good news is we're picking up Murray's trail, but you know my brother, right?'

'Well, a bit.' Cullen yawned. 'I could really use you here, mate. How long's it going to take?'

'This is a piece of string case, Scott.'

'Strings, threads. You and your metaphors.'

'You know what I mean. Could be a month, could be over in an hour.'

'What's happening in an hour?'

'Nothing. Look, I'll call you back later today.'

'Right.' Another sigh-yawn. 'Craig, if there's anything you need, give me a shout, okay? The case is logged, and there's a local Inverness cop assigned to it. Oh, he's on leave today.'

'Shows how high a priority this is, doesn't it?'

'Look, Craig, you've got a conflict of interest here, so don't do anything stupid. You can use police resources if you need to, but don't take the piss.'

'Does that mean Methven doesn't know?'

'I told you not to take the piss.'

Hunter dipped his spoon into his porridge. 'Oh, and if I were you I'd check out the Crafty Butcher podcast.'

'What? Have you finally cracked?'

'I'm serious. It's a craft beer podcast presented by the King and the Billy Boy. The King as in—'

'Elvis?' Cullen gasped down the line. 'You're kidding me.'

'Like I say, check it out.'

Cullen laughed. 'I'll put you back on with your lover.'

'Wait a sec. Can you run a check for me?'

'Here we go. I already regret my hollow offer of help.'

'Oil rig called the Osprey Alpha. It's possible Murray visited it.'

'Okay, I'll get someone to have a look into it.'

'Cheers, Scott. Is that going to be Elvis?'

'Aye. Call him, not me. And good luck finding Murray. I mean it.'

More muffled chat and Chantal was yawning down the line, like she'd not stopped during Cullen's chat. 'He's grinning like he's—Craig, what did you tell him?'

'I gave him a podcast recommendation, that's all.'

'Right. Do I want to know?'

'Probably. Anyway, what's on the docket today?'

'Breakfast with a load of mouth-breathing arseholes, then as much sleep as I can manage, then back to taking statements and all the crap you usually get on these cases. Never rains, Craig. Never rains. And I don't know Perth at all.'

'You've surely been?'

'Is there a reason to go to Perth?'

If there was, Hunter couldn't think of it. 'Sounds like you're getting on with it, though.'

'One way of looking at it.' A pregnant pause. 'Good luck today. Hope you find him. Love you, bye.'

'Love you too. Bye.' Hunter ended the call and rested his phone next to his empty bowl. They were saying they loved each other so casually now. Almost like they'd stopped meaning it. Or maybe they'd gone from infatuation to true love.

'What's not to understand?' Jock's voice tore out across the quiet room. The elderly couple looked at Hunter then at the door as Jock stormed in, fists in pockets, shaking his head. 'Drip, ideally from ground beans. Got it?'

The Polish waiter stood next to him, frowning at his notepad. 'Baked beans?'

'*Coffee* beans.' Jock pinched his nose. 'Christ on the flaming cross. Filter coffee. Four mugs of it. Black, big jug of milk on the side.' He stretched out his thumb and fingers, indicating a pint-sized vessel. 'If it's from beans, great. If you've just got pre-ground, that'll do.' He smiled at the waiter. 'You got that?'

The frown betrayed any certainty, but the waiter gave a nod and walked off.

Jock sauntered over and sat, slapping that morning's *Press and Journal* onto the white tablecloth. 'Craig.'

'Morning.' Hunter poured himself another mug of tea before Jock got in there. 'You not having breakfast?'

'Just coffee.'

'Sure that's wise after last night?'

'It's my fasting day.'

Hunter let out an involuntary groan. Fast train to hangry central.

'Got to keep in shape, son.' Jock patted his flat stomach. 'Six hundred calories today.'

'That's it?'

'It's got other benefits too. Like low blood sugar and what have you. Sure you'll be getting all that with your hocus-pocus martial arts I saw you doing this morning.'

'Tai chi.'

'Whatever. You look like an idiot doing it on Cromarty beach at the crack of sparrow fart. In the dark.'

'How did you see me, then?'

Jock tapped his nose and looked around the room, smiling at the elderly couple.

'When did you finish up last night?'

Jock dropped his surveillance of the room and picked up his paper. 'Chucking-out time.'

Hunter sighed. 'You started drinking at four and you were on the randan until the back of eleven?'

'Midnight.'

'We're here to look for my brother.'

Jock lowered his paper enough to scowl at Hunter. 'While you were back in your room speaking to your Asian babe, I was chatting to—'

'My *what*?'

'You know, your bird.'

'My *bird*?'

'Calm down, Craig.' Jock tossed his paper on the table. 'No need to be such a snowflake.'

Hunter gritted his teeth.

Jock leaned in close, mischief twinkling in his eyes. 'So I was chatting to these lassies who work in the solicitors. They didn't see Murray, but they backed up that Fiona lassie's take on things. Saw her chatting to some boy and twatting him one. She's a feisty one, that's for sure.'

Hunter nodded slowly. He should've done that himself, canvassing locals for additional verification of the tale. But he didn't, instead heading back to his room. And not even speaking to Chantal, only one text back from her: *Busy*

The waiter came over with a tall cafetière, the plunger at full reach, the coffee darkening the water almost black. 'Is this what you want?'

'It'll do, thanks.' Jock smiled at him, giving a good measure of the famed Hunter charm that hadn't been passed down to his oldest son. He shoogled the cafetière, round and round. 'This country's going to the dogs.' Then he plunged it and poured some out into a mug. A waft of bitter steam spread across the table as he tipped in enough milk to turn the coffee muddy brown. 'What happened to employing staff who could understand what you wanted, eh?'

'I don't understand what you want, so what chance has that poor lad got?'

Jock muttered something under his breath as he slurped at his mug. 'Decent coffee, though.'

'You're seriously fasting today?'

'That a problem?'

'When you don't eat, you're like a bear with a twelve-pint hangover.' Hunter rolled his eyes. 'Oh, wait...'

'It wasn't *that* much last night.'

'Wasn't it? You were throwing them down your neck.'

Jock took another sip of coffee. 'I think we should get on this Fiona lassie's boat and see for ourselves.'

'I'm not trespassing on a bloody oil rig.'

Jock grinned. 'Chicken?'

'No, it's illegal. And I'm not paying her two hundred quid until we know for sure Murray was there.'

'How do we go about doing that, Sherlock?'

Hunter picked up his phone and called Elvis.

Unlike his bosses, Elvis still picked up. 'What's up, you fanny?' Sounded like he was in a café. Probably with Chantal's group eating a hotel breakfast.

'Just wondering if you'd spoken to Cullen yet?'

Elvis sighed down the line. 'Right, well aye.'

'What's that supposed to mean?'

'I'm doing some digging just now while I'm at my corn-flakes.' Elvis crunched and sooked. 'Thing is, it's not a simple story. You got a pen?'

14

Hunter let the automatic gearbox do the heavy lifting as he slid along the main road, lined with mature beech and oak, all seeming wild and natural to his untrained eye.

The Crafty Butcher bled out of the speakers, the only thing that seemed to pacify Jock. How the roles were reversed...

Bain: 'So, if you were thinking about New World hops in a no-deal Brexit world, would you stock up now?'

Elvis: 'Of course, Bri—Billy. You don't know how it's going to go. Nobody does. And as a hardcore home brewer, I don't want to run out of galaxy or citra hops in November as I'm putting together my Christmas IPA. Do you?'

'See, I'm thinking I might try going back to traditional British hops, make some lovely real ales.'

'Old-school. I like it. Very hard to source, though.'

Hunter reached over and killed the stereo. 'Nice car, have to say.'

'Never scrimp on your motor, son.' Jock yawned into his fist, all that caffeine still not beating its way through the hangover. 'Where the hell are we?'

Hunter floored it to climb a gradual hill, powering down the middle road through the wide Black Isle. According to Jock's satnav, the Cromarty Firth was a couple of miles north, the Moray Firth five or so south. This definitely seemed the road less travelled.

The road dipped down to an ancient gatehouse glowing in the morning gloom. Hunter slowed by the entrance and let a bus past, sitting there, the indicator ticking away. Down in the lowlands, the gatehouse would've been turned into a family home a long time ago, but this looked like it still guarded the stately home beyond from the hoi polloi. Shit, it did—a checkpoint blocked entry.

Hunter slid across the road and waited by the barrier.

'Sure this is the place, son?'

Hunter scanned around, looking for any way through. 'That's what my source told me.'

'Your source?'

'A cop mate. He got me the registered address of the owner of that rig Murray went out to.'

'This is all a bit too professional for you. I was expecting you to get that daft wee bugger to take us out there at first light.'

A bright light clicked on and a man stepped out of the front door, brandishing a clipboard, his muscular frame barely contained by his dark-grey suit.

Hunter wound down the window on Jock's side and leaned across to hold out his warrant card. 'Police. Looking for the Oswald Partnership.'

The guard clicked his tongue a few times. 'Okay, follow the road round through the trees. The receptionist will be waiting for you.' His accent was southern English, big hints of Thames Estuary but some Midlands too. Way out of place up here.

The barrier rumbled up.

'Thanks.' Hunter doffed his imaginary cap and drove through. The road narrowed to a single track, twisting through banks of rhododendrons and Scots pine.

A red squirrel darted across and Hunter hit the brakes. The car braked hard and the squirrel skipped off up a tree. 'Holy shit, I've never seen one of them before.'

'Shut up.'

'I'm serious.'

Jock shook his head, but didn't say anything.

Hunter drove off and the trees separated into a wide opening. A hulking country house was perched on top of a small hill overlooking a loch, and the road led into a half-full car park in front of a modern office building, 'Oswald Partnership' etched in bright orange on grey slate. A Victorian factory clock hung from the modern gable, reading 07:12.

Hunter parked in a guest space and hit the power button. 'Need you to stay here, okay? I'm a police officer. This is my job.' He fixed him with his hard-cop stare but it didn't seem to make any difference to Jock. 'Besides, I'm "playing the daft laddie" here.'

'Aye, well you're shit hot at that.'

'Stay here.' Hunter jabbed his finger at Jock. 'I mean it.' He got out of the car and, wonder of wonders, Jock stayed, hidden behind his broadsheet newspaper. Hunter walked across the car park towards the office, already busy for this early on a Tuesday. From somewhere in the woods behind, came the deep rumble of machinery. Probably a tree-felling operation. He stopped by the entrance to let a small Fiat past —two mid-twenties women singing along to a Beyoncé tune —then he stepped across the wet flagstones and pushed through the heavy metal door.

The place felt way too busy for this early an hour.

Inside, it was like an expensive restaurant. Granite flagstones lined at the edges with purple striplights, their glow running up the wooden reception desk and meeting at the Oswald Partnership logo.

A slim Asian man in shirt and trousers stood up with a broad smile. 'Hi, how can I help?' Didn't look like a security guard.

Hunter stepped over to the desk. 'Looking for an Iain Oswald.'

'I'm afraid that Lord Oswald's rather busy today. If you'd phoned ahead, we—'

'It's a police matter.' Hunter held out his warrant card. 'An urgent one.'

'Edinburgh police? Interesting.' The receptionist picked up a smartphone, tapped the screen and put it to his head, still with the same vacant smile. He turned away, speaking in a mutter, then back with the same smile. 'He'll see you now. Callum will show you through.'

A door flew open and a burly security guard sashayed through, his fluid movements belying his size. Callum was yet another big guy in a sharp suit — shirt open to the neck, wiry sandpaper hair poking out. He gripped Hunter's hand in an iron handshake and walked over to a wide doorway, where he swiped a card through a reader. The door clunked open and he led Hunter into a half-full open-plan office, the kind you'd see anywhere. Banter, chatting, phones ringing, coffee smells. And still Callum didn't speak.

'Bit taken aback by how many people you've got here.'

Callum didn't answer, instead marching over to the far side, where another office overlooked the loch. And he literally marched—the guy had definitely seen some time in the military. He opened the door and popped his head in, then came out with a thumbs up and let Hunter enter. Callum followed, though. Harder to play the daft laddie with an audience.

A man reclined on an office chair, feet up on an ornate mahogany desk, talking on the phone. 'Well, I'll see what we can do about that.' God knows where these guys were tailored, but he had the best-fitting suit of the lot of them. 'Of course.'

By the window, a middle-aged woman, looking Hunter up and down. Mustard-brown polo neck, checked skirt and knee-high boots. A small toy dog in her arms. She held out her hand, like she expected it to be kissed. 'Lady Margaret Oswald. How do you do?'

'DC Craig Hunter.' He shook her hand softly. 'I'm looking for Lord Oswald?'

'My husband's on a call with some clients from the Gulf. Terribly busy time.'

'Right, I'll phone you later. Thanks.' Oswald hung up and stood, hand out. 'DC Hunter?'

Hunter took it, like shaking hands with a drunk puppy compared with Callum's iron grip. 'Should I call you Lord Oswald?'

'Of course not! Lord Oswald was my father.' Oswald

slumped in his chair with a loud crunch and a happy smile. 'Please, call me Iain.'

'Okay, Iain.' Hunter took one of the chairs in front of the desk. 'Thanks for seeing me at short notice.'

'Happy to help the police at any time.' Oswald gave his wife a smile. 'I'll catch you over at the house, dear.'

'Very well.' She hugged her dog tight and left the room.

Oswald gave Callum a nod, but it didn't mean 'leave us to it'. The big guard stayed by the door, hands clasped behind his back. 'So, Detective Constable, what brings you here?'

'I gather you're the owner of Osprey Alpha?'

'Well.' Oswald nodded slowly. 'Legally, it's a complex arrangement involving—' He smiled. 'Let's just say that yes, I am the legal owner. My father built up this business to refurbish the rigs back when the oil boom started, with my assistance of course. But I'm sure you're aware the North Sea oil supply is dwindling?'

'I've heard mention of it.'

'It'll hit the Scottish economy hard, particularly Aberdeen. We've almost run out of viable oilfields and there's so much competition from fracking, and what have you, that the remaining ones are becoming uneconomical. And this climate crisis is pushing people towards electric cars, wind turbines and so on.' He paused to lick his lips, possibly aware of some tendency to digress from the point. 'Anyway, we now decommission the rigs as well as refurbishing them. As someone who's proud of what this tiny nation has achieved, I find it profoundly heart-breaking when we do, but I'm glad to be able to assist the tidy-up operation and restore the region to nature.'

'Very noble of you.'

'Glad you agree.' Oswald shuffled some papers into a pile and stuffed them into a drawer. 'Now, how can I help?'

'I'm working a missing persons investigation. A man from Edinburgh disappeared while he was up here.'

'And why should I know anything about that?'

'Because I believe he went aboard your oil rig.'

'I see. Well, oil rigs are extremely dangerous sites, especially those in the process of decommissioning. People shouldn't be snooping around them.'

Hunter sat back in the chair, eyes narrowing. 'Name of Murray Hunter.'

'Ah.' Oswald picked up a newspaper. 'I saw the notice in this morning's *P&J*. Murray Hunter, last seen in Cromarty. Says a PC David Robertson is investigating, though. Why is a DC Craig Hunter from Edinburgh showing up?'

'He was my brother.'

'And are you here officially or trying to railroad me, mm?'

'This is an official investigation, sir. I'm assisting PC Robertson. You're welcome to contact his sergeant.'

'Look, I don't mean to get off on the wrong foot, Constable, but, like I say, oil rigs are incredibly dangerous places. The wind alone... If your brother indeed went up there, it's just possible he was whipped off to sea. And most of the equipment requires formal training.'

'I want to get aboard Osprey Alpha and see for myself.'

'Oh.' Oswald swallowed. 'Well, I'd need to check.' He looked over to the door. 'Callum, can you...?'

The goon finally left the room.

Oswald seemed to relax, but only slightly. 'It might be possible for you to have a wee look, but it'd have to be supervised, of course. Only thing is, my guys are working fourteen-hour days just to clear this backlog, so it might be a while.'

'Why have you got an office full of people when you really need engineers to service oil rigs in the firth?'

'Because...' Oswald laughed. 'Listen, the grunt work is done by third parties. Here, it's all sales and relationship management. And there are relationships governing a lot of people to keep sweet. We've got three rigs sitting at Invergordon that are due in the Gulf urgently.'

'Is Osprey Alpha one of those?'

'I'm afraid it isn't, which is why it's the most hazardous. There's a lot of machinery that's incredibly dangerous in the wrong hands.'

'Sir, it'd really help my investigation if I could get up there. I just need half an hour to look around.'

'Look, it's strictly off limits until my guys can run a full inspection. And that's where our priorities have to lie.'

The door opened and Callum marched in, charging over to Oswald's side of the desk. He whispered something, and not just a few words. Sentences, paragraphs.

Oswald nodded and patted Callum's arm. 'Okay, thanks.' He grimaced at Hunter. 'Osprey Alpha is going to the dry dock at Invergordon for a full decommissioning next week. It was in the Buchan oilfield, which ceased production last year. One of the older fields out in the North Sea, a site where the operator used underbalanced drilling to allow them to keep extracting long after anyone else would bother to. As is common, that can result in extensive corrosion to the drilling equipment and to the platform itself.'

'Which means?'

'Well, I'm afraid that I can't allow anyone up there.'

'Not even your own men?'

'Well, I just don't have the resources. Like I say...' Oswald wiped a bead of sweat from his forehead. 'I'm sorry, but it's just too dangerous. I have three guys insured to go on a rig like that and they're all needed on critical tasks.'

'Thanks for your time.' Hunter stood up with a smile and passed over a business card.

Oswald inspected it, then gave Hunter a sympathetic look, his forehead creasing in all the right places. 'I'm truly sorry, though. If your brother has been up there and has perished, then I'll do everything I can to support your investigation.' He pinched his brow. 'Let me see what I can do. We might have some flex. Can I ring you?'

'I'd appreciate that, sir. I'll await your call.'

Oswald uncapped a fountain pen and scratched a note. 'And I'll also double security on Osprey Alpha to make sure no further incursions happen.'

Hunter smiled his thanks, but he knew that'd make his Plan B much less likely to succeed. And much more urgent.

HUNTER GOT in Jock's car and eased the door shut, resisting the temptation to slam it. He knew they were being watched, so didn't want to give anything away.

'Well? Did the daft laddie get anything?'

Hunter sat back and pressed his head against the rest, drumming his fingers on the wheel. 'Not sure.' He looked across the car park to the office. 'He'd heard of Murray. It was like he was expecting me.'

'That'll help fuel your James Bond fantasies.'

'Very good.' Hunter looked over at Jock and tapped the *Press and Journal*'s front page. 'He said there was an announcement in the paper.'

'Ah, right.' Jock flicked through the pages. 'Saw it myself. This your doing?'

'It's standard procedure. Once it's on the system, the press office issue it.'

Jock folded his paper up and dumped it in the door pocket. 'So, can we go up onto the platform?'

'Nope.'

'He refused the daft laddie?'

'I felt so bloody stupid in there.' Hunter rubbed his neck. 'Either something's fishy here and he's buying time, or Murray died through misadventure up on that rig.'

Jock nodded along with it. 'So what now?'

Hunter tried slumping further back in the chair, but couldn't. 'Well, we could wait around until Lord Oswald calls me and lets us on the Osprey Alpha.'

'You don't seem too happy about that.'

'We could be talking weeks. And what will we do in the meantime? Even the prospect of sitting in a café with you grumping about how hungry you are is—'

'I'm fine.'

'Aye, bollocks you are.' Hunter looked over at the office again. The sun caught the glass as it rose.

'So you want to just head up there and have a look ourselves?'

'It might be incredibly dangerous up there, but it's where Murray was last seen.' Hunter hit the start button and put the car in drive. 'Call Fiona and get her to meet us at the harbour.'

15

Hunter pulled up his hood and trudged along the Cromarty shore. Despite the early morning calm, the wind and rain were now brutal, like the sea was emptying onto land, and Noah's flood was starting today. Out at sea, waves climbed two metres high. And they were going out in that... 'I need you to behave here, okay?'

'*Behave*?' Jock looked round, his face lashed with rain, his hair plastered to his head in a severe parting. 'What do you think I'm going to do?'

'I mean it. Fiona is helping us here. She isn't working for us. Our priority is looking for Murray, not being a dickhead to him.'

'A dickhead?' Jock stepped over the low wall. 'Eh?'

'Just keep the heid.'

'I always bloody do.' Jock stomped off towards the jetty.

Fiona crouched low by a small motorboat and, unlike Jock in his leather jacket, she'd dressed for the weather, just a small hole in her hood where her bright blue eyes poked out. Hungry eyes. 'You got the money, bud?'

Jock looked round at his son.

Hunter handed her a hundred quid, folded in a roll.

She didn't even have to count. 'We said two.'

'You get the rest when we're back here, safe and sound.'

'Wanker.' Fiona pocketed the cash in her waterproof trousers. 'Come on, then.' She hopped into the boat.

Jock reached out to Hunter then took his time lowering himself into the boat, swaying around like he was ten-pints drunk. Not that Hunter had ever seen that... He sank into a seat out of the rain. 'So, hen, why didn't you go to the cops?'

Fiona looked round, eyes full of fury. 'Eh?'

Hunter hopped in and grabbed hold of Jock before he did any further damage to their relationship. 'Jesus, I told you not—'

'Are we walking into a trap here?' Jock was reaching past Hunter, giving the full force of his anger to Fiona.

'I'm not doing this out of the kindness of my heart.' Fiona was untying a rope. 'If you want to pay more, then maybe I'll start caring about your—'

'Stop!' Hunter nudged Jock with his elbow, blocking him from getting at Fiona. 'I told you about being a dickhead. Any more and we're going out without you.'

Jock's eyes bulged. 'Don't be an arse, Craig.'

'I'm not the arse here. I warned you, and you're close to the final straw.'

'Fine.' Jock looked at Fiona with the expression that had melted Hunter's mother's heart way too many times. 'I'm sorry, okay? I'm just worried about my boy.' He sat again. 'Now, can we get going?'

Fiona went back to untying her rope, and gave Hunter a thunderous stare. 'Is he always like this?'

'This is him on a good day.' Hunter sat next to Jock, giving him another warning glare.

Fiona turned on the motor, which gave with a belch of diesel fumes, and they shot off across the pitching waves onto the Cromarty Firth. The boat rocked and rolled, fast then slow, then slow then fast and—

Hunter lurched, then tipped his head over the side and vomited, his porridge looking like it'd barely been digested.

Jock clapped his back, roaring with laughter.

THE OSPREY ALPHA loomed out of the sea like a giant kraken, ready to swallow them up and take them down into the depths.

The further they'd gone down the firth, the less the boat pitched around, the less the waves foamed and leapt up at them. Hunter still felt sick, still had acid burning his throat and mouth.

Jock stroked his arm, a rare sight of parental concern. 'You okay, son?'

'I've never been in a boat before.'

'What? That's bollocks.'

'Funnily enough, my old man never took me out when I was young.'

Jock muttered something under his breath. 'What about in the army?'

'Not in my training, no.' The boat tipped again and

Hunter felt his stomach turn upside down. He leaned over the side, staring deep into the brine, but nothing came up.

'Christ, son, you should've just skipped breakfast and saved yourself the hassle.'

'This isn't funny.' Hunter couldn't even look round at Jock. Another dry heave, but still nothing.

THEY APPROACHED the column of oil rigs, which seemed impossibly tall this close. The dirty spray of rain obscured any names or signage and all four looked identical. Lights glowed high up the nearest and one further over. From the nearest platform, a walkway ran out across the water, stopping about a hundred metres away from another, darker rig, just leaving a sharp drop into the sea. Behind, a low town spread along the coastline.

'Invergordon.' Fiona was following Hunter's gaze. 'Bandit country, bud. Full of third- or fourth-generation Weegies. Lads who left Govan to work up here. Now it's the only place where that work still exists. Try to avoid going anywhere near.'

'Will anyone spot us?'

'In this?' Fiona winked at him. She clapped his arm, her grip lingering maybe a bit too long. 'Get yourselves ready.' She steered them towards the oil rig, the one past the end of the walkway. The platform loomed above them, dark against the pale-grey sky, concrete legs covered in barnacles and other shells. No signs of life up there, no lights and none of the industrial grinding coming from its neighbour. She stopped at a small jetty next to one of the legs and moored the boat. A narrow steel ladder, rusted to a coffee brown, ran up to the platform, which seemed like miles above their heads. A massive winch hung over, with a giant hook to scoop supplies up. Probably not even connected to the power.

Fiona stood, hands on hips. 'Right, I'll wait here for you.'

'Oh no, you bloody don't.' Jock stood over her, like he was trying to intimidate her, though the rocking of the boat was undermining the effect. 'Last time a Hunter came here, the boatsman came back without him. You're going up there first.'

'This isn't part of the deal.'

'He's right.' Hunter stood next to Jock, arms folded. 'You're coming with us.'

'Christ.' Fiona finished hitching the boat to the side, shaking her head and moaning under her breath. 'Seriously, another hundred bar and I'd be happy to come up with you.'

Jock grabbed her arm. 'You're already getting paid enough for this.'

'Bloody hell.' Fiona set off up the ladder like a monkey climbing a tree, hands and feet barely touching the rungs.

'Okay.' Hunter went next. He placed one hand, then the other, on the slimy metal— it felt like it'd been underwater for years. As soon as both feet were on, he started to feel better. More stable and above the level of the waves. Felt less like he was going to throw up again. 'See you up there.' He started climbing and soon got into a rhythm—left, right, left, right, left right. Looking north, another four rigs forming a procession to Invergordon, the town's lights flickering in the morning grey.

His foot slipped, and he pulled his body close to the

ladder while he caught his breath again. He looked down at Jock, only a few rungs above the jetty. Hunter must've done at least thirty. Good progress. He started up again.

What the hell was Murray up to, coming up here, just for his YouTube channel? Poking around a derelict oil rig with torches and cameras to get kids to sit through adverts and pay off his colossal mortgage? Who was Hunter trying to fool? Murray was earning so much he'd just paid cash for the house.

And where the hell was he? Were they going to find his body at the top?

Hunter clambered up onto the platform that marked the halfway point and waited in the spitting rain. The wind was stronger now, pushing with a force he hoped he could overcome, but he was getting less and less sure. Thick rain poured down on the firth, blocking the view back to Cromarty. The view down the Black Isle towards Dingwall was clear, but the North Sea was a wall of grey, like the elements didn't want anyone heading out there.

The metal rang out in a slow rhythm and Jock's head peered over the top, a few jerky movements bringing the rest of him up and over. He collapsed to his knees, breathing heavily, his face screwed tight. 'Christ on the cross.' He gulped in more air, then frowned. 'Is that Tain over there?'

Hunter followed his gaze across the land to the north. Nigg, or whatever it was called on the map. 'Don't be daft. There's a ton of hills between here and Tain.'

'Swear I can see it.'

And you can see pink elephants, you old lush.

Hunter didn't say it.

'That lassie's got a bloody cheek. Another hundred quid

to go up there?' Jock grabbed the up ladder and set off ahead of him, taking it slow and not very steady.

'Keep the heid, Jock.' Hunter followed him up, settling into a much slower groove than when he'd been unhindered, but maybe a steadier one. And the stronger wind meant that slow was a better idea.

'Should've gone to the police when she heard what happened to Murray, I swear. She knew, didn't she?'

Hunter was catching enough to get the general drift, but the occasional word was swept out to sea.

'If anything's happened to my boy, I'll drop her off the bloody side.'

'In front of a police officer?'

'Maybe I'll drop you as well.' Jock looked down, grinning. His eyes bulged and he looked up again.

'Don't even joke about it.' Hunter had to slow his rhythm again. Left hand, left foot. Right hand, right foot. Over and over, until Jock slipped over the edge. Then it was Hunter's turn to climb over the last rungs onto the platform.

Up here, the wind screamed in his ears. The rain battered his face, making it a struggle to keep his eyes open. His jacket was nowhere near up to the task and he was already soaked.

The platform was deserted and a lot bigger than Hunter expected. Grey sheet metal covered in rust and giant bolts where equipment had been locked in, but was now mostly missing. Painted white signs pointed to the helicopter platform, but even that had been taken away. The winch's cable swung in the gale, and the only other thing standing was the living quarters, according to the signs, a two-storey grey block almost indistinguishable from the sky. Four CCTV cameras, but none had the telltale red blink, and two had their cables severed.

Hunter had a flash of the video in Murray's notes. It was here. The live feed had broadcast from here.

Fiona shrugged her shoulders. 'Okay, so what's the plan?'

Hunter didn't see many options. And he didn't know what he expected, maybe Murray running towards them as they came over the top. 'Let's start with the living quarters.'

'That's pretty much where we'll finish.' She set off, stepping slowly through the maelstrom.

Hunter followed equally jerkily, too busy keeping the icy rain off his frozen cheeks to check on Jock.

Fiona stopped by the door.

Someone had snapped open the padlock. Murray? Or someone else?

'Let me.' Hunter eased the door open and peered inside. Looked like a canteen, pretty large too. Mercifully free of any wind or rain, but it stank of rust and rotting meat. Rows of bolted-in tables and seats ran down the middle. A bar and serving hatch occupied the far side, though the window through to the kitchen was boarded up. Old-school CRT TVs hung from the ceiling, their power cables dangling free. Hunter hadn't seen any satellite dishes outside, but that's how they'd while away their weeks at sea, watching satellite football in here. That and the pair of table tennis tables in the corner, a bat still resting on a ball on one side. A smashed-in fruit machine lurked in the other corner. Either someone had lost big style or just wanted to destroy something.

'Jesus, it's all pish lagers.' Jock was inspecting the taps, his face as sour as the beer he'd been drinking the previous night. Didn't stop him tugging on one, though it ran dry.

'Stop it.' Hunter waited until Jock looked over, then followed Fiona over to the door marked 'Quarters'. Through it, the corridor split left, right and straight ahead, with a staircase leading up. He took a look up the stairwell, but it seemed just as dead as the mess hall. 'Right, let's split up. This floor, then regroup and check upstairs.'

'Suits me.' Fiona walked through the door on the right, leaving it hanging open.

'Born in a bloody barn...' Jock scowled but didn't rush over to shut the door behind her. Maybe betraying a fear of what might be behind it. 'Right. Back here in ten, okay?'

'Works for me. I'm going to keep a close eye on her.'

'Wise.' Jock took the straight-ahead corridor.

Hunter followed Fiona. The first door hung open. Empty, just a bunk bed screwed to the wall, the lower mattress full of exposed springs, the upper intact but heavily stained.

Fiona winked at him. 'Fancy a bunk up?'

'Seriously? I'm hunting for my brother here.'

'Come on, I'm a girl, you're a boy...'

The sink was dry, but no doubt pissed in more times than in Scott Cullen's flat.

'Look, I'm in a relationship.'

'Don't know what you're missing.' She sauntered off out of the room.

But Hunter saw something in her. Spending fortnights at sea, the only woman on a boat. She didn't seem to shag around, but she must've put up with so much hassle. And this is how she dealt with it. Teasing.

Hunter followed. He tried the door across the corridor

and got the same result. The next door was a shared bathroom. Mouldy curtains hung over two baths. Two shower stalls were smashed in, the precious pipework long since removed. Two toilet cubicles with dry bowls. The fractured remains of sinks—someone had gone to town on them with a sledgehammer, leaving broken porcelain all over the floor.

'You finding what you expected?'

'Not really.' Hunter went back out into the corridor and crept up to the end, ten more bedrooms on either side, three more bathrooms. A door led out to the other side of the platform, just a narrow walkway leading to a ladder down.

No signs that Murray had been here, no signs that anyone had for a long time.

'Come on.' He led Fiona back to the meeting point, taking it slow and double-checking the bedrooms and bathrooms again. No sign of Jock, but still three minutes to go.

'Maybe I'll try it on with your dad.'

'Seriously?'

'He's a good-looking guy.' She looked anything but relaxed, her nervous gaze sweeping around.

'Come on.' Hunter opened the door leading straight on.

'Look at the state of this.' Jock stood in a doorway halfway up, sifting through a box. 'Christ, they've got all flavours here.'

Hunter joined him. DVD cases and magazines. Porn. Lots of porn. 'Jesus.'

'No internet out in a North Sea oilfield, son, so you have to keep it old-school.'

'Take your word for it.'

Fiona ambled up the corridor towards the window at the far end.

Jock frowned, staring into space. 'Here, maybe they're Murray's jazz mags. Normal straight stuff. Just like his old man.'

'What, a wanker?'

'Shut up, Craig.'

'What's the big deal with him being gay, anyway?'

'He's not gay!'

Knowing not to argue with him when he was like this, Hunter checked down the corridor. 'You found anything else?'

Fiona was looking through one of the doorways. She turned to shrug.

Jock inspected a magazine. 'Hard to get past this little treasure trove. Reckon I could get a few quid for this lot on eBay.' He kept flicking through. 'Christ, you don't get many of them to the pound.'

Hunter checked the next room. A backpack rested against the wall next to the bed. He opened it and found another cornucopia of pornography. He took it back out to the corridor. 'Here's another load.'

But no sign of Jock.

Hunter looked both ways, fearing the worst—his father hunched over a bathroom sink, a jazz mag in his left hand and—

But Jock came out of the next doorway and thumbed back into the room.

Hunter took it slow and walked in. Jock had dumped his porn collection on the lower bunk but a sheet of paper lay where the pillow should be. A message, dated last Monday:

'Murray, I'll meet you back at the cottage—Keith.'

'Who the hell is Keith?'

'No idea.'

Hunter checked the note again. 'This not being our Murray is way too much of a coincidence. And last Monday...' He let out a deep breath. 'Where the hell is he? Is that—'

Footsteps thumped towards them. Fiona, running, eyes wild. 'There's a boat on its way over!'

16

Hunter shot through the canteen and stopped by the door to the platform to peer out. The sky had brightened to brilliant blue, the grey pushed over to the mainland.

Fiona joined him and pointed over towards the other rig. 'See them, bud?'

Hunter squinted, struggling to see what she was on about. Then he caught it. A speedboat, the noise muted by the roaring gale, but the bright-white slipstream glowed in the murky green-brown water. Just one, though, and it slipped out of view under the rig.

Meaning it was going to moor.

Meaning someone would come up.

Hunter checked around. Shite—four CCTV cameras. Shouldn't have assumed they were all as dead as the rest of the rig. 'How do we get back to your boat?'

'This way.' Fiona pushed through the door and snaked

off across the platform, keeping low, but she didn't have much to hide behind.

Heavy breathing announced Jock's presence. 'What's going on?'

'Someone's come over. We need to go.' Hunter pushed Jock through the door. 'Hurry!' He set off after his father, but Jock was slow, and still carrying his porn haul.

Hunter snatched it out of his hands and tossed it behind them. 'Jesus!'

'Why the hell did you do that?' Jock's legs slipped from under him, and he crashed onto the platform with a damp thud.

Hunter reached down to help him, but Jock was a dead weight. 'We need to hurry!'

Jock rolled to his side, then got up on his knees. 'Why did you—'

'Come on!' Hunter grabbed his arm and yanked him, fast-walking through the heavy wind and across the slimy platform. God knows what it was like out at sea, probably had secure walkways to stop this nonsense.

Fiona stood by the ladder, pointing down. 'Big guy climbing up that leg.'

'Just one?'

'Right.'

Hunter peered down the ladder. A man mountain winched himself up the ladder—a different technique from Fiona's spider-monkey one, but just as fast. Clang, clang, clang, clang. 'You recognise him?'

'Nope.'

'Hide.' Hunter pointed to a low wall by the nearest leg

and dragged Jock over, pinning him down and covering his mouth with a hand. He waited, listening to the clanking.

The guy appeared over the edge of the ladder. He was huge and didn't seem perturbed by the gale. Black fishing gear, glistening with rain. He tugged his hood down. Completely bald head, almost pink from the cold. He scanned the area, looking right at them.

Shite!

Hunter ducked low and listened hard again, but the wind and rain were too loud to hear any footsteps. Could be standing over them, could be miles away. He sneaked another look.

The guy was by the door to the crew quarters. 'You!' He stormed towards them. 'You're trespassing.'

Hunter tried to show his warrant card, but his hands weren't doing what they told him to. 'I'm a cop.'

The words didn't seem to make any odds. 'Have you got a search warrant?' Slight Russian accent. 'This is private property.'

'Do you work for Lord Oswald?'

'What are you doing here?'

'Looking for my brother. Murray Hunter.'

The guy reached into his pocket and pulled out a gun. 'You are going to—'

Then he toppled forward.

Jock stood behind him, lugging a length of metal pipe. 'Take that, you prick!'

Hunter let out a breath. 'Jesus.'

'The boy pulled a gun on you!'

Hunter searched the guy for ID. Nothing. He scanned around the deck. 'Where is his gun?'

Jock frowned. 'Lost track of it.'

Hunter grabbed the guy's lapels and checked his wound. Blood and already showing signs it'd bruise. He was out of it. Hunter slapped him. But the guy didn't wake up.

'There's more boats coming here!' Fiona was shouting over the screech of the wind. 'We need to go!'

Hunter patted him down and found a phone in a zipped-up map pocket by the collar. He checked it. Locked, but it clearly wasn't his. The background was a photo of Murray Hunter and a man with a soul patch, hugging on some beach somewhere.

So Murray had been there. And this guy either had Murray's phone, or he had his friend's. Assume it was Keith.

Hunter stared at their attacker and wanted to drag all of the information out of him. Find out what he knew about Murray. But he'd pulled a gun on them and if his mates were as hostile, then they were in deep shit. No chance he could get him down the ladder, even if he weighed as little as Fiona.

She waved a hand in front of his face. 'Come on!'

'Go!' Hunter grabbed Jock and hauled him over to their ladder, pushing him to go first.

The old bugger stepped over and eased himself down, even slower than his walking pace.

Fiona went next, and Hunter stood there, watching for any more predators, the polyrhythmic clanging from below. Then he grabbed the ladder and followed Fiona down, both having to keep to Jock's slow pace. Still, no man left behind. Seemed to take forever, keeping his head looking up as he descended, but he soon reached the halfway point.

Jock was already on the second section.

Fiona stood there, fists clenched. 'Bud, this is worth—'

'Keep going!' Hunter pushed her towards the ladder.

'Hoy!' The guy was at the top, staring at them from above. 'Stop!'

Hunter didn't answer, instead rushing down the ladder, climbing fast.

A gunshot rang out, echoing like it was fired into the sky rather than down at them.

Hunter's left hand slipped and he fell, but he caught himself on the lower rung. He stopped to look back up.

The man slid down the upper ladder at a rapid lick, but no sign of the handgun.

Below, Fiona's boat started up.

Hunter set off again towards the jetty—fast, fast, fast.

The metal clanged. Above, the man was on the lower ladder now, heading right for them.

Hunter tried to go faster. Not long now. But the guy was closing on him. He let go with his right hand to reach down, but his foot slipped and he tried to correct his grip. His other foot squeaked away from the metal and he plummeted to the jetty, landing with a crunch.

The air flew out of his lungs. Stars spun in front of his eyes.

He tried to get up but couldn't.

The man was almost down at Hunter's level, powering down a ladder like nobody should be able to, at least nobody that size. Each rung, he seemed to grow.

Hunter rolled over and pushed up. His ribs felt like someone had tried tearing them out with pliers, but had given up halfway through and left them all broken and twisted. He got up to standing and rested against a pillar.

The boat was ten metres away. Fiona was pleading with him. 'Come on!'

The man jumped the last few metres, landing with a clatter.

Hunter stumbled towards the boat and toppled in, landing on the floor. If it was called the floor. He didn't know. His ribs burned and the stars were still spinning.

The engine revved and the boat rumbled off across the water. 'Shite!' Fiona kept looking behind her. 'Who the hell is that?'

All Hunter could do was lie there, panting hard and heavy, his chest burning. He checked across his chest for telltale holes or blood. Nothing. Just sweat and hair.

Hunter pushed himself up. Two speedboats shot towards the oil platform. 'Can we get away from them?'

'On it.' Fiona pulled a handle and their boat blasted through the waves.

Hunter looked back towards the rigs but couldn't see any sign of approaching boats, not that his eyesight was up to much. Saw double, quadruple, octuple of everything. And the stars were denser, more tightly packed and swimming faster. He let himself take a breath, but it hurt like someone was stabbing his chest. His heart was thudding, his whole body shaking like it hadn't since Kandahar.

He knew what he needed to do to calm down, but the prospect of a boat filled with gunmen ploughing towards them meant he couldn't bring himself to do it.

A speck appeared in the distant foam. Was that a boat? No, it was a seal coming up to eat. Of all the times to see that.

Hunter gave another scan of the horizon and decided they were clear. The boat's diesel fumes stung his nostrils.

Salty tang on his lips. He turned to face the land Fiona was navigating them towards.

The wide sandy beach sprawled ahead of them. Dark clouds blocked out the sun, a faint disc hanging above the town. The lights of Cromarty glowed in the grey morning. Behind, the Sutors were a grey-blue, those giant hills guarding the narrow entrance to the firth from the sea.

And he was back. Heart rate back to seventy. Under control.

Unlike Jock, who couldn't keep his manic eyes from the distant threat. 'The bastard had a gun!'

Fiona was remarkably calm, steering them towards the small harbour, her singing lost in the engine drone. Hunter kept catching snatches of melody and she could carry a tune, but he had no idea what it was. Probably some sea shanty.

Jock stuffed his hands in his pockets. He was shivering and trying to hide it too. 'Did we learn anything?'

Hunter sat up and tried to process everything. His lizard brain had been in charge, focused on getting them the hell out of there. And now... Now it was for the mammalian brain to process everything, to plot out moves and strategies, to rationalise everything, to connect dots.

And that part had very little to offer.

He let out a slow breath, keeping his focus on the horizon. 'All we've got from our excursion is the possibility that Murray might've been there. And the name Keith, I suppose.'

'He *was* there.' Jock reached into his pocket and his shaking hand held out the paper with the message.

Hunter took hold of it. It wasn't evidence anymore, but it

was information. Intelligence. A lead. Hope. He tried to swallow it down.

Jock shook his head. 'Craig, something's happened to your brother on that rig. That boy meant business. I mean, you've got all your ninja stuff, but you were lucky I found that pipe because if I hadn't, you'd be in the water.' He swallowed hard. 'And I'd have no sons left.'

Hunter struggled to wrap his brain around the reality of Murray being dead. Before, it'd been a prospect, but that armed numbskull drawing on a police officer? It was real now.

'I don't know what happened up there, son, but your brother had a habit of finding trouble. Or it found him.'

Hunter looked at the note again. 'Any idea who Keith is?'

'Your guess is as good as mine, son.'

'You were staying at Murray's house for two weeks and he didn't mention a Keith?'

'Your brother doesn't exactly confide his deepest, darkest secrets to me.' Jock stood as they came in to the jetty, keeping perfectly still against the rolling waves.

Hunter stared off at the distant oil rig, hazy and blue. Maybe the guy was just working on another rig, finding out who was trespassing on their property. But in no way would anyone doing that shoot at a cop. He looked over at Fiona, who was mooring the boat to the wharf. 'Did you get a plate off the boat?'

'A *plate*?' Fiona roared with laughter. 'It's not a car.'

'So what is it?'

'You're looking for the boat's name. And theirs was covered. Whoever they are, they don't want to leave a trail.'

'You recognise them?'

'Afraid not. It was a Bayliner 2855, unless I'm very much mistaken. No idea where they're docked, mind. Cost you fifty grand if you could find one.' Her gaze narrowed. 'Look, can I stay with you guys? I don't feel safe after what happened to Shug.' She looked back out to sea. 'That big guy must've killed him too.'

'Figures.' Jock frowned at Hunter. 'You think those guys worked for that Oswald boy?'

'I need to find out.'

17

Jock drove along the road, his podcast blasting out. Fiona was in the passenger seat, staring out of the window. Down on the beach, a couple walked their dog, tossing a tennis ball into the surf at high tide. The dog was having the time of its life. Dropping the ball at the man's feet and rushing for it as he hurled it into the brine. A red car followed the curve to follow the road along the river.

No sign of any armed Russian operatives.

The guy was hard as nails. And skilled. Hunter assumed the accent was Russian, but he heard so little of it he couldn't be sure. Could equally be Israeli, Ukrainian, or any flavour of eastern European, either inside the EU tent or outside.

Hunter's phone rang. Chantal's grinning face beamed out, snapped late at night when they'd been drinking. She looked happy. He answered and she sounded anything but. 'What's up?' Her yawn rattled the speaker.

'Morning.' Hunter touched his ribs and the bruises bit

back. Didn't feel like he'd cracked anything, none of that tell-tale ache, but it didn't stop it hurting. 'How you doing?'

'Not good. Barely slept and I've got two missed calls and five texts from you. And Scott wants me and Elvis to interview someone assaulted by an Albanian.'

Albanian?

Did that hang together better? Most of the heroin in the UK was run by them, sometimes in tandem with Turkish gangs. The Met closed down a gang in Southend the year before, tied to some assassinations in London.

'Sorry.' Hunter focused on a Range Rover behind them, the gunmetal catching the sparse sunlight. 'We went out to this oil rig and—'

'CRAIG! What the hell were you doing on an oil rig?'

'Long story. We were following my brother's trail to—'

'Jesus Christ!'

'But we found a message to Murray from someone called Keith and...' Hunter got the sheet of paper out of his pocket. Next to Keith's still-locked mobile. 'Someone was there and they... we got away.'

'You can't help yourself, can you?'

'This was...' A sigh eased out of his lips, giving only the mildest jab of pain. 'No, you're right. I can't.'

'Did you speak to the owner?'

'First thing. He told us not to go.'

'Wonder why...' Another rasping sigh. 'I'm coming up there right now.'

'Chantal, it's fine. We got away.'

'No, it's not. I'll speak to Scott, get some time off and get the train or I can hire a car. Shite, I'll even get the *bus*. You can't go up on oil rigs, you stupid bastard. You can't get into fights with people and—'

'Can you get Elvis to check who owned the boats that chased us?'

She paused, air rattling her microphone. 'I'll ask him. But seriously, do I need to—'

'No. Look, I shouldn't have told you.'

'No, you arsehole, you should've. Like you should've told me about your father not being dead. Christ, Craig. What's up with you?'

'I'm sorry.'

'And if this was the other way round, you'd just tell me it's all fine?' She left a space he couldn't honestly fill. 'I'll speak to Scott. Don't do anything stupid in the meantime.'

'Seriously, I'll be fine. Don't come. Okay?'

'Craig, is there something else going on?'

'Of course not. Look, can you look into that Oswald guy for me? I get a bad feeling about him.'

'A hunch, great.'

'Chantal, my brother went up on his oil rig and went missing. I did the same and some big security brute chased us off.'

'And you're heading there now?'

'If Oswald knows where Murray is or what's happened to him...'

'Makes sense, I suppose.'

'Thanks. Love you.'

'Mm. Love you too, Craig, but you push it at times.' And she was gone.

Fiona craned her neck round, a mischievous grin on her face. 'That the ball and chain?'

'Her name's Chantal.' Hunter watched the Range Rover overtake them.

'So what the hell are you going to do, big guy?'

Hunter didn't know. Assume him and this Keith went to the rig and someone got kidnapped. By Oswald's people? Or by some Albanian gang? Or aliens? Or nuclear-powered Aztecs or Incas?

'Here we go.' Jock slowed for the gatehouse entrance to the Oswald estate. The guard took one look at them and waved them through.

Through the trees, Hunter watched the building. Seemed even busier than first thing. Smokers outside the front door.

A Range Rover was parked nearby, and a big lump got out the driver's side. The guy from the oil rig.

'Turn round.'

Jock glanced at Hunter. 'Eh?'

'Turn round. Leave.' Hunter tried to disarm him with a smile. 'That's our friend from the oil rig.'

'He's a henchman working for that Oswald boy?'

'It's likely.'

'So let's pile in there and grab him.'

'Not the smartest move, Dad. There's a possibility Murray's alive. We bring that guy in, there's no chance we'll find him.'

Jock cleared the gatehouse and took a hard right, back towards Cromarty. 'So the trail's cold?'

The trail wasn't as cold as he'd thought. If they could find Keith, or Fiona's mate who took them to the rig, then maybe—

'So this Lord Oswald boy is involved?'

It was hard to tell. Very hard to tell, but it felt like he was hiding something. As well as knowing more than he should, he was evasive. It felt like too much of a stretch, at least with the information to hand.

Hunter looked round at Jock. 'Involved in what, though?'

'Drugs, people trafficking. Could be anything.'

'Why would someone like Oswald need to run a drug operation?'

Jock's nostrils flared. 'You need to listen to me, son. That boy shot at us!'

'Look, don't mention that to anyone, okay?'

'Why?'

'Just trust me.'

'Fine, but I think we should get over to that boy's office, pin him to the table until he spills.'

'Aye, that's exactly what'll happen.' Hunter rolled his eyes.

Jock glared at Fiona. 'What about you, toots? You know this guy?'

'Never heard of him. Toffs like that never speak to the likes of me. And please don't call me toots in front of him. He'll get jealous.'

Jock laughed. 'Where we headed?'

THE MOWAT BREWERY Coffee Shop was all hard edges— wooden tables and chairs, granite slabs and bar—and the sound echoed like a dub techno twelve inch.

Fiona led Hunter over to a table, away from Jock and the rest of the beer fiends. 'What we doing here?'

'One, I need that old git to get some food in him before I kill him.' He nodded over at Jock, shovelling beer nuts into his face as he soaked in the laughter from his sudden best mates. 'Two, I need to think through what to do now.'

'Isn't Jock right? Shouldn't you go in there?'

'If he's right, then I don't want to admit it to him.'

Fiona laughed just as a waiter appeared with their drinks. Hot chocolate for her, tea for him.

'Thanks.' Hunter nodded him away, then poured a cup for himself. Jock was supping a coffee at the bar. No doubt being tempted by a brewery tour, though it was surprising he hadn't already tried to organise a piss-up. 'Fiona, you said you haven't seen Shug since last Sunday, right?'

Fiona sipped from her mug. 'Right?'

'But you said you'd spoken to him.'

Fiona blew on her hot chocolate but didn't take a sip. 'Right, so I got a WhatsApp off him a few days ago.' She took another sip and grimaced. 'Shug was saying he's away, wouldn't tell me where. Just abroad.'

'Abroad?'

'Shug's a bit of a shagger. Always heading to Thailand, if you catch my drift.'

'Great. You think he's there?'

'Could be. Or it could be someone else has his phone. Didn't stack up and, until I see the boy with my own peepers, I'm not believing anything. I mean, you could check flights to Bangkok, right?'

Hunter held out his hands. 'Can I see your phone?'

'Rather you didn't.' Fiona slurped at the hot chocolate.

Hunter snatched the phone off her. The screen was filled with a photo of his arse as he bent over to tie his laces.

'Really?' She was blushing.

He switched apps and found the recent message from Shug. Unanswered. But it showed Shug as being online.

Fiona
Hey boy, u ok?

Shug
Why wouldn't I be
Lol

Hunter started typing, trying to copy Fiona's clipped style:

Oil rig shite?
Cop here asking about the boys

Ffs
Shite
What did you say????

Relax bud
Said nothing
But one of your boy's is missing
Any ideas?

Best keep you out of it

Cheers
So?

So whit?

What should I tell the pricks

Nowt

Cops bud
Not taking piss off for an answer

Lol
Sod it

Then it said 'Shug is typing...' but no message.
Hunter let out a sigh and walked over to the window. The
smartphone buzzed again.

Shug
Took the pair of them to the oil rig and they went up but
only the mate came back and he was freaking out

That matched what they knew so far.

The hell happened up there bud?

This boat came out of nowhere
Thought it was the coasties
Started ma engine
Shot off
But this Keith kid was climbing down the ladder
Went back for him
Then pissed off again

Didn't say what happened but took the boy back to Crom
Kid said he was leaving
Not seen the dick since mate

                                        Say where?

No idea

                                        You go to the cops?

Kid told me not to
Should of seen him dude
Shiteing it
Got to land and he shot off like bat oot ay hell

                                        Where you at?

Left these camera things in the back

        Hunter stared at the screen, trying to keep calm.

                                        Cameras?

Heid ones
Like mountain bikers
Or canoers
Or porn lol

                                        You still got them?

Aye

Going to sell them but
Bloody hell
Pure shiteing it about the boys in the boat

Cops after them bud

Christ's sake
Must of seen mah name on boat reg
Be turning up at mah door any day noo
Well ahm long gone
Long! Gone!

Where u?

Walls have ears Fi
Ah'll call when ah'm back

Mind if I look at the cameras?

You wantin to get into porn eh lol

LOL
Maybe
Girl needs to earn a crust
Bud I'll see if there's anything I can give the pigs
Throw them off your scent eh?

Good idea
Keys under the gnome

18

'That's it there.' Fiona pointed out of the window.
A ramshackle cottage on the right, one-and-a-half storeys, bare stone, with bay windows downstairs and squat dormers poking out of the roof. Either side of the door, a thin strip of unruly plants passed for a front garden.

Hunter drove on down the narrow street, past more fishing cottages like you'd find in any town or village north of Edinburgh. Fortrose could be Forfar, Forres or Fort William.

'We not stopping, bud?'

'Not outside, no.' Hunter pulled up at the stop junction. Not much traffic, just a tractor parked outside a Co-op that looked more like a house than a shop. He pulled into the car park and killed the engine. 'Stay here.'

Fiona was in the passenger seat, tapping away at her phone. 'I'm looking after *him*?'

Jock was in the back seat, drinking a massive coffee from a paper cup. 'Good point. Why are you still here?'

'Like he's letting me go.' Fiona went back to her phone. 'He's chaos, bud. He can't be controlled.'

Hunter waited until she looked up. 'You're crapping yourself, aren't you?'

'Thinking you pair are my best bet. Strength in numbers, bud. Plus my name's mud in Crom just now.'

'Well, just keep an eye on him.' Hunter turned round and locked eyes with Jock. 'Same with you. Stay with her and make sure she doesn't bolt.'

'Sure thing, son.' He slurped coffee, oblivious to what else was going on.

Hunter got out and walked over to the corner. The tractor trundled past, belching out fumes. The hoodie-wearing lump saluted a dapper gent outside the Co-op. Hunter crossed and walked up Shug's street. Only a couple of parked cars on the road, and nowhere near enough room for a porch let alone a drive.

Halfway up, he bent to tie shoelaces that didn't need tying. Gave him a chance to scope the area better than the cursory glance before.

Shug's small cottage wasn't directly overlooked. Over the road, a side-on bungalow sat in some actual garden, surrounded by a tall wall. Looked like a clone further up.

Both neighbouring cottages looked post-war rather than two centuries old.

A silver Range Rover slid past.

Hunter couldn't figure out if it was the one he saw in Cromarty. Unlikely. Or extremely likely. That was gunmetal grey, but then so was the sky. Now the sun was out, that could lighten to silver.

Either way, he set off again towards the cottage, but he knew there wasn't a front garden, meaning any gnomes were round the back. A drive led to a garage behind the left-hand neighbour, with a gate into Shug's garden.

Hunter opened it with a squeal, walking into the garden like he was here to water Shug's plants while he was off shagging half of Thailand. He stopped by the garden hose and looked around for anyone who might've heard. Nobody even who cared. Over the hedge was a grand old house, maybe a manse or just a wealthier local, but no sounds of kids playing or anyone gardening. Not the season for either.

He spotted a row of gnomes. Not what he'd expected. They wore bondage gear and demonstrated sexual kinks: one was being whipped by another one; one wore a gimp suit; another was hanging from a noose, wearing fishnets, with an oversized lemon in his mouth; and the last one held a candle to his exposed genitals.

And his candle hid a key.

Thank god for vice-signalling sexual deviants.

Hunter walked over to the back door and unlocked it. Another look around, no sign or sound that he was being followed. He carefully unlocked it and nudged the door open. Again, listening hard. Inside, the walls were covered in all of the deviant artworks you'd expect. The tennis girl scratching her arse. Charlie the Seahorse smoking a spliff. A Del Amitri album cover blown up to Ao.

A harsh rubbery smell he couldn't place. Given the gnomes, he didn't want to.

The place was an absolute midden, stuff lying everywhere: CDs lying on DVD cases; clothes on the kitchen floor; a week's worth of dirty dishes. Hard to figure out if it was a life lived in chaos, someone who'd split in a hurry, or if someone had cased the joint before Hunter.

A few open cardboard boxes lay on the kitchen counter. Box one had packaged Funko Pop dolls, squished-down versions of Iron Man, Captain America and other Marvel superheroes. Next box was filled with more Funko Pops, this time from *The Walking Dead*.

The third box had a GoPro camera inside.

He knew he should go, but Hunter popped the front panel and unlocked it. He'd used a similar device in his fell running days, a birthday present from Murray, and this wasn't so far advanced that he needed to consult a manual. The screen showed a list of video files. He opened on the last one.

Video started playing, filling the screen. Whoever wore it crept across the rig platform, without anywhere near as much wind as he'd faced that morning. The camera seemed head-mounted, but that bit lower than you'd expect. They came at the crew quarters from a different angle than Hunter and Jock had, and entered via the corridor Jock was supposed to search, where they'd found the note.

Keith—assuming it was him—ran along it, passing the room with Jock's porn, and into the recreation area. The sound swelled, the tiny speakers nowhere near good enough to reproduce the detailed room noises. Keith chanced a look backwards and started writing the note to Murray. He left it on a bed, then slipped out and raced along the corridor. He stopped by the door and peered out. No sign of Murray now. So he walked onto the main deck. He peered down and Shug's boat was still there, but he was leaving.

Keith ran after him, sliding down the ladder like a fireman. Guy was clearly in the top percentile of physically fit. Where Hunter had been in his squaddie days.

The boat was now twenty metres or so away. Shug spotted Keith's waving arms and seemed to think it through.

Keith looked into his hands—clutching a giant block of white powder; cocaine, maybe, or pure heroin—then at Shug coming back.

A voice called from above and he looked up. A man was up on the platform, with Murray. Looked like the same guy who'd shot at Hunter, who Jock twatted with that pipe.

'Here, get in!' Shug's boat was down at the jetty. No time to dock, just rocking with the waves.

Keith gave Murray a final wave then jumped in the boat, landing on his side and looking back as they shot off around the oil rig.

A speedboat was moored at the far side of the rig, the same one that chased them, or at least the same model.

The video stopped and Hunter played it all through. The video tallied with what Shug told them over WhatsApp.

That block of drugs, though? Jesus.

Hunter played the second-last file.

Murray swung round, pointing his camera back out to sea.

'There's enough here for, like, ten shows.' That voice again, peering into the crew quarters, looking exactly as Hunter had left them that morning. The ping pong table, the games machines, the copious pornography, the TVs. 'Hello?'

He walked through the door, taking it much slower than Hunter had when they'd visited, and stopped at the pinball table. A hand reached over and pulled the lever, then let it go again. He crouched low and flicked the power but the table stayed dead. Then he walked over to the bar and fiddled with the dry taps just like Jock had. Seemed bored, if nothing else.

He walked back to the crew quarters and took the left fork. He stopped dead and crouched low. Inside the first room was a pile of cardboard boxes that hadn't been there that morning. Keith sidled up to one and eased the packing tape off. He pried the flaps apart but the camera took a while to resolve the image.

Blocks of heroin, hundreds of them, just like the one he had on the other video. But so much of it.

'Hot shit.' Keith took a bag and turned it round in his hands. 'There's at least a hundred bags here. This is over a kilo. Smack or coke, Muz. Must be billions of quid.'

The camera pointed over at the door back to the deck, but it was shut and rattling in the wind.

Keith sighed and walked over. He stopped dead, then the camera swung round to point at a man still standing out on the oil rig platform, his features hidden in the darkness, the camera struggling to cope with the bright sunlight coming from behind.

Hunter pressed pause, his heart fluttering. He could make out the face.

Murray.

But he was holding his hands up. The trail was heating up again, but Hunter couldn't see who was pointing the gun at him.

Hunter hit play and Keith seemed to put his head to the door, like he was listening. Heavy footsteps pounded past.

A man's voice. Either the microphone didn't catch it or the speakers couldn't reproduce it accurately, but it was hard to figure out what was being said.

'—You are not supposed to be here. As much as I would like to kill you, I have a much better plan. We are going to have so much fun.'

The video cut off. No more footage to check.

Hunter replayed the last snatch and felt like he'd been punched. It confirmed his worst fears. Murray was possibly dead.

Definitely.

Probably.

I punch Murray in the arm, harder than I meant to. It makes him cry. Murray tries hitting me back, but I'm too big and too strong for him. I do that thing he hates, where I grab his head and he's punching and punching but he can't hit me, so he cries even more.

I hold him there really long, his crying getting worse and worse, then I let him go, and he scurries off inside.

Crybaby, running to Grandpa.

Hunter stared around the grotty kitchen, counting the glasses in the cupboard, the cups on the mug tree, the plates on the rack. Back in the here and now. No time to visit the pharmacy yet. He found a clean-enough glass in a cupboard and poured some water. He sipped it.

How the hell had that happened? Two idiots mucking about on an oil rig and they stumble across a shit-ton of drugs.

Did Lord Oswald know what was going on? Was he behind it?

Those rigs sat there for a long time, for months or years, waiting their turn to be refurbished or dismantled. Perfect place to hide a pile of drugs as nobody in their right mind would even consider going up there. Just a pair of idiot urbexers, or a desperate brother and father.

What the hell now?

Hunter looked around the empty cottage. Nothing more to see here. That video camera was the only connection between Shug and Murray. He needed to find Keith. Assuming he was still alive, he'd know more.

Big if.

A shadow passed under the front door. Someone outside.

The handle rattled and the goon from the oil rig stood there, peering in.

19

Hunter sneaked over to the back door and tried to open it without making a sound. Almost succeeded, just a slight click. He pushed himself against the side wall, clutching the GoPro to his chest, and peered back inside.

The goon was now snooping around Shug's kitchen. Gloves on, a mask covering his mouth. An expert. How the hell had he found Hunter?

Hunter set off across the garden but the GoPro slipped out of his grasp. He reached down to pick it up. Caked in mud.

Shite and shite again.

He crept through the gate, then darted down the path onto the street. A mid-grey Range Rover was parked a few spaces down. So it *was* the goon who had been following Hunter and staking out the hotel.

Hunter settled into a casual walk, just a normal guy out for a stroll, carrying a muddy head-mounted camera. Back to the crossing by the Co-op and the Range Rover still hadn't moved.

He didn't even take a knife and jab it in the tyres.

Fiona was leaning against Jock's Passat, sucking deep on a cigarette and messing about on her phone.

'Get in.'

She looked up. 'Huh?'

'In!' Hunter got behind the wheel, and dropped the camera on Jock's lap.

'Well?' Jock didn't look up from his paper.

'I'll show you later.' Hunter jabbed the ignition and put it in drive. Fiona was taking an age of man to buckle up. 'Right now, I need to get away from that guy.' He pulled off into the slipstream of a tractor, heading towards Cromarty on the road to Rosemarkie.

And he spotted the Range Rover in the rear-view, indicating left at the Co-op.

'We're being followed. Buckle up.' Hunter stuck the Passat into sports mode and floored it, whizzing round the tractor. Another one rumbled towards him and he sneaked in just before it hit. The speedo kept climbing, hitting eighty, ninety.

'Christ, son, this is overdue a service!'

'Well, I'm putting it through its paces now.' Hunter spotted an opportunity up ahead—a walled garden selling plants, followed by a lane signposted towards a brewery. Last place Jock should go, but beggars couldn't be choosers.

The Range Rover was stuck back in the convoy, weaving out, but the oncoming traffic stopped it closing.

Hunter swung round a bend and lost it. He took another left and shot down the lane without losing much speed.

Seventy, eighty. Another lane at the back of the walled garden. He pulled into it and hit a three-pointer, aiming back onto the road.

Then he waited, window down, listening for a roaring engine.

'What's going on, Craig?'

'Shhh.'

'Don't you—'

Hunter reached round and covered Jock's lips with a hand. 'Just two minutes' silence, that's all I need.'

Jock shook his head.

And there it was, the roar of a heavy diesel engine. The Range Rover shot past, a scream of silver and diesel.

Hadn't spotted them.

Hunter listened to it disappear, the sound becoming thinner and more diffuse.

'Who was that?'

'The arsehole on the oil platform. He was in Shug's cottage.'

Hunter snatched Fiona's phone from her.

'What the hell?' She clawed at the air. 'I need to tell Shug—'

'You're telling him nothing. Radio silence, okay?' Hunter checked the messages on the screen. Still showed the last one he'd sent to Shug. So either they'd kept quiet, or Fiona had deleted any subsequent exchanges. 'There's something going on here. He's been staking out the hotel and now he's rooting around Shug's. Are you leaking to him?'

Fiona just shook her head.

Jock was dicking about with the GoPro. 'These things are those fancy ones you put on your head?' He stuck it on and started adjusting the camera. 'Like in those pornos?' He clicked his fingers. 'What do they call it? Point of view.'

Hunter grabbed the box and spotted a tag inside.

Keith Wilson, Inverness.

Mobile number below. He got out his own phone and checked it. The same number Hunter had dialled earlier.

He called Cullen. Voicemail. Probably in an interview or just avoiding him now.

What now?

Got it.

He spotted Keith's phone in the tray under the car stereo. Still unlocked. But Keith's.

He called PC Davie Robertson again, tapping his fingers off the wheel.

It was answered with a mumbled, 'What?'

'It's Craig Hunter. Need your—'

'You know what time it is?'

'Sorry if I've just got you out of your bed, but—'

'Aye, you have. Mate, you never done nights?'

'Too many to count.' Hunter sighed. 'Look, I need to know everything about the case.'

'Why, what have you done?'

'Nothing yet. But my brother... Listen, did the name Keith come up?'

'Keith?' A long yawn. 'Well, had a few calls from a Keith Wilson in Inverness, looking for someone called Murray.'

'You didn't think to add this to the file?'

'Hold your horses. Not my fault. We get these calls all the time, sure you've had your share?'

'Suppose so.'

'Besides, you don't know if this is the same one.' Another

yawn. 'Lad kept calling the station, saying he was tracking down who'd taken Murray. He said he's onto something. Asking us to look into Albanians in the area.'

'Albanians?'

Fiona looked round, frowning.

'Right. Guy was obsessed. Dunno. He was supposed to come into the station with some evidence he'd found, but he never showed up.'

'You got an address for him?'

HUNTER DROVE THROUGH INVERNESS, one dual carriageway leading to a roundabout and on to another dual carriageway.

'Tell you, this used to be a nice town.' Jock sat in the passenger seat, gripping the oh-shit handle above the door, shaking his head. 'Now it's like *Stirling*.'

'What's wrong with Stirling?' Fiona was in the back seat, arms folded like she had no idea what to do without her phone.

'If I need to explain it...'

Hunter locked eyes with Fiona. 'Jock's just hangry.'

'Hangry? What the fu—'

'It's a portmanteau of—'

'I know what it is! I'm not hangry!'

'So why are you shouting, bud?'

Jock turned his ire to Fiona. 'You try fasting!'

'Rather just not eat shite the other five days of the week.'

'Enough!' Hunter pulled onto Caledonian Road. 'Have a look for the house.'

Fiona pointed over the road. 'That's it there.'

'You been here before?'

'No. Well. Got a buddy in number forty. Lives in Fort William now.'

Hunter got out onto the street and leaned back in as cars whistled past. 'Stay with him. Call me if you see a grey Range Rover.'

'You've got my phone.'

'Jock can call.'

Jock looked at him, pleading. 'Come on, Craig, let me come with you.'

'If the worst's happened, I need to preserve evidence.'

'Sod this for a game of soldiers.' Jock got out of the car. 'I'm coming!'

'No, you're not.' Hunter blocked his path. 'I've joked about you being hangry, but you're acting like a cock. Get some food in you and then you can maybe come with me. Corner shop, now.'

'Right.' Jock staggered up the street, dragging his right leg behind him.

Hunter shifted his focus to the back seat. 'You okay?'

Fiona gave a shrug. 'Bit spooked, like.' She sat there like a stroppy teenager, arms still folded. 'Can I get my phone back?'

'I don't trust you.'

'Man... I've helped you, haven't I?'

'Let's just say the jury's out. After this, I'll drop you in Cromarty.' Hunter passed over her phone.

'Thanks.' She bit her fingernail. 'I'd rather take my chances with you and the GILF.'

'GILF?'

'Grandfather I'd Like to Fu—'

'Behave yourselves, right?' Hunter grabbed the keys then set off down the street.

Number fifty-six was a small semi-detached house in a street of similar houses. Some had swipes of paint, others had stayed in the same default seventies roughcast job. Keith's home was better tended than the rest. Instead of a feral garden, the front yard was covered in decking, with wild bushes growing among pot plants thriving in the sun. He walked up the path and tried the doorbell.

Nothing. No sounds, no lights.

Not a good sign. Hunter's stomach started rumbling. A mix of hunger from the up-chucked porridge and sheer nerves.

He looked back down the street. No Range Rovers. No pedestrians either.

He tried the door and it nudged open. The butterflies did somersaults. A radio played out New Order somewhere inside, thin and distant.

'Hello?'

No response.

The butterflies flapped their wings.

Hunter stepped into the house, straight into a living room-kitchen with an oven-hot temperature. The kind of heat he associated with assassins and torturers or, worse, stag weekends in the Algarve. Bright, the curtains open wide. Bottle-green futon, metal coffee table, beige designer armchair. Tasteful artworks. No sign of anyone, no sign anyone had been in for a few days.

The rank smell of rotten meat hit his nose, followed by a dessert of mould spores. The kitchen was small, barely enough units to put a week's shopping in let alone hide a body.

He went through to the hallway. No staircase, so just a single floor. Two doors off. The first was a bedroom, a massive bed almost wall to wall. Made, though, sheets tucked in tight like a good squaddie. An iPhone charger on the bedside table, next to a blue pack of condoms and a tube of KY jelly.

Back in the hall, Hunter caught a fresh waft of the smell. He stepped into the bathroom. Sink and toilet, ice white, dry as a bone. The shower unit was off to the side.

Hunter opened the unit door.

A dead body lay in a pool of blood. Naked and male, eyes wide open and staring at Hunter. One gunshot wound in the forehead, two in the chest.

20

H unter stood there in the roasting hot bathroom, trying to process it. As mangled as the body was, it matched Keith's description and the photo on the phone's lock screen.

The voice on the video echoed round Hunter's head.

'You are not supposed to be here. As much as I would like to kill you, I have a much better plan. We are going to have so much fun.'

He fought through the revulsion, trying to stop slipping into old habits.

Grandpa's lying on the floor, gasping, clutching his chest. His face is pale like Skeletor and he's staring right at me. 'Please, son! Get your father!'

Centring himself. Taps, brushed chrome. Sink, ice white. Radox shower gel, the alpine scent lingering and mixing with the rancid stench of death.

Okay, back.

He looked at the body again. Glass bricks stacked at the

side of the shower stall, distorting the light from outside. No other way to describe it but an assassination. Someone had done this deliberately. Meaning there was a clear reason for this guy's death. Assuming it was Keith, then it had to relate to Murray's trip to the oil rig. Right?

If they couldn't kill Murray on the rig and leave his body, they felt they could do it to Keith here.

Two questions, then.

First, why did they kill Keith?

An assassination was easiest behind closed doors. Lure them in, strike, leave. Some forensic traces left behind, maybe, but the most efficient method by far. They banked on the body not being found for a while. Keith and Murray worked in a strange world, as likely to be breaking into derelict buildings in the Scottish Highlands as in Germany, California or Japan. So he had no close ties, nobody who'd check in on cats or dogs, not even hens like Murray. Just an empty shell of a house in the arse end of Inverness.

Second question—what the hell happened to Murray?

Hunter had drawn a fresh blank. A dead body closed off intelligence avenues.

A dead body was something he should call in. Call Cullen.

Now.

Do it.

Only option here.

Hunter got out his phone and called Chantal. Still voicemail. Then he tried Cullen, and got his voicemail again.

So, who now? Control?

Wait—Methven. The new boss. He still had his mobile number on there. The dial tone was harsh in his ear.

Another call bounced to voicemail. But a delay, like it was a conscious decision rather than phones-off protocol

He could picture the scene. Chantal leading the interview, Cullen sitting next to her, opposite a suspect and their lawyer. Methven all puffed up like a senior investigating officer should be, standing in the obs suite, playing pocket billiards, sipping strong coffee and wanting to jump in and tell Chantal how to do it properly.

Hunter retried the number, but it bounced to voicemail even quicker.

Elvis!

Hunter hit dial and it rang and rang. Until: 'Alright, Craigy boy, your prostate finally exploded?' Sounded like he was in a car, driving. Slight distance meant he wasn't behind the wheel.

'No, mate. I've...' Hunter took another look in the shower and got a wave of revulsion. 'I've found a body.'

'What?'

'A dead one, Paul.' Hunter sighed. 'Look, is Cullen there?'

'No, mate. You're on speaker and I'm with Methv—'

'Constable, what the sodding hell are you talking about? A *body*?'

'I'm in Inverness, sir, and... I've found a dead body. He's been murdered, sir.'

'Where are you?'

'Caledonian Road.'

The squeal of brakes and a roaring engine. 'Two minutes.'

'What?'

'We're in this infernal sodding city.' And Methven was gone.

Okay. They're on their way here. Only thing worse than waiting was—

Don't think about that.

Hunter tried to occupy himself. Another search of the dingy flat, but nothing obvious jumped out at him. Outside, he stood in the doorway. Watching, waiting, guarding.

The street was quiet. A young mother pushed her baby along the street, reaching a wriggling finger in to pacify the child. At the corner, an old man stood while his dog peed against a tree.

Then sirens, blaring not too far away. A flash of blue as Methven's Range Rover swung round the corner and hurtled towards him. The one Range Rover Hunter was glad to see. He ran down to the kerb, waving his arms.

Methven pulled up on the road, two-thirds in a space, the rest sticking out onto the street. Methven hopped out, flanked by Elvis and Bain.

Hunter couldn't look at the house, his stomach churning. 'I've secured the property, sir. Only one entrance.'

'Excellent.' Methven opened the boot and tossed a crime scene suit to Bain.

The numpty dropped it on the pavement and nodded at Elvis. 'Pick it up, Constable.'

'Sergeant!'

'Sorry, sir.' Bain reached down for it himself, snarling at Elvis.

Methven tore on his suit like the inverse of him tearing off a wetsuit at the triathlon Hunter had competed against him in. 'Have you got an ID for the victim?'

'I think it's probably Keith Wilson, the owner.'

'Only probably?'

'Need someone to ID him.'

'Can I ask what you're doing here, Constable?'

'Working?'

'DI Cullen said you were back in Edinburgh.'

Hunter looked around but couldn't see Cullen. He hated winging it at the best of times. 'Following a lead, sir.'

'You were supposed to be in sodding Perth, but you've been keeping DI Cullen in the sodding dark, haven't you?'

'No, sir, I've—'

'Purple sodding buggery, Hunter!' Methven jabbed a finger at him, tapping the end of his nose. 'You've gone rogue on me for the last time.'

'Sir, I've operated under DI Cullen's instructions. Check with him.'

'I sodding will.' Methven was suited up first. 'Okay, I'm going in.' He snapped on his mask, but it didn't cover the glower he directed at Bain. 'Sergeant, hurry up.' Then he trained his ire on Elvis. 'Constable, you're on crime scene management.'

'Gaffer.'

Methven gave a firm nod, then set off inside the house.

Bain was taking his time suiting up, eyeing Hunter. Creepy little bastard was completely bald now, his ill-advised beard now trimmed away to a shiny smoothness. God knows where he'd stopped shaving, probably like a baby all over. 'Could do without this shite.'

Hunter was barely aware of the sound of another car parking. A hand gripped Hunter's arm and pulled him away.

'Come on, Craig.' Cullen, jaw clenched tight. 'Need a word.'

Hunter stepped away from the bollocking. 'I tried to cover for you with Crystal, but I think you better 'fess up.'

'Shite.' Cullen ran a hand through his hair, upsetting the pristine gelwork. 'We could lie and—'

'No, Scott, we can't. You're a DI. Tell him the truth. Besides, you're allowed to manage a caseload. Just say this is part of it. It's not a million miles from the truth. You got Buchan to log it.'

'Fine. You're not as daft as you look.'

'Mate, I'm not in the mood for this.' Hunter couldn't help but laugh. 'Why are you here, anyway? Where's Chantal?'

'She's still in Perth.' Cullen took his arm and led him away from the gate.

Bain entered Keith Wilson's home, leaving Elvis standing outside the house, arms folded, trying to look intimidating but... Looking like Paul 'Elvis' Gordon.

'And why are you in Inverness?'

'We're investigating a murder.'

'I know that. I'm on the case as well.'

'Following a lead.' Cullen sighed. 'The victim has connections here.'

'What's his name?'

'Alistair McCoull.'

Hunter frowned. It rang a bell. So much noise in his head from the case and the still-rattling ribs and his missing brother and a dead body. But that name... Wee Ally? 'Wait, does he co-own the *Pride of Cromarty*.'

'What?'

'It's a boat. Co-owns it with a guy called Shug.'

'Hugh "Shug" Mowat, right.' Elvis yawned into his fist. 'A

person of interest on our case. We're heading up to Fortrose to pick him up, then you called.'

'Good luck. He's gone to ground.'

'Let's take a step back here.' Cullen leaned back against his Golf. Newer model and a GTI this time, but the same manufacturer as ever. 'How do you know Shug?'

'He took Murray out to an oil rig.' Hunter bit at his thumbnail, then pointed at the house. 'Murray and the owner of that flat. Probably the body in the shower. Guy's disappeared, but left behind a GoPro.' He struggled for breath. Saying it out loud made it seem all the more real. 'Scott, I think that's my brother's boyfriend in there.'

Cullen just nodded like he knew Murray was gay. 'I don't like your brother's disappearance intersecting my case.'

'Ally McCoull is only a tangent. Co-owned a boat. He was an assassination, right?'

'Shot through the head, mouth and heart.'

Hunter frowned. 'Same here.'

'Seriously?' Cullen swallowed. 'Not so much an intersection, then. Christ.'

'Tell me about him.'

'Guy lives in Perth, worked at General Accident, then when it became Aviva or whatever. Retired five years back and bought a boat up here with Shug Mowat. Shug is our chief suspect.'

'I don't think he's your guy, Scott.' Hunter huffed out a breath and nodded at Keith Wilson's house. 'In there, that's not a fisherman's work.'

'Right.' Cullen stared over at the house, eyes twitching. Probably running the same calculations as Hunter, assessing the same probabilities and motives. And giving up in the same way. 'What a mess.'

Fiona got out of Jock's car onto the street and lit up a cigarette. She waved at Hunter but didn't seem too curious. At least she hadn't run off when she saw the cops.

'Who's that, Craig?'

'Fisherwoman from Cromarty. She's helping us.'

'Us?'

'Me and my old man.'

'And where is your old man?'

'Shit.' Hunter left Cullen and crossed the road. He looked in the car. No sign of Jock. 'Oh, Christ.' He walked over to Fiona. 'Where is he?'

'He came back, took my phone, spoke to someone, then cleared off in a hurry.'

'Didn't say where he was going?'

'Nope.'

Hunter just bloody knew it. The hangriness in the past always led to one thing—Jock storming off.

21

'I 'm supposed to believe this heap of shite?' Bain was interviewing, sitting at a twisted angle opposite Hunter. Kept slapping a hand to his head and it was really getting on Hunter's nerves. 'You must think I came up the Clyde in a banana boat.'

'It's the truth.' Hunter stayed in the same position. Arms folded across his chest, legs locked together at the ankles. 'And I only care if DI Cullen here believes it.'

Bain bristled, his top lip twitching. Hunter never thought he'd miss the moustache, but there you go. 'Let me get this straight, you just found the boy's address, aye?'

'No, PC David Robertson gave me it.'

'So you went to this address and just happened to find him in the shower, dead?'

'I know what you're trying to do here. You went inside that house with DCI Methven, so you'll know he looks like he's been dead for days. I was with Chantal all weekend. Have you tracked my father's phone?'

'Could your old man be involved?'

'Excuse me?'

'Well, he seems to have shat it and pissed off as soon as we showed up running blues and twos.'

'He was staying at my brother's home near Galashiels until yesterday morning.'

'That right, aye?'

'You got evidence that he wasn't? Have you tracked his phone?'

'We did, aye. Turned off first thing this morning.'

Hunter stared at him for a few seconds. 'He's a big fan of your work. Your podcast.'

Blushing hard, Bain twisted round to focus on Cullen. 'What do you think, Sundance?'

'It's DI Cullen.'

'Sorry there.' Bain cackled out a laugh. 'Force of habit.'

'Right, Craig.' Cullen leaned forward and clasped his hands together. 'Your dad's missing, for reasons, but we've got this Fiona. How does she fit into this?'

'She... knows Shug and Ally McCoull. And she...' Hunter assessed the risks, 'came up with...' *Sod it, tell the truth.* He leaned forward, clasping his hands just like Cullen. 'Fiona took me and Jock out to an oil rig. The last place Murray was spotted.'

'That where you found the video?'

'No, that was Shug's cottage in Fortrose.'

Cullen leaned over to Bain and whispered in his ear. Bain got up and left the room.

Hunter waited for him to go. 'Scott, what the hell's going on here?'

Cullen sat back and rested a foot on his thigh. 'I can't do

you any favours here. Just because we go back a few years and you let me stay on your sofa in my hour of greatest need. Any of that.'

'I wouldn't ask you to.' Hunter tried to swallow but his mouth was bone dry. 'Have you watched the video?'

Cullen nodded. 'You think your brother's dead?'

'I do.' There, he'd said it at least. 'But I need to find his body. My mum deserves a funeral.'

'And your dad?'

'Just his own.'

Cullen laughed.

Hunter locked eyes with him, showed how desperate he felt. 'Scott, I've been phoning you and Chantal, but—'

'Interviews, Craig. You know the drill. That's what led us up here.'

'What's Fiona saying?'

'Square root of bugger all. You sure she's not involved?'

Hunter processed it. There were a few avenues that led to her being involved, but many more that didn't. Still didn't exonerate her. And nothing explained that big lump being one step behind Hunter at all times. 'I don't know. If she's quiet, I'd say it's because she's scared.'

'Why would your dad run?'

'Search me.' Hunter felt a tingle up his spine, almost made him shiver. 'In my youth, the problem wasn't Jock leaving so much as him coming back.'

'Come to think of it, you've never talked about him in all the time I've known you.'

'There's a good reason for that.' Fire surged through Hunter's veins. 'I wish he was dead, Scott. He's an arsehole.'

'But is he involved in a double murder?'

'It's probably a triple.' Hunter sat back and clamped his hands on his thighs. 'He's a dodgy git, Scott, but that's it as far as I know.'

'So why's he run off?'

'He hates cops. Even me.' Hunter let go of his thighs. 'Look, Scott. I got shot at when I was on the rig.'

'Why doesn't that surprise me?' Cullen rolled his eyes. 'What happened?'

'That's it. We were rooting around, this boat came over. Big foreign guy came up. Could be Russian, could be Israeli, could be Albanian.'

'Albanian?'

'I don't know. Chantal told me you were interviewing someone but I don't want to—' Hunter sighed at Cullen's sudden texting. 'Yep, you're jumping to conclusions.'

'Worth checking out, Craig.' Cullen looked up. 'Any idea who this guy is?'

'No idea. Jock thinks Oswald's involved, but—'

'Who's Oswald.'

'Lord Iain Oswald. Owns the rig. I want to speak to him.'

Hunter leaned forward. He was getting sidelined in his own case. Typical Cullen, always wanting to be front and centre of anything.

'I can't believe you went on an oil rig.'

'Come on, mate. If Michelle went missing and you found out she'd been—'

'I get it.' Cullen walked over to the door and opened it. Bain was standing outside like he'd been eavesdropping. 'Give me a minute.' He left and shut the door.

Hunter sat on his own—time and space to think. Time and space he didn't want to think in. He needed to be out doing something. Finding Jock, finding Murray's body. Anything but sitting there, staring at his own reflection in an Inverness interview room that stank of boiled fish. Rancid boiled fish.

The door opened and Chantal stepped inside, pulling it shut behind her. 'What the hell, Craig?'

Hunter got up and tried to kiss her, but she pushed him away. 'What's up?'

'A dead body? What the hell is going on?'

'Chantal...' Hunter felt like he'd been kicked in the stomach. Pain stabbed across his ribs like hammers on piano strings. 'My brother's probably dead. I've just found his boyfriend's body. And you're not answering my calls.'

'I was driving!'

'And you can't pair your phone to the car?'

'With four DC passengers and the constant stress of you going all smoochy, smoochy on the line? Aye, right.'

'But I needed your help. My brother's dead.' The air escaped his lungs, squishing him dry. Tears stung his eyes, his nostrils burning.

'Aw, shite.' Chantal rushed over and held him as he cried, her hand smoothly caressing his back. 'I'm sorry.'

Hunter wrapped his arms around her and held her close. 'It's okay.' He brushed tears away, not that he was scared of her seeing him like that, just... 'I've no idea where Jock is.'

'He's run away?' She looked up at him. 'Oh Christ, Craig. As if I wasn't getting enough of a bad vibe off him.'

'There's a reason for that. He's a racist alcoholic who's completely incapable of—'

'It's not that. Bain's got a hard-on for him. Saying he's connected with the case. Trying to paint him as a suspect.'

'Bain's got previous for that.'

The door opened, Cullen this time. 'Chantal, you're up. Get the tape running.'

'Sure thing.' She kissed Hunter on the cheek and whispered: 'Love you, Craig. Sorry about all this. We'll find your brother, okay?'

'Love you too.' He let her leave.

Cullen held the door for her. 'So, big guy. You want to watch?'

THE OBS SUITE, a tiny room filled with monitors and recording equipment, stank even worse of fish, like someone had steamed off rotten haddock in there. The source seemed to be an old-style TV in the corner. Hunter opened it. It wasn't a TV, but a battered old microwave. Inside, a plate full of cod loins rotted away. He shut the door and tried not to think about it.

Which proved next to impossible.

On his small monitor he saw Chantal sitting opposite Fiona in a large interview room, much bigger than where Hunter had been processed by Bain and Cullen.

The obs suite door opened and Elvis waltzed in. 'Craig, my man.' He screwed up his face. 'Jesus, you should get yourself checked. That's *vile*.'

'It's that microwave, not my guts.' Hunter tried to deflect any blame onto the animal who'd left festering fish in there. 'How's your podcast?'

'My— What?'

'Never mind.'

Elvis scowled at him. 'She's quite tidy, isn't she?'

'So's your wife.'

'Sod off.' Elvis stretched out. 'Seriously, what do you know about my—'

The speaker erupted. 'When is this starting?' Fiona was slouching, looking bored rather than frightened. Clearly not her first rodeo.

'The tape's running.' Chantal pointed at the recorder. Actually a tape machine, doubling up in case the ancient technology broke. 'He'll be here soon.'

Cullen entered the room in a flurry of suit jacket and stubble. 'Miss Shearer. Sorry for the wait.' He rested his coat on the back of his chair and sat. 'You okay?'

'I need to get back to Cromarty.'

'All in good time.' Cullen rasped his stubble, loud enough for the microphone to pick up. 'But first, I'd be grateful for your help with something. We're looking for a mate of yours. Guy called Shug.'

Fiona sniffed. 'Right.'

'You help us find him, you get out of here, then you can get back up the road to Cromarty. How's that sound?'

'What's he supposed to have done?'

'You know an Ally McCoull, right?'

'Aye, Wee Ally.'

'Tell me how.'

'Well, depends on what you want to know, bud. He's a bitty older than us. Think he came from Crom originally but lives down in Perth now. Owns a boat in Cromarty.'

'Sure it's not co-owning a boat?'

'Aye, with Shug.'

'And that's Hugh Mowat?'

'Think so.'

'To your knowledge, do they ever argue about the boat?'

'Not that I heard.

Mate, you're going to need to tell me why I'm here.'

'Okay.' Cullen drummed his fingers on the table, the sound popping the obs suite speakers.

Elvis burped. 'Sorry.' Then again. 'God that fish is minging.'

On-screen, Cullen gave Fiona a pistol finger. 'We believe that Shug, as you know him, or Hugh Paul Mowat as Her Majesty's government does, visited an address in Perth on Friday and murdered Alistair McCoull.'

'What?'

Cullen turned to face Chantal, his expression one of extreme worry. 'Am I not speaking clearly enough?'

'I can hear you just fine. Need me to see if DC Hunter or DC Gordon are hearing this through there?'

'Nah, I'll take your word for it.' Cullen looked back at Fiona. 'Must just be your ears that are the problem.' He gave a pause. 'You know anything about that murder?'

'Woah!' Fiona raised her hands, like she was calming a wild horse. 'No way, man!'

'Well, we've got a huge issue here.' Cullen clapped his hands together and screwed his face tight. 'Two dead bodies. One in Perth, and one here in Inverness.'

Fiona frowned. 'That boy died?'

'What boy?'

'Keith.' Fiona deepened her frown. 'That big lad, Craig, he brought us here looking for a Keith. That who he found in the flat?'

Cullen nodded.

'Christ.'

'We've still not managed to identify the body, but we think it's him. He seems to have lived a fairly hermitic lifestyle. No personal photos. In fact, no personal possessions other than... Well.' He flashed a cold smile. 'You know anything about his death?'

'I'm way out my depth here, bud. I took Big Craig and his old boy up to the rig, just to help out. But if they're killing people...'

'You think *they're* killing people?'

'Isn't that what you're saying here?'

Cullen sat back, his nostrils flaring. Or at least it looked that way on the grainy monitor. Either way, he was clearly flustered and frustrated. 'I need to speak to Shug.'

'Shug's not a killer.'

'Okay, but I can't just take your word for it, can I? He's our chief suspect in Ally McCoull's murder. We believe he was in Perth on Friday to meet someone. Same day Mr McCoull was killed.'

Fiona seemed to shrink in on herself.

Cullen and Chantal exchanged a look.

Hunter stood up and got a fresh blast of stale fish. 'Bollocks to this.' He walked over to the door.

Elvis grabbed his arm. 'Craig, mate, if you go in there, Cullen will go *tonto*.'

'Like to see him try.' Hunter brushed him off and walked out into the corridor. Hard to figure out which door led to the interview room. He tried the first one and got a cleaning cupboard. Next door was the right room.

Cullen looked over at him with a dark scowl, then went back to glaring at Fiona. But he didn't seem to have anything to ask. That or Hunter had thrown him off his train of thought.

Hunter sat next to Fiona. 'Alright, let's cut the bullshit here. Last time you saw Ally McCoull was in the pub in Cromarty last week, right?'

'Aye?'

'You got barred after you attacked Ally, didn't you?'

'What?'

'We'll get a statement from the barman. Get a few regulars to back it up. Then we'll start going through your comings and goings since then. I suspect there's a big gap around Friday night, right?'

Fiona shook her head, hard. 'No!'

'Look, the sooner you stop clowning around here, the sooner you'll get home.'

Still nothing, just shaking her head.

'I know the guys you hang out with on the boats. Real hardened types. Probably a few of them have done time. Given you some advice. Don't get a lawyer in. Keep quiet, see what the cops can make stick. I get it. But right now, you're not my focus.'

'I helped you, bud. Took you out to that rig.' Fiona looked at Cullen, sly like she knew she was getting Hunter into trouble. 'And this is how—'

'I appreciate it, but we did pay you for your trouble. And for what it's worth, I don't think you killed Ally. We just need to find Shug. That's it. When we do, you're out of here. Deal?'

'Right.'

'Okay, so I know you've been messaging Shug on Whats-App. What's your passcode?'

'Like I'm telling the cops that.'

'You can walk away...'

Fiona sighed. 'Christ's sake. Passcode is 1688.'

Cullen rolled his eyes. 'Rangers fan?'

'My dad was. It's his boat. But it's no use while your old man's in the wind.'

'What do you mean?'

'Well, he swiped my phone, didn't he?'

Hunter groaned. 'I gave you it back. Shite. Why did he take it?'

'Your old man said he needed to check in.'

'Who with?'

Fiona shrugged. 'Didn't say. He called someone, then dashed off.'

Meaning the old rascal had nipped away with the only solid lead they had in either case.

'Where's Jock's car?'

Chantal frowned. 'Downstairs.'

22

'Oh my god.' Cullen was in the back seat of Jock's car. 'What on earth is this?' He held up a torch. 'Is it what I think it is?'

Hunter could only nod. He leaned into the car. 'Can I help?'

'Help? Craig, you just barged into that interview without permission. You broke my strategy.'

'Didn't look like you had one there, mate.'

'And now I've got your dad's Fleshlight all over my hands.'

'Hope he's cleaned it.'

'That's... Ugh.' Cullen got out of the car with a grim expression. 'Craig, I'm your superior officer, so you need to defer to me.'

'You're one to talk.'

'Do as I say, not as I do.'

'You found anything in there?'

'Just your father's sex toy.' Cullen shut the car door and leaned against it. 'He got any family up this way he could run to?'

'On Mum's side, but nobody close. Jock never talks about his side, but he seems to know a hell of a lot about Cromarty.'

Bright headlights lit up Cullen like a police helicopter. A minibus pulled up outside the station and people started getting out. Big men, athletic women. All in suits. Could tell a mile off they were cops.

Chantal stopped checking in Jock's boot to look over. 'Who's that?'

'The Livingston MIT.' Cullen put his hands in his pockets. 'After Craig found another body, we needed more skulls. Inverness are up to their nipples and Glasgow have, well... it's Glasgow. So Methven pulled in virtually all the favours he's been building up for the last couple of years.' He smirked, like he wanted to say something he shouldn't. 'So, aye, they're helping out too. And I've got to brief them about this murder.'

'Sorry for barging in, Scott.'

'Don't mention it. I'd rather my subordinates jumped in and were right, than were wrong or kept it to themselves.' Cullen set off. Or tried to.

Hunter grabbed his sleeve. 'Are you doing anything about the drugs haul?'

Cullen glared at Hunter's hand. 'There's another minibus halfway up the A9 full of my old drug squad buddies. We'll dig into it.' He patted Hunter on the back. 'Just find that phone, okay?' He left them, walking over to the minibus. Slowly, like he was looking for someone.

A tall woman stepped down from the vehicle, her dark hair hanging loose in a lopsided ponytail. Looked slimmer than Hunter remembered. DS Yvonne Flockhart. Hunter's ex. She made a beeline for Cullen and they embraced. Not the hug of colleagues, but of lovers. Lingering fingers stroking fabric with a shared intimacy. Intensely staring into each other's eyes.

Hunter's gut lurched, the butterflies twisting and turning down there. 'What the hell?' His fists were clenched. 'Sleazy bastard was sleeping in my flat for *four months* while he was shagging my *ex*.'

Chantal rolled her eyes. 'Who are you more jealous of?'

'What?'

She pinched his cheek. 'Winding you up.'

'Don't.' Hunter spotted some fury in her eyes. Her insecurity, deeply hidden beneath all that bluster and arrogance and cool. He pinched her cheek this time. 'Look, it's not the fact they're an item. I don't care. I've got you. I win.'

She shook her head. 'You know how to charm a girl.'

'It's the subterfuge. Or it's that Scott can't talk to me about his life. I thought we were over it. I mean...' Hunter sighed. 'That messed me up for years. Losing my girlfriend because she'd... It stopped me being able to trust anyone. You helped me get over it. I'm not angry anymore. It's just... stupidity.'

Chantal shot him a warm smile. 'Come on, let's find that phone.'

'I'm worried what else we might find in there.' Hunter got in the car and sat on the driver seat. Still spotless. Jock's two newspapers sat on the passenger seat. Hunter popped the glovebox and a box of ribbed condoms tumbled out, along with a copy of the *Times*. Hunter opened it and a porno mag was rolled up inside. All those trips to the newsagent. The guy was a sex addict.

'What?' Chantal was in the back seat, rooting around under the seats. 'You got something?'

'Nothing.'

'This is creepily clean and tidy, Craig. Given the state you leave our flat in, you clearly didn't inherit his OCD.'

'Organised to the point of psychopathy, right?' Hunter popped the hatch between the seats. 'I see what you mean.'

Chantal opened the central console.

'Scott's already—'

'Why would you put a torch in—' She scowled. 'Oh my God.' She gritted her teeth, looking like she was going to be sick, and slammed the lid. 'Well, there's no phone.'

Hunter took one last look around the cabin. 'Nope.'

'You got any idea where he might be?'

'None.'

A big sweating lump came over, hands in pockets. 'Which one of you is Cullen?'

'Him.' Hunter pointed at the embracing couple, got a rabbit-in-the-headlights look from Cullen. 'Why?'

'Got a guy upstairs wants to see him and a Craig Hunter?'

HUNTER FOLLOWED Cullen through the station, desperately needing another coffee. Or his bed. Definitely needed something to eat.

Cullen stopped by the door. 'Who is it?'

'No idea, mate.'

'You first.' Cullen beckoned him into the room.

Hunter entered.

Lord Oswald sat there, dressed to the nines. Tweed flat cap, Barbour jacket, pink shirt, red trousers. 'Ah, Inspector.' He gave a curt smile to Hunter. 'And you've brought a friend. Of course, the matter at hand pertains directly to him.'

Callum, his assistant, stood over his right shoulder, hands in gloves, his black suit paired with a dark-grey shirt and tie.

Cullen took his time sitting, his usual trick while he tried to own the room and everyone in it. He beckoned for Hunter to join him, then smiled at Oswald. 'How can I help?'

Hunter stayed standing by the door, trying to size up Callum's threat level. He reckoned he could handle him, if anything came of it, not that it was likely to in a police station.

Oswald gestured at the chair opposite. 'Please, sit.'

'I'm good.'

'Well, then.' Oswald tensed his forehead, then focused on Cullen. 'I wish to make a formal complaint about Mr Hunter here and his father for trespassing on an oil rig presently under the care of my business.'

Cullen nodded slowly. 'Is that so?'

'I have evidence of this trespass.' Oswald reached into his jacket and produced an envelope, which he placed on the table in front of him. Just that bit too far away for Cullen to reach. 'This packet contains CCTV footage of Mr Hunter here and his father aboard Osprey Alpha this morning.' He tapped the envelope. 'Please ensure, as his superior officer, that he's taken to task for this.'

Cullen looked at Hunter but didn't seem to know what to do.

Hunter walked over and grabbed the packet, then started leafing through it. Grainy black-and-white shots of him, Jock and Fiona, both as a group and after they'd split up. At least three of Jock sifting through the pornography.

'He was trespassing, Inspector.'

'I was following a lead in a missing persons case. You'd refused access.'

'Which is entirely my right. It's an incredibly dangerous place.'

'Filled with a shitload of heroin?'

Oswald laughed. 'What the *hell* are you talking about?'

'Let me guess, that's nothing to do with you?'

'Good heavens, man, I'm a respectable businessman.' Oswald scowled at Cullen. 'Now, given he's admitted to trespassing, can you please prosecute him and his father?'

'See, we have video evidence of the drugs. Boxes of heroin.' Hunter waited for any reaction from Oswald, but the guy was good. 'Thing is, when *we* went up to the rig, the drugs were gone.'

'Inspector, I insist you prosecute them.' Oswald leaned forward, keeping his voice low. 'When I warn people off trespassing, they usually comply. When your chap here came to see me, I just *knew* he'd go up there. It was written all over his face. And there's a CCTV system. It was merely a case of watching them stagger around in the wind. It'd be amusing if it wasn't so illegal. Now, are you going to prosecute them for me?'

Hunter rested on the table with a grin. 'Something missing from this lot, though.'

Oswald looked baffled, his mouth hanging open. 'Excuse me?'

'Well, you've got me and my father. There was someone else with us.'

'There are three people in the photos. One of them is a local fisherwoman.' Oswald rolled his eyes. 'You saw fit to bring two members of the public along with you.'

'Okay. I meant someone else. You sent your goon after us.' Hunter held his hand above his head. 'Big lump, foreign accent.' He nodded at Callum. 'Even bigger than him. The guy who shot at me.'

Cullen said nothing.

Hunter looked back at Oswald. 'He looked pretty handy. And I'm pretty sure he's responsible for the murder of—'

'I have absolutely no idea what you're talking about.'

Cullen joined Hunter in standing. 'Sir, can we access your CCTV remotely?'

'Certainly.' Oswald clicked his fingers at his assistant.

Callum nodded and pulled out an extra-large Samsung smartphone. He held it out to them, showing footage of Hunter and Jock cocking about on the rig, blown about by the wind, shouting at each other as they tried to leave.

The attacker appeared at the edge of the screen, climbing up a ladder. Then his whole body, before he slipped up and over, then disappeared off to the side.

Hunter snatched the mobile off him and hit pause, then wound it back. Not a great image, but good enough. 'That's him.'

Oswald stared at the screen. 'Well, I've never seen him before in my life.'

'He doesn't work for you?'

'Absolutely not.' Oswald waved a hand at his lumbering goon. 'Gentlemen, this is my head of security. Callum McBeth.'

Hunter focused on him. 'And let me guess, you've no idea who this guy is, right?'

'Of course he doesn't.'

Hunter shot Oswald a glare. 'I'm asking him, not you.'

'No idea who he is.' Callum had a thin and shrill voice, like he'd lost both bollocks in a freak gardening accident as a youth.

'But you've seen him?'

'Just on that video.'

'So if you gave us full access to your CCTV, we wouldn't see him taking all the drugs off the rig? Wouldn't see him—'

'We've lost the footage.' Callum folded his bulky arms but his suit didn't pucker at all, just stayed at the perfect fit. 'We had a break-in at the weekend and someone took the servers.' He pointed at the ceiling. 'I'm working with your colleagues in Inverness on floor three.'

'Just so happened, right?'

'Our theory is it's an inside job. I'm interviewing all of our employees.'

'Sounds like you know who's involved.'

'Not yet.' Callum licked his lips. 'But we had a report of two people up on the rig the week before. Headed up myself but certainly didn't see any giant boxes of drugs. No sign of them. Which is why we installed the security system. Not that it's doing us any good.'

'Mate, we've got video evi—'

'Craig.' Cullen shot Hunter a warning glare.

Oswald got to his feet, pocketing his smartphone. 'Inspector, are you going to charge him with trespass?'

Cullen lifted his shoulders. 'This isn't my remit. I'm a murder squad detective and so is Craig. He reports to me, that's true, but this is a local policing matter. Suggest you file a complaint with the front desk.'

CULLEN STOPPED in the corridor and opened a door. 'In here.' He held it for Hunter, then shut it when Hunter was in the room. 'If it turns out little Lord Fauntleroy back there isn't involved in all this, I don't know if I'm going to be able to protect you.'

Hunter stormed over to the window and looked out. Cracking view up to the castle, a Victorian military stronghold rather than Edinburgh's ancient landmark. 'I'm looking for my brother, Scott. That was his last known location.'

'Very noble, mate, just watch where you're looking.'

Hunter turned to face Cullen. 'You think I'll get done for this?'

'Probably. I'll help you any way I can, but he's got evidence you were up there where you shouldn't have been. Whether you go down for it, that's not for me to speculate on. But you're on my time and your brother's case is now part of mine.'

Hunter felt a surge of relief. 'I appreciate it.'

'First, you think that security guy's lying about the lost CCTV?'

'Undoubtedly. But we'd need a warrant to get access to their logs, by which time they'll make their servers disappear, assuming they haven't already.' Hunter held Cullen's blue-eyed gaze. 'The way I see it, I think someone's using Lord Oswald's rig to smuggle heroin into the country. Possibly with his knowledge, possibly without. The guy on the rig was hardcore, Scott.'

'I've done my time in the trenches on drugs cases over the last few years. You wouldn't stick that amount of smack on an oil rig you weren't in complete control of.'

'You think I'm on to something?'

Cullen spent a few seconds thinking it through, staring up at the ceiling. 'Craig, you know I'm an ambitious prick, so tell me if this is my ego getting ahead of me.'

'No, it all works. At least in my head.'

'Okay. We need to find this guy who attacked you. Get him in a room, see what he knows.'

'Guy like that won't speak.'

'He might not, but he'll be on a record somewhere. And either someone he knows talks, or someone who knows him will.'

'That's pretty dark.'

Cullen shrugged. 'At least two murders here. I'll get as dark as I need to.'

Hunter leaned back against the door. 'We still need to find Fiona's phone. And my old man.'

Cullen nodded. 'Right. Let's go back to first principles. Flush him out.'

'And how do we do that?'

Hunter had him. Cullen stood there, hands in pockets. Kept starting to say something, then stopping.

'Boys!' Chantal came over, holding a note in a gloved hand. 'This is from your old man.'

Hunter read it:

> Sorry Craig
> Need to get back to Cromarty
> Love,
> Daddy

23

Hunter pulled up outside the Cromarty Hotel and waited. The TDI engine in Jock's Passat had kicked the arse of Cullen's Golf GTi. That or Hunter's driving skills had been the difference maker. 'Daddy... Jesus.'

Chantal was in the passenger seat, arms wrapped around her torso, scowling at everything she looked at in the pervert's vehicle. 'Where the hell is he?' She did a lot of listening.

The town was lit up for the impending night-time, but the sun was still up, hanging over the horizon above distant hills Hunter didn't know the names of.

'Right, then.' Chantal put the phone to her ear. 'Methven.' That's all she needed to say.

'Come on, let's go.' Hunter got out into the cool night air and waited for Chantal to join him before locking the car with the remote. He set off to the front door, but took one last look at the Passat. 'That's an expensive motor, isn't it?'

Chantal opened the door. 'Can be, why?'

'It's just...' Hunter frowned before stepping inside. 'How the hell does he afford it?'

Chantal's turn to frown. 'You lead on, I've got a call to make.'

Hunter nodded, not wanting to even know who the call was to, then entered the hotel bar. The exact same array of drinkers as when they'd checked in almost twenty-four hours ago.

The barman was standing back, thumbs tucked into an apron emblazoned with the logo of a brewery Hunter couldn't even read. 'Can I get you, mate?'

'I'm staying here with my old man. You might remember him?'

'Hard to forget, son. Trying to order a pint when he came in at two this morning. Nae danger.'

Hunter rested his hands on the bartop. 'Trouble is, I haven't heard from him in a few hours. He been in today?'

'Not that I've seen.'

Hunter leaned in close. 'He's not quite got all of his marbles and he's had heart troubles. Any chance I can get a look in his room?'

The barman looked over and nodded at a man slightly raising his pint glass. 'Be a sec, Sid.' Then back to Hunter. 'Pal, I can't just—'

'I'm a cop.' Hunter held out his warrant card. 'I don't like to play it like this, but I'm worried about him.'

The barman sighed. 'Let me pour this pint, then I'll get you the cleaner's key.' He took a fresh glass and started pouring Best into it.

The door clattered open and Chantal stumbled in,

scowling back at the entrance. Didn't even elicit a look from the drinkers. Which surprised Hunter—maybe it was more enlightened up here, but down in the central belt, an Asian-Scot, especially a female one, entering a pub would've got a fair amount of interest. She walked over and took Hunter's hand, then whispered in his ear. 'I checked. Your father owns the car, assuming he's John Edward Hunter.'

'Jock for short, aye.'

The barman handed Hunter the key. 'Here you go, son.'

'Thanks.' Hunter led off to the stairwell. 'He definitely owns a 68-plate Passat?'

'It's on a lease, but he's the legal keeper.'

Hunter held the door for her. 'Curiouser and curiouser.'

HUNTER KNOCKED ON THE DOOR, making the 'Do Not Disturb' sign sway a little. 'Jock?'

Silence.

In another room, a vacuum rumbled away. Sounded like it was upstairs.

He tried again. 'You in, Dad?'

Still nothing from inside.

Hunter unlocked the door. 'One last chance, Jock.' He waited, listening hard. Then he was struck with the fear that his father might be dead in there. One body tended to lead to multiple bodies, at least in his mind. He jerked the handle and opened wide.

Empty.

The double bed was made, the pillows puffed up almost like nobody had slept there. But Jock's dark purple sleep mask lay on the chest to the left, resting on his Kindle. His suitcase sat on the luggage rack.

Hunter looked in the bathroom. Everything was dry. Just some obsessively placed toiletries. Razor, shaving foam, can of deodorant, toothbrush, small toothpaste.

'He's not been here since breakfast.'

'Seriously, this is how tidy he is?'

'You saw his car.'

She snarled. 'And his sex toy.'

'Where the hell is he?'

'Step back, Craig. You were in Inverness and he ran off when he saw our cars. Where else could he have gone?'

'Back to Murray's, but that's hours away. Train to Edinburgh, then down to Gala. Taxi to Murray's.'

'We could check.' Chantal walked over to the window and looked out. 'Who's that guy? The Irish one?'

'Right. Warner.' Hunter folded his arms and played it through. The trouble with an estranged father—other than the father bit—was the estranged part. He just didn't know enough about the old bastard to be able to second-guess his movements. He squatted and started sifting through the luggage, hoping for no more sex toys. 'If I was to give him the benefit of the doubt, I'd say he's looking for his missing son.'

'By running from the cops?'

'Well, exactly. There's a lot of doubt and hardly any benefit. But I don't know... I mean, he's always been a shady git. Always up to his hooky little tricks. But running from the cops? That's extreme, even for him.'

'Maybe he thinks we'll slow down his search?'

'But I found Keith before he knew.'

'Just before Scott and Crystal turned up, though.'

Chantal turned away from the window. 'We had intel that Shug was in Inverness. Dead end, though. Hence Cullen and Methven hanging around and trying to blame each other. Your phone call was a bolt from the blue. Saved both their arses.'

Always the way. Hunter took another look around the room. 'Come on, he's not here.' He left the room and locked the door behind Chantal. Then followed her downstairs.

HUNTER STEPPED out into the cold again. The sun had slipped below the horizon and the sea breeze had picked up, flinging a discarded newspaper around the turning space. He unlocked the Passat but didn't get in.

The assumption that Jock would return to the hotel had fallen apart. Hunter had no clue as to where he was or any idea why he'd run from the cops.

Hunter couldn't help but shake his head. 'I just want to find my brother.' His throat felt tight as he dialled Fiona's number.

And Jock actually answered. Sounded like he was driving, but the engine was that bit louder and that bit further away. Given Hunter was resting against his car, that was yet another mystery. 'Where are you?'

'Son, I need to lie low for a bit, okay?' Click and he was gone.

'Bastard hung up on me.' Hunter tried again, but it went straight to voicemail. He opened the car and got in, slamming the door behind him.

Chantal sat on the passenger seat like she was at a

crime scene. Up ahead, the local service bus trundled down the road from Fortrose, headlights on, a few passengers standing to get off. 'He's a bloody depraved pervert and...' She nudged his arm. 'Why aren't you listening to me?'

'Got an idea.' Hunter put the car in gear and drove off, pulling up outside the pizza restaurant, with a good view of the square outside the hotel and across the beach. He dialled a number. It was answered. 'Elvis, need you to ping a number for me.'

'I'm not just here for the nasty things in life like a blocked drain...'

Hunter read out Fiona's number.

'Right. Got it. He's moving fast, slipping between cell towers like nobody's business.'

'Knew it. He's on the bus. Where is he?'

'Just by Cromarty. Tell you, the brewery there is top notch.'

'Thanks, mate.' Hunter killed the call. 'Come on.' He got out and set off back to the hotel.

One last look and the place was still quiet and dark, but the dim lights of a bus in the distance. He let Chantal go first and followed her, waiting by the window and peering out.

A man hopped off the bus and bounded over to the hotel. He jogged towards the building and shot up the steps, slowing as he neared the top. Hunter stepped over to the doorway and waited at the side.

Jock blundered through, unfolding his keys and scowling.

Hunter grabbed his shoulder, spun him round and pinned him to the wall. 'Oh, look, there he is.'

'Ah, shite.' Jock stopped wriggling. 'Craig, son, I need to get out of here.'

'Where's the phone?'

'Right.' Jock reached into his pocket for a blue-silver Samsung. 'Here.' He passed it over.

Hunter unlocked it. 'You've been messaging Shug, pretending to be Fiona. She just gave you her passcode?'

'I can guess most people's based on a few questions. Yours is 4781.'

'Jesus.' Hunter felt himself blush as he checked the messages.

Shug
Crom harbour
Quarter to six
Be there or be a prick

Half an hour.

24

Hunter sat in the car and checked the dashboard clock. 17:40, and no sign of an early appearance by Shug, unless he was watching from afar.

'Cullen's late.' Chantal leaned forward to stretch out. 'We should've put the meeting back.'

'No chance of that, hen.' Jock in the back, his foot jiggling like he was playing in a ceilidh band. Or he was bursting for the toilet. Like a small child. 'One-time deal. Someone like that gets in touch with info you want or need, you don't get much say in when you meet.'

Chantal twisted round to frown at him. 'What exactly was your plan, then?'

Jock sat back, arms folded. 'Listen, that laddie knows what happened. I was going to go to town on him.'

Chantal looked round with a sneer. 'With your Fleshlight?'

Jock shrugged. 'How the hell did you find that?'

'Not exactly well hidden, was it?'

'Why did you run?'

Jock shrugged. 'I didn't want to get caught up in a load of nonsense with the police.'

'You're sitting in a car with two cops.' Hunter twisted fully round to face him. 'Besides, you didn't know I'd find a dead body in that flat. You didn't know the cops would be a couple of minutes away.'

'I just needed to get out of there, son. Don't need any noise from the cops.'

'What have you done, Dad?'

Jock slumped back in his chair. 'I'm living in my car.'

'It doesn't look like it. It's too tidy.'

'Well, I don't exactly want to put up a sign saying "Man sleeping here, come and steal his valuables", do I?'

Chantal smirked at him. 'Who would steal a used Fleshlight?'

'Shut up about that. Christ!' Jock let his seatbelt whizz up. 'Look, I'm a tidy man, and I clean up every morning. And I've a special cleaner for that thing. I've got a sleeping bag and one of those sleep pillows for the planes. Then Murray let me stay at his for a bit while things blew over.'

'What things?'

'Never you mind.' Jock tapped at the window. 'Looks like Shug's not turning up. Five minutes late now. That Fiona lassie said he'd be bang on time.'

'Fiona knew about this?'

'Well, I sounded her out about Shug. She wasn't exactly full of great chat. Think she's got a thing for me. I'm sick to the back teeth of daddy issues.'

'No, you exploit them.' Hunter scanned the area. The sweep of the coast, down to the small harbour. Nobody around in the early evening gloom, not even dog-walkers. He got out his phone and called Elvis. 'You guys on your way over or what?'

'Got a wee bit of a problem, Craigy boy. Sheep all over the road. Can't get through.'

'You're kidding me.'

'Wish I was. We're doubling back to the A9 and taking the low road. Be another fifteen minutes.'

'Bloody hell.' Hunter tightened his grip on the phone, felt like snapping the bastard thing. A few deep breaths and he was calm again. 'Can you track a number for me?'

'Sure. Got my laptop primed and ready. What is it?'

Hunter read it out.

'My reception's not the best up here in the boonies, let's see.' Clicky clacky sounds. 'Aha, got it. One potato, two potato, three potato and bang. Well, it looks like it's in Cromarty. And it's moving. If I was a betting man, I'd say it's near the pub. That help?'

'A bit, aye. Cheers, Elvis.' Hunter hung up. 'Shug's here.'

'Thought you'd be able to track his phone down to the inch, son?'

'Doesn't work like that. We're not CTU.'

'CT-what?'

'It's a *24* reference. Never mind.' Hunter got out of the car. 'Let's split up and find him. Jock, you stay here.'

'What? I'm not—'

'Last time, you buggered off with a stolen phone. Stay here and behave, okay?'

A nod and a grunt from Jock, then the old git tugged his jacket collar up and sat back.

Hunter locked the door this time, then followed Chantal

towards Big Vennel and the high street. 'He's going to screw this up, isn't he?' He sighed. 'Just like he's screwed everything else up in his life.'

On the high street, a pair of male smokers lurked outside the pub, eyeing up an office worker heading home. No sign of Shug, not that they had much to go on other than a sketchy drunk Facebook photo.

'Right, you go that way.' Chantal set off towards the pub, leaving Hunter to head towards the art centre, to where he'd tailed Fiona the previous night. The short side roads were mostly empty, just a couple of businessmen getting out of their cars in the pale streetlight glow. He called Chantal as he walked. 'You got anything?'

'Not yet. You?'

'Still nothing.' Hunter looked back the way and spotted her talking to the woman with the heels. 'Keep me posted.' He ended the call and dialled Elvis again. 'Can you get me an update on that phone's location?'

'Checking... It's not moved yet, Craig.'

'Still near the pub?'

'Aye, as far as the tech will let me see. You know, if I had access to the GPS...'

'Can you?'

'Ha, good one.'

Chantal was talking to the smokers outside the pub, but their body language didn't look encouraging.

Hunter was outside the arts centre now. No ceilidhs tonight, not even a candlelit yoga session. Down the street to the shore, Jock sat in the car stretching out his back, the window cracked open and his sharp breath puffing in the air.

No Shug. And no other possible routes. So he doubled back towards the pub, rounding the bend again.

Chantal was hammering towards him, chasing after someone. Shug, presumably, though the light was so low he couldn't see who.

Hunter darted towards them, his boots clomping off the road, rattling his fragile ribs.

Chantal caught up with Shug, but he darted away from her grasp, kicked her in the shin and pushed her over, sending her tumbling into the pub doorway, then bombed towards Hunter.

Hunter closed on him, but Shug cut down a side street towards the shore. A stark choice—Shug or Chantal?

Hunter raced over to help her up from the doorway, yelling, 'You alright?'

'Get him!' Her shout echoed round the street.

'Right.' Hunter sprinted off down the vennel, his boots slapping off the cobbles now, his breath coming slow and hard, but digging into his ribs. 'STOP!'

Shug was fast, short and lithe, head ducked low, and outpacing Hunter, gaining half a stride with each one of Hunter's. He spun out at the end of the street, turning right, and Hunter pushed hard, rounding off the corner, and stopped dead.

Jock stood over Shug, now lying on the ground. Jock knelt low and grabbed Shug by the throat. 'Right, you little shite. Where the hell is my son?'

Shug tried kicking him away but Jock held him fast, pinned to the pavement. 'Get to France!'

Hunter elbowed Jock out of the way and caught a sickly smell. Dogshit. He gripped Shug by the wrist, yanking him up to standing, and saw a smear all up his back. He let out a deep sigh, even though his breathing was still racing.

Chantal jogged over, dabbing her mouth with the back of her hand.

Hunter gave her a nod, still holding on to Shug. 'You okay?'

'I'm fine.' Chantal slowed to a leisurely stroll and put her phone to her ear. 'Thanks for the backup, Scott. We've got Shug.'

Hunter turned on Jock. 'I told you to stay.'

'Well, I've got two pairs of keys, haven't I?' Jock stared at Shug. 'And I wanted to sort this pervert out with my own two hands.'

Shug bristled. 'Who you calling pervert, you old wanker?'

'Leading my son astray!'

'Mate, they were the ones leading me astray. Pair of them, snorting amyl nitrate. Couldn't keep their hands off each other's cocks, kept trying it on with me. Not my scene.'

Jock wrestled free and stomped towards Shug. 'You come here and say that!'

Hunter grabbed Jock by the shoulders. 'STOP!'

And he did.

Hunter focused on Shug, trying to ignore the reek of dog muck. 'Tell me everything you know about Murray Hunter.'

'Like I told that old prick, you can get to France.'

25

The interview room still stank of boiled fish, but it was getting worse. Rotten, boiled fish. That could play to their advantage this time. Maybe. But it was masked by the cloying reek of dog shit. Shug sat there, in a fresh tracksuit, still somehow stinking of it.

Hunter leaned forward, catching his shirt button on the edge of the table. 'We're looking for a Keith Wilson.' He let the name settle in the air and in the interviewee's mind. 'You seen him recently?'

Shug sat back, cleared his throat, then took a long sip of water, slow and careful, while he stared at Cullen, then at Hunter. Under the harsh strip lights, his weaselly features were lined with creases and cracks. Not so much a lived-in face, as a long series of stays in grotty hotels. All this time, he'd not even looked at Hunter. Didn't seem the sort to defer to official hierarchy, so maybe there was something else in his reticence. Like knowing what happened to Murray.

Shame, or guilt maybe. 'No idea what you're talking about, pal.'

'Know anything about Keith's death?'

'Now hold on a minute!' Shug raised his hands high in the air and shot a dark glare at Hunter. 'What the hell are you talking about?'

'Sure you don't want that lawyer in here?'

'Quite sure, pal, quite sure.'

Usually it was a blessed relief to be without a snidey little bastard in a cheap suit, but when someone was this deep in trouble, a lawyer could help coax out the truth in exchange for something useful for their client. Then again, Shug didn't seem to know how deep in the shit he was.

'You know where Murray Hunter is?'

Shug frowned, running a hand over the salt-and-pepper stubble. 'The actor?'

'What?'

'You know, the comedian boy.' Shug started clicking his fingers. 'In that *Absolutely* show. Mind it? Back in the eighties?'

'Different spelling.' Cullen leaned forward, a subtle flash of his eyebrows telling Hunter that he was taking over. 'That was Moray as in the firth. This is Murray as in David Murray. Used to own Rangers.'

Shug rolled his eyes. 'I'm not a hun, pal.'

'Right.' Cullen nodded slowly. 'So, is it Ross County or Inverness Caley Thistle?'

'Aye, good one. Not been arsed with football in many a year. Used to be a Celtic fan, as it happens, but...'

'But you gave that up for heroin.'

Shug gave Cullen a long hard look. 'Do you want me to help you or what?'

'You know which one it is, so let's cut to the chase. Last week, you took two people on your boat out to an oil rig in the firth.'

A shrug. 'So you say.'

'We've got evidence of it, you need to—'

'I didn't kill him.'

'But you know who did, right?'

'You seem to have the wrong idea about me, pal. I'm just a fisherman with a sideline in boat tours.'

Hunter nodded at his bony arms, covered in tiny pinpricks. 'Which doesn't explain the track marks.'

Shug started rolling down his left sleeve.

'The way I see it, something happened on that oil rig.' Hunter waited until the right sleeve covered the scabbed-over dots on Shug's skeletal forearm. 'Now, we have video evidence that you were on the rig with them.'

'Like hell I was!'

'You were on the jetty.'

Shug slumped back in his chair and shoved his hands in his pockets.

'Despite running from us, you're here as a potential witness, not a suspect.' Hunter screwed up his face, started tilting his head from side to side like he was weighing something up. 'The way it's looking, though, I think we should rethink that approach.'

Shug picked up his water again, his hand shaking slightly. He didn't speak.

Hunter glanced over at Cullen. 'What do you think, Inspector?'

Cullen sat back and folded his arms, twisting his lips as he thought. 'I agree with your assessment. Way I see it, he's just a fisherman caught up in something here. Something he didn't expect.' His pause let Shug nod a few times, but he clearly didn't realise he'd stepped into a trap and the snare was biting into his leg. 'But he's hiding something from us, isn't he? And I'd *really* love to know what. Because if we found out from someone else the information he's keeping back, then that really wouldn't look good for him, would it?'

Shug still kept quiet.

'Of course, if that something implicates him in a murder, then—'

'I wasn't involved in anything like that!'

Cullen nodded slowly. 'So how about you tell us exactly how you are involved?'

Shug gasped out a sigh. He stared up at the ceiling, the lights shining on his neck and showing a diagonal slash across his throat from his right ear. 'Sod it.' He settled back in his chair and hugged his arms tight around his skinny frame. 'I took those two loons over to that rig, okay? I waited there for them while they went up, but a boat came over. I was about to hightail it out of there when I spotted that Keith boy coming back down the ladder, absolutely shitting himself. He got in and told me to go. So we did.'

'He say what happened to Murray?'

'Said nothing much, pal.'

Hunter decided not to press it now, just keep him talking. 'Where did the boat come from?'

'From the Invergordon side, but I couldn't say exactly where. Got a few suspicions.'

'Any you'd like to share with us?'

'Nothing you'd find useful.'

'Keith didn't bring anything back?'

Shug snorted.

'We know he found drugs up there.' Cullen thumbed at the door. 'I've got five drugs squad guys just arrived from Edinburgh. Specialists. If you tell us something useful about what Keith found, you can walk out of here a free man.'

Hunter nodded along with Cullen's words. 'Just the truth, that's all we want.'

Shug took a few seconds to think it through, his finger tracing the line on his neck. Then he nodded. 'So, this Keith lad found a load of smack on the oil rig. He grabbed a couple blocks when he ran off.'

'A couple?'

'I saw two. He might've had more. I don't know.' Shug scratched at his right arm. 'I helped him test the purity. This stuff was like the pure driven snow, I tell you.'

'You used it?'

Shug looked away, calculating the odds. Same as every heavy user. His freedom to inject and shorten his lifespan versus admitting his habit and doing time, even if in rehab. 'A spoonful of sugar, pal.'

'So you're an addict?'

Another nod, much shorter and more subtle than the others.

'It's quite common among the fishing community, but you know that. We won't report you to anyone.'

'Okay, so I'm a smackhead.' Shug seemed to deflate as he spoke, like he was at a Narcotics Anonymous meeting. 'I injected on shore leave, then popped methadone when I was out at sea. But that work's dried up, so...'

'So you're just taking heroin all the time?'

'Apart from when I take people out on the boat.'

Hunter tapped a shoe off Cullen's foot, indicating he was taking over again. This wasn't a drugs bust, it was locating a person of interest in a double murder. Probably a triple. 'So what happened to the rest of Keith's heroin?'

'Sold it.' Shug had the thousand-yard stare of a wine or coffee connoisseur. 'Well, I took a chunk of it, kept it for my own supply. Shit's so pure it'll keep me going for months. First lot I took, I was strung out on the floor, man. Total Kurt Cobain shot. Felt just like the first time I tried smack. It's what we're all chasing.'

'And the rest of it?'

'Keith wanted nothing to do with it. Said it was covered in blood.'

'But you wanted everything to do with it, right?'

'Right. Met this geezer in the pub one night. Kid was from Edinburgh but laying low in Cromarty. Daft prick was giving it the chat, trying to impress people. Not sure how low you can lie when you're telling complete strangers you're a dealer, but he was. And he was keen to get hold of all that gear and had the money to hand, so...'

'How much did you get?'

'Twenty grand. Know it's worth a lot more, but it's nice to have the cash now. Pay off some debts, get some work done to the *Pride of Crom*. Maybe let me buy the other half off Wee Ally.'

Hunter decided to keep the news of Ally's death away from Shug just now. 'And he just happened to have twenty grand on him?'

'Well, it was in his caravan. Drove us down there. Boy

had it in an Adidas sports bag. Dude like that, he'll have an emergency slush fund, won't he? Enough to keep him going long enough that the heat dies away.'

'He give you his name?'

'Nope. Just took his cash and buggered off.'

'He say where he was taking the heroin?'

'You messing with me? I barely ask my punters where they want to go on my boat, let alone where a dealer's taking a load of smack I don't want to know anything about.'

Hunter decided to hit him with it. 'Any idea why someone would murder Alistair McCoull?'

'What?' Shug's pale face lost a few more shades. 'Ally?' His gaze shot between them. 'Ally's dead?'

'Murdered. At his home.'

'Christ.' Shug huffed out a sigh and started crying. 'Man...'

And they weren't getting any more out of him.

HUNTER STOOD in the obs suite and sipped the machine coffee, black with three sugars. Felt his teeth lose a few layers of enamel. He looked over at Cullen, sipping his own coffee, but staring at Shug on the monitor. 'So my brother's dead?'

Cullen clamped his shoulder. 'You okay?'

'I just want to find who did this.'

'Well, that confirmed the drugs were real and now we know what happened to them.' Cullen rested his cup on the table. 'And we played well together in there. Just like old days, but more effective.'

'Thanks.'

'What are our options here?'

Hunter took another sip. 'Find the dealer, find the smack.'

'And what does that give us?'

Good question. Hunter needed to find Murray. Was chasing down a heroin deal likely to do that? 'The pharmacology could be interesting, could tie it to a known dealer, someone we could shake down.'

'That's one for the drugs squad and it'll take days.' Cullen tossed his empty cup in the bin, leaving a trail of black dots on the inside. 'You really think your brother's caught up in this narcotics operation?'

'Caught up, aye, but involved? No. All we've got is a smackhead fisherman's word for what happened. That GoPro gives a part of the story, but who knows where it leads.' Hunter rested the cup on the table. 'We need to speak to this dealer. If we can tie the drugs to an ongoing operation, that might give us a lead.'

'Let's back up a bit here.' Cullen picked up his cup and took a long slug. 'What have you got so far?'

'Well, my brother's boyfriend's dead, murdered in his flat in Inverness. Shug took them out to that rig, where they found a ton of heroin. Keith swiped a couple of blocks and escaped. Shug sold some to a mystery dealer and went to ground. We were really lucky to catch him.'

'Two deaths in such a short space of time has to be linked, right?'

'I'd say so. Shug was hiding out. We thought he was abroad, but he was somewhere local. Say whoever killed Murray identified Shug's boat. They've got a name, so they murder the co-owner in Perth. I saw someone at Shug's cottage in Fortrose looking for him.'

Cullen focused on the screen again, on Shug scratching at his arms.

The door swung open and Elvis stepped in, crowding an already full room. 'Ah, Craig, there you are.'

'Alright, Elvis. What's up?'

'See your old man? There's a missing persons report on him.'

26

Jock was in the station canteen, chewing hard and noisily, his lips slapping together. A plate of six sausages sat in front of him, artfully drizzled with brown sauce. He looked up at Hunter and said something, but it was just meaty mush.

Hunter took the seat opposite, leaving Elvis standing like an idiot. 'Thought this was a fasting day.'

'Aye, well. Laddie behind the counter said they had a load of sausages going off. Needs must, eh? Besides, I've acted like a bit of an arse today. Running from the cops and that.' Jock frowned at Elvis. 'You're the boy from the Crafty Butcher podcast, right?'

'Eh.' Elvis frowned, his lips shifting between a smile at being recognised, and a scowl at being recognised. 'Crafty what?'

'You heard it, Craig, didn't you?' Jock stabbed a sausage-speared fork at Elvis. 'I know it's you, son. Recognise your voice a mile away. You really think Stone is the best brewery in the world?'

'I never actually said that.'

'Give us a minute.' Hunter waved Elvis away, then focused on his dad. 'Jock, why is there a missing persons report out on you?'

Jock put another sausage into his mouth, whole, and took ages to chew it. 'You tell me, son.'

'According to this,' Hunter unrolled a sheet of paper, 'one Kirsten Turnbull of Wallyford has reported you missing.'

'Wee place near Musselburgh. Used to be a mining—'

'I know where it is.' Hunter stabbed the paper. 'Who is she?'

Jock went for another sausage.

Hunter swatted the fork away and it spilled across the plate, then clattered to the floor. 'I'm serious here. If there's a missing persons report on you, then I've got to follow up with the investigating officer.'

'Fine.' Jock reached across to the dirty plate diagonally opposite and inspected the soiled fork. 'I got kicked out by my girlfriend.'

Hunter got a vision of Kirsten Turnbull as yet another middle-aged siren tempting Jock away from his mother, yet another woman with problems he was more than happy to exploit for free bed and board. 'What did you do?'

'Women don't understand me, son.'

'I'll say...'

'That's why I was staying with your brother. I mean, I was sleeping in my car before that, but at least I've got one boy who still cares about me.'

Hunter narrowed his eyes.

'But Murray said it was temporary, just while he was busy and away. And I knew Kirsten would understand in time.'

'Or there'd be another Kirsten? Maybe a Borders one in Galashiels or Melrose or Hawick?'

'Hawick? Christ, I've got standards.' Jock scowled. 'Women love me, son. Not much I can do about that.'

'Same deal as with Mum? She feeds you, lets you sleep in her bed until you piss her off and she kicks you out? Same every time. Right?'

'It's love, son.'

'Love. Right.'

'I mean it.' Jock grabbed Hunter's wrist and looked at him with the frenzied eyes of the born-again. 'Kirsten's one of those exotic dancers.'

A groan escaped Hunter's lips. 'You're in love with a *stripper*?'

'That's a bit harsh.'

'But she takes her clothes off for money?'

'Well, aye.'

'Christ.' Hunter couldn't help but shake his head. Usually it was parents disappointed with their children. 'How old is Kirsten?'

Dad looked away. 'Twenty.'

'You're sleeping with a twenty-year-old?'

Jock speared another sausage with a dirty fork he'd taken from someone else's plate. Manky bastard. 'Knew you wouldn't understand.'

'Jock, she's sixteen years younger than *me*!' Hunter shook his head. 'Jesus, she's young enough to be *my* daughter let alone yours.'

'Come on, Craig, that's—'

'Where does she work?'

'Wonderland in Edinburgh. Over on Lothian Road.'

Someone behind Hunter laughed. 'That's Cullen's favourite place.' Elvis.

Hunter shot him a glare that would read 'piss off' to most people. 'Are you still here?'

Elvis shrugged. 'Place is under new management. Last owner was murdered. Some London boy owns it now. Much classier than it used to be.'

'The lassie's in love with me, son. I mean, she's got really bad daddy issues.'

'Grandaddy issues, more like.' Elvis laughed again.

Jock rocked forward, chuckling as he chewed his latest sausage.

'Elvis, when I told you to give us a minute? Piss off.'

'Keep your wig on, jeez.' Elvis walked over to the coffee machine and started jangling coins in his pocket.

Hunter leaned in close to Jock again. 'So why did Kirsten report you missing?'

'Because she's so much younger than me and doesn't know what to do.' He belched into his fist. 'Back there, I grabbed that wee lassie's phone and called Kirsten, but she knew it was me and begged me to come home, so I hung up. Then I decided to find Murray myself, so I called Shug, got him to agree to meet.'

'So you ran away because of a combination of commitment phobia and hanger?'

'I'm not—' Jock pushed the plate away. 'You had the car keys and I'd forgotten about the spares I keep in the glovebox until you locked me in.'

'Well, you've made a right mess of this.'

'Son, I'm sixty-four, like in that Beatles song. Well, your mother and me, we don't meet or greet each other anymore. But Kirsten, it's freaky as hell. I mean, she's paid to strip for all sorts. Businessmen, boys from the rigs, joiners, milkmen. Tinkers, tailors, soldiers and maybe not sailors.' Jock bellowed at his own joke. 'But that sort of girl's usually really cynical and clued up, right? Knows her onions, knows how to exploit the rubes in there. Been doing it since she was sixteen and knows how to do it, but she's crazy about me. Will do anything for me. And I mean *anything*.'

'I don't want to know.'

'Cooking and cleaning, not just the sexy bedroom stuff. Or kitchen worktop. Or Cramond Isle.'

'Jesus! Stop!'

Jock brushed a hand across his lips. 'Look, son, I couldn't handle her. I panicked and ran. I'm forty-four years older than her. It's not right. So I was sleeping in my car, then I met up with your brother for a beer a few weeks back and he let me stay in the flat above his garage if I looked after his chickens.' He put his fork down and pushed his plate away. 'Look, I don't know if I love her. I mean, I loved your mother and I made a cat's arsehole of that. I bugger everything up. I upset your mother. I screwed up you and your brother.' He brushed something out of his eye. 'Now I'm worried about messing up Kirsten.'

'Oh, shite, she's pregnant, isn't she?'

'Sorry, son. It's not my finest hour.' Jock slumped back in his chair. 'Shug know anything?'

'Of course he didn't. He's a smackhead. Kept going on about Keith selling that block of heroin to his dealer.'

Jock frowned. 'He say who the dealer is?'

'No, why?'

'What did he say about him?'

'Just that he was from Edinburgh and was hiding out in Cromarty for a while.'

Jock nodded slowly. 'I've got an idea who might know.'

27

Hunter gripped the wheel tight, keeping the Passat on its lead, taking it nice and slow, crawling along Cromarty's high street. 'You awake?'

'Course I'm bloody awake.' Jock burped and let out a sausagey mist.

'So where is it, then?'

'Left there.'

Hunter knew the vennel. 'This is where Murray was staying, right?'

'Right.' Jock folded his arms. 'It's the American couple I was talking to in the pub.'

'You could've told me this back in Inverness.'

'Aye, and you'd have come here without me. We're looking for my son as well as your brother.'

Hunter tore his door open and stepped into the dim lane. He headed round to Jock's side, the seaweed reek hitting his nostrils, soon buried under his father's overpowering aftershave, even at this hour. 'Why them?'

'When you were out trying to find that Fiona lassie, I was drinking with them. They told me they were much more into substances, if I caught their drift, but they were running low. Asked if I knew anyone who could help out. Said they'd been speaking to a lad they met in the boozer. Said he was from Edinburgh.' He shook his head. 'The way those Yanks say Edinburgh, I swear...'

Cullen's Golf slid along the lane, quiet as a fox, and parked behind them. Elvis got out, tucking his shirt into his trousers.

Cullen got out next. 'Do you know the dealer?'

'A drug dealer? Come on. Hardly.'

Hunter focused on Elvis. 'Keep Jock in the car.'

'Craig, you're not my boss.'

'This isn't a professional thing. If he goes walkabout, I will break your legs.'

Elvis swallowed hard. 'Christ.' His eyes pleaded with Cullen.

'Stay here, okay?'

'Right...'

Jock winked at Hunter then beamed at Elvis. 'You tried that blonde in the hotel down the front? It's a gorgeous pint.'

And just like that, Elvis got in the driver's seat. 'Oh? Do tell.'

Cullen walked over to Hunter, shaking his head. 'This the place?'

'Aye, assuming they're in.' Hunter followed him over to the house and knocked on the door. Just like the previous night. Felt like months ago.

No answer. Lights on, though, and music playing. The

Cure. Chiming bass guitar, pounding drums and guitars floating in the ether.

'What's the play here, Scott?'

Cullen tried the door. It was open. 'Nothing ventured.' With a shrug, he sneaked in, drawing his baton.

Hunter realised he was flying blind. No cuffs, no baton.

In the kitchen, the music switched to a Depeche Mode song.

The American couple were at the kitchen table, Randy hunkering low to snort a monster line of coke off the woodwork. 'Oh my Christ! This is good shit!'

The woman rested her glass of red wine and took the rolled-up banknote off her husband, her hungry eyes sparking at her own line. Then she looked right at them. 'Holy shit!'

Cullen had his warrant card out. 'Police!'

Wine splashed everywhere, sluicing the cocaine down the lines cut around the table edge.

'SHIT SHIT SHIT!' Randy ran off.

'Got him!' Hunter followed, taking it slow.

The big guy was halfway up the stairs, staring back, face red, eyes wild. Looked like he was going to have a heart attack. 'GET BACK!'

Hunter stepped onto the first step. 'Just need a word, sir.'

'PISS OFF!'

'Come on, sir, it's all right. We'll turn a blind eye to the drugs.'

'NO!' And he turned and clattered up the steps.

Nowhere near as fast as Hunter, though. He closed the gap to two steps then reached out and grabbed the big guy's T-shirt, right in the middle. He held him there.

Randy slipped and fell backwards, his bulk crashing through Hunter and sending them rolling down. As they went, Hunter tried to keep hold of him. A knee caught his gut, but he didn't let go, instead wrapping his forearm around Randy's throat.

Then he lost the grip as he ended up on top, then another revolution and he was on the bottom and couldn't see anything. He gripped hold of fabric and a ripping sound cut the air, then a big hairy arse filled his face, Hunter's cheeks touching sweaty bum.

He wrapped his arms around the American, just about interlocking his fingers around his obese waist. 'Stay still!'

Randy was a wriggler. Kicking and elbowing.

'Stay! Still!' Hunter twisted round and pulled his arm up into a half nelson. Then he got the other one round to complete the move, pushing Randy flat against the stairs. 'You going to stop trying to get away?'

A muffled, 'Yes!'

'I'll let go and you can sit up but if you run I will take you down again, okay?'

'Submit!'

Hunter let him go.

The big man eased himself into a sitting position. Looked like he had a few bruises coming. His coke mania seemed to have diminished slightly, though his rage was still boiling away.

'It's Randy, isn't it?'

It seemed like a shrug. Hard to tell.

'Need you to answer a few questions about those drugs.'

Randy just shook his head, breathing hard and heavy. 'You can't do this!' A jab of the finger. 'I know my rights!'

'This isn't about the drugs.'

'You just said it was!'

'It's about who you got them from.'

'No way, man. No way.' Randy pulled a zip across his lips.

Hunter wasn't getting any more out of him. Not here and not like this.

He grabbed his arm and pulled him to standing. 'Right, you're coming with me.'

HUNTER SAT Randy by the kitchen table, now spotless and glistening. 'Sit there.'

Elvis was ringing out a cloth in the sink, shaking his head and scowling. The music had shifted to New Order, playing at a lower level. One of their dancier songs.

Cullen was standing behind the American's partner, hands on hips. 'Where did you get the coke?'

'Like I'm telling you that.' Randy shook his head. 'Son of a bitch.'

Cullen gave Hunter a flash of the eyebrows as he sat.

'This is barbaric.' The big man sat back, eyes swivelling in his head. The coke mania was still clinging to him. 'I want you to speak to the goddamn embassy!'

'The ambassador's people are going to tell us to charge you with drug possession.'

'This is goddamn outrageous.' Randy slammed a meaty fist off the table, rage burning in his eyes. 'You bust into our apartment and bring us in here?'

'Sir, we witnessed you taking a controlled substance.

Class A too. I don't know what that's like back in the USA, but—'

'Goddamn make me sick, you limey asshole. We bailed your asses out in the Second World War and we've helped your sorry asses ever since. And this is how you repay us?'

'Sir, you're barking up the wrong tree.'

Randy tried to flip the table. But the weight of Cullen and Hunter held it in place. He yelped—all he'd got was a sore wrist. 'You asshat! This is outrageous! You can't do this to Uncle Sam!' The coke was talking. Shouting. Screaming.

Hunter gave him a smile. 'You're from Philly, right?'

That seemed to knock Randy off balance. 'So?'

'The next time you'll see the city of brotherly love will be 2026. Class A possession with intent to supply carries a minimum seven-year sentence.'

'Supply?'

Hunter held up a bag containing over a hundred pills. 'That's a lot of ecstasy. And I found a lot of cocaine in your—'

'Goddamnit!' Another pounding on the table. 'I'm not a drug dealer!'

Cullen sat back, nodding and smiling. 'It's not for us to assess. We merely supply the facts to the procurator fiscal— that's the district attorney in your language, Randy—and her team determines the charges. Given the mountain of evidence there, I suspect any jury will find you guilty.'

Randy slumped forward, head in hands. 'Goddamnit.'

'Of course, if you said you'd never take drugs again, we could be lenient.'

'Piss off.' He didn't look up at them.

'And if you helped us track down who you got the drugs from, well...'

That got him. 'Well what?'

'Well, we can see what we can do about forgetting what we saw. Or we can wait for the forensics guys to—'

'Forensics?'

'They're on their way here to tear this place apart.' Cullen pointed a finger pistol at him. 'But if you tell us what you know about the dealer you bought the drugs off...'

Randy took one look at his wife, then sighed. 'Listen, we spoke to this guy in the pub one night. Shug? Is that even a name?'

'It's Scots for Hugh. Like Dod for George.' Hunter gritted his teeth. 'Or Jock for John.'

Randy nodded like he followed it. Maybe the gravity of the situation was getting through to him. 'Well, Shug said his guy had gone to ground and passed us to this dealer he'd just met. We bought a load of coke and ecstasy from this dude. Now we're running low and—'

'What?' Hunter shook the bag. 'This is running low?'

'Sure. Not the X, but the coke is like one night left.' Randy rubbed at his nostrils, his eyes darting around like he wanted to shove some more up there. 'I really wanted some ketamine to take the edge off this high, but he's gone to ground.'

Hunter walked over to the stereo and killed New Order. He stared hard at Randy, trying to keep him focused. 'What was this guy's name?'

Randy broke into a broad grin. 'I am not saying shit, man.'

Cullen gave Hunter a long hard look, then flicked his head towards the doorway. 'What a bloody mess.'

Elvis joined them, shaking his head. 'Boy's away with the bloody fairies.'

Cullen pinched his nose. 'Does anyone know where the drugs squad are?'

'Stuck.' Elvis started picking at his teeth. 'Heard there's a big accident on the A9. Three-car pile-up just north of Dunkeld.'

'So I need an Inverness cop who knows any drug dealers in Cromarty. Christ, saying that out loud makes it sound that bit more impossible.'

Elvis clapped his hands together. 'Leave it with me.' And he left the house.

Hunter stared at Cullen. 'Let me nail him down.'

'No violence.'

Randy leaned against the table, completely wasted, and not elegantly. The guy was barely hanging together, eyes rolling around.

Hunter crouched low, going to Randy's eye level and slapped the fat guy on the back. 'Randy, I need to speak to your dealer.'

'He's back in Philly, dude.'

'Your one here. The one who gave you the ecstasy and the cocaine.' Hunter leaned in close. 'I'll maybe get you some ketamine.'

Randy frowned. 'That guy.'

'You going to tell me his name?'

Randy shrugged. 'Why should I?'

'Listen to me.' Hunter held his gaze for a few seconds. 'Your country might specialise in brutal incarceration, but it's no picnic over here. Especially for the amount of drugs you had in this house.' He pointed over at Dani. 'And your better half will serve time in Cornton Vale, a women-only prison. It's not pretty there.'

Randy snorted. 'This you saying you'll drop the drugs charge if I talk?'

'You'll get a fine and a criminal record. But that's it. You can get back home on your scheduled flight.'

Randy sank back in his chair, exhaling softly. 'But a record?'

'Sorry. You can't possess that much coke and get away with it. Them's the breaks.'

'The drugs are all mine, right? Dani had nothing to do with it.'

'Okay, deal. So, I need your side of the bargain first. Where is he?'

'So I texted this guy at lunchtime, said we needed more stuff. He texted back, said he can't come up to Cromarty, but we can go to him.' Randy looked around the room. 'Get me my cell.'

'Why?'

'Because he gave me his address, dumbass.'

Hunter stood up tall and reached out a hand.

Cullen held up an evidence bag, not looking too sure he should comply. Then he pulled out a swanky smartphone covered in so many stickers you couldn't tell which brand it was. 'What's the passcode?'

'Face ID, dude.'

Cullen pointed the phone at Randy then looked back at it. 'That's got it. He give you a name?'

'Called himself Mick.'

Cullen tapped and swiped at the screen. 'Here we go.' He held up the phone to Hunter, showing a WhatsApp chat:

Mick

Ashworth's Caravans, Kingussie

Call me when you get there

28

Hunter tore off a large chunk of battered haddock and bit into it. Tangy and a bit stale, but the only thing in the chip shop, and boy did he need his protein. And eating fish wasn't like eating meat, was it?

The caravan site seemed normal to him. No swimming pool, no pub, not the sort of place the average gangster would hide out in. Elderly couples sat on their verandas playing cards, even in this weather. Rain battered the windscreen, thick and heavy. Deep bass pounded from somewhere. Close to pub chucking-out time, so he was expecting a few lads to make a trip to the Co-op off-licence and 'all back to mine'.

Maybe it was perfect for hiding out, even if you weren't a gangster so much as a mysterious drug dealer.

On the back seat, Elvis let out a burp, followed by a soggy fart.

Chantal scowled at him, still barely halfway through her own fish supper. 'You don't exactly get any better, do you?'

'Can't improve on perfection.' Another burp. 'Look lively.' He pointed to a set of approaching headlights. 'That the locals?'

Hunter looked over at Cullen's car, parked a hundred metres closer, and got a flash of lights. 'Looks like it.' He refolded his food and stuffed it in the door pocket. 'Let's go.'

Chantal shook her head. 'I'm finishing this.'

'Suit yourself, Sarge.' Hunter winked at her and got out into the heavy downpour. He was drenched in seconds. He tugged his collar up and hurried over to Cullen's car.

Cullen got out of his Golf. 'Where's Chantal?'

Hunter nodded at the Passat, just as Elvis got out, and cleared his throat. 'Keeping up a recce.'

'Right.'

'Cracking chips these. Cheers, Scott.' Elvis took another mouthful and rolled his wrapper into a ball. Hadn't thought what to do with it, so just held on to it.

Bain got out the far side and waved at the oncoming squad car. Hunter would love to have been a fly on the wall for that journey down the A9.

A local cop got out of the car. No partner, just him. Resource cuts being what they were up here, that made sense to Hunter. And the guy was a giant. Late twenties, a slightly darker shade of stubble than Cullen, and with legs long enough to outrun a racehorse. The rain didn't seem to bother him either, probably used to the onslaught. 'Well, how can I help you at this late hour?'

Cullen joined him by the driver's door, hoisting a brolly above his head. He'd need much longer arms to get it over both their heads. 'PC Robertson?'

'Davie.'

'Call me Scott.' Cullen shook his hand, but didn't introduce the rest of the ragtag squad.

Hunter barged between them. 'We spoke this morning. You're running the missing person investigation, aren't you?'

'You'll be Craig, then?'

'Right.'

'Sorry for radio silence. Night shift this week. And we've got no end of trouble up here. All the cutbacks mean I can cover anywhere from Dunkeld to Thurso, if I'm not careful. Sorry about your brother.'

Hunter nodded his thanks for the little Robertson had achieved. 'I'll assume you know nothing. An intelligence source pointed us towards a person of interest staying in one of the caravans. Name of Mick.'

'Mick?'

'That's all we've got. I need him safe and sound, okay?'

'Okay.' Robertson put his ringing phone to his ear. 'Aye, Andy. See us? Right.' He hung up. 'Owner. Andy Ashworth. Good lad.'

A squat man walked over, dressed for the weather, unlike the rest of them. Hood wrapped around this face, a couple of blonde curls poking out, darkened by the rain. 'So eh, Alex, how's it going, eh?' A nasal whine. Rural Perthshire if Hunter had to put money on it, each ehh stretching out. 'How can I help?'

Robertson folded his arms. 'Looking for a Mick.'

Ashworth nodded. 'Eh, caravan thirty-seven's owned by an Edinburgh guy. Steven West. Not seen him in, eh, months, but there's a guy called, eh, Michael staying there.'

Cullen pointed at Elvis. 'Get the address off him then put

in a call to Inspector Buchan in Edinburgh, get units to pick this Steven West up.'

'Can you bin this for me?' Elvis passed his wrapper to Ashworth. 'Buchan's not speaking to me.'

'What?'

'I beat him at chess and—'

'So call Lauren Reid. Call anyone. Just get someone to pick him up.'

'Boss.' Elvis walked off, phone to his ear.

Robertson stepped in close to Cullen and Hunter. 'Drug dealer? Sure?'

'That's what our intel says.'

'Well. Holidays, weekend golfing. Not drugs.'

'People golf up here?'

'*Decent* courses.'

'Take your word for it.' Cullen gestured for the team to huddle round him. 'Okay, we need to surround the caravan and take him for questioning. Craig, you're with me on entry. Bain and Chantal.' He smiled at Bain. 'Brian, can you find Chantal and guard the rear exit?' Then he smiled at Robertson. 'Constable, can you and Elvis keep—'

'Elvis?'

'DC Gordon.' Cullen looked over at him, still on the phone. 'You two keep a wide perimeter in case he makes a break for it. Might be an idea for you to have your engine running.'

'Got it.'

'You got any lads who could offer support?'

'Not here. One car north of Inverness. Two south.'

'But that's hundreds of miles!'

Robertson gave a flash of eyebrows.

Cullen clapped his hands together. 'Right, let's do this.'

Hunter followed Cullen over to the caravan. 'This going to work?'

Cullen glowered. 'Got to.'

'That's shite logic, Scott.'

'You're telling me.'

Bain dragged himself away from the gossip.

Cullen stopped by the pebble path outside the static caravan. Dim lights inside, the faint rumble of the TV and the smell of almost-burnt toast.

Hunter smiled at Chantal as she headed round the back of the caravan with Bain.

Brighter lights flicked on inside.

Hunter pulled Cullen down into the flooded flowerbed, his thighs getting a splash of cold water. The curtain twitched. He whispered, 'Well, there's someone in there.'

'Okay, let's just brazen this out.' Cullen walked up to the caravan's door and knocked on the plastic. 'Police!'

'No!'

Hunter recognised the voice, but couldn't place it.

Cullen hammered again. 'Sir, I need you to open up.'

'No!'

Dim headlights lit up Cullen. A car drove up the thin path. Hunter squinted through the rain.

A dark Range Rover. The guy from the Osprey Alpha was behind the wheel, caught in a flash of headlights from the side. 'Scott, that's the guy from the oil rig!'

'Get him.'

Hunter spun round the side of a thick tree, trying to circle the back of the car. But it squealed off through the park. He got out his radio. 'Hunter to Robertson, get after that vehicle!'

'On it.'

The local squad car whooped its siren in the dark night and sped off after the Range Rover.

'Shite!' Cullen's voice.

Hunter swivelled round. Cullen was in the flowerbed again, flat on his back.

A shadow caught in the bright light from the caravan door. Mick, running for it.

Hunter hauled Cullen up to standing, then sped off deeper into the caravan park. Hunter motioned for Cullen to take a right and head Mick off at the pass. He chased through darkness cut apart by shafts of light from caravan windows.

And he lost him.

Right at the edge of the park. A wall blocked exit or entry. Tall slats, interlaced enough to let the light in. He looked back the way, knowing he must've missed him somewhere. The last four caravans were arranged in a diamond, like a little village square. Benches sat outside. One had a long veranda. Bingo—Mick was up there, hiding from the light.

Hunter stepped towards him, taking it slow and quiet.

And Cullen blundered over, splashing in the puddles. The guy spotted Cullen's approach and shot towards him, eating up the distance before Hunter could let out a warning shout. Mick punched Cullen in the face, then a swift knee in the bollocks and Cullen went down.

Hunter didn't have time to see if he was alright, just

focused on keeping pace with his target back through the caravan park.

Bain and Chantal closed in on him from the other side. Mick stopped dead and the three of them circled round their prey. A flash of light and Mick lurched at Bain, who tripped over and landed in a paddling pool, ice-cold rainwater splashing out.

'YOU BASTARD!'

Hunter thundered after Mick and his feet started sliding on the muddy grass, but he wasn't letting the last lead in finding his brother—or what was left of him—get away.

The target was running towards a car, hand above his head and clicking a remote. The lights flashed. He got to the door and tore it open.

A fat smudge shoulder-barged Mick, cracking his head off the frame. Both of them went down.

Hunter caught up.

Elvis lay on top, rummaging around for spilled handcuffs, just out of reach.

'Here.' Hunter grabbed them and passed them over. 'Good work.'

Elvis got up and helped Mick to his feet. The light from the caravan caught his pale skin.

Hunter let out a deep breath.

'Mick' was none other than Derek Farrell, the drug-dealing rapist they'd been hunting for months.

29

Cullen winced with each step towards them. 'You got him?' He was still clutching his groin.

Hunter nodded. 'It's Derek Farrell.'

'Should I know that name?'

'I presume you DIs have a newsletter that covers wanted criminals, one you're supposed to actually read?'

'I'm not in the mood.' Cullen let out a deep breath. Looked like his eyes were watering and not from the rain. 'Swear, I'll never have kids now.'

'That's a good thing for the human race.'

'Craig, I mean it. The number of times I've seen Methven get clocked in the nadgers... Christ. Where is he?'

Hunter pointed off into the distance. 'Robertson and Elvis are taking him to Inverness. Robertson lost the guy from the rig.'

'Right.' Cullen got out his radio. 'And definitely can't place the guy's accent?'

'Could be anything, mate.'

'Okay. Sort that rabble out in there.'

'Boss.' Hunter stepped into the caravan, dripping wet, and joined Elvis in the living room.

Surprisingly nice. A long kitchen table set between Shaker units. In the corner, an L-shape sofa sat around a giant wall-mounted TV showing some aggressive beachside porno.

'Get that off.'

Bain was rooting around in the kitchen. He was still soaking wet, shivering, shaking his head. 'Eh?'

'The... Never mind.' Hunter hit the power button.

'Got something.' In a gloved hand, Bain held up a block of drugs very similar to the one on the GoPro footage.

Hunter took a long look at it. Pure white powder, too clean to be coke, but not dirty enough to be heroin. Certainly not street heroin. The evidence trail wasn't dead yet.

Bain walked over to the bathroom, giving the place a quick scan. 'Nobody's flushing anything down the toilet. Okay, toots, you want to do the other room? Check nobody's torching a stash.'

Chantal left him and entered the bedroom. Then stopped dead. 'Craig!'

Hunter walked over.

A girl lay on the bed, half-dressed. Biting a gag and mumbling. Eyes wide, but out of her head on something. Maybe roofies, maybe something even worse. And she looked young. Barely fourteen, let alone sixteen.

HUNTER ENTERED the private room and gave the doctor a stern look. 'Can you give us a moment?'

He nodded and followed them out into the hospital corridor, giving Chantal a nod. 'Sergeant.'

'How is she?'

'Well, we've completed a rape kit, but that's up to your lab to process.'

'I'll get it fast-tracked.'

The doctor nodded. 'Sadly, even your fast track goes round the houses.'

'Found out what she's on?'

'Vodka, judging by the smell. Her blood alcohol level's still high. And I suspect it was spiked too.'

'Rohypnol?'

'Be a while before I can confirm, but you'll know as well as I do that date rape drugs like that don't persist in the bloodstream. We might have caught this early, though.'

Chantal smiled at him and patted his shoulder. 'Can we have a word with her?'

The doctor took his time considering, then folded his arms. 'I am concerned for her wellbeing.'

'I've had training, sir. Until Friday, I was in the Sexual Offences Unit and—'

'Fine, fine.' A flash of a smile. 'I trust you.' He snorted, then sloped off down the corridor.

Hunter took a deep breath and braced himself. Never got any easier.

Elsa lay on the bed, staring up at the ceiling. Didn't seem anywhere near as out of it as back in the caravan, and she didn't seem to have woken up to the truth. And Christ did she look young.

Hunter sucked in another breath and followed Chantal in. 'Hi there. My name is Craig. This is Chantal. How you feeling?'

Elsa glanced at them. A smile danced across her lips, then disappeared, replaced by a frown. 'What do you want?'

Thirteen and she'd already sussed out the world.

'We wanted to ask you about Derek Farrell.'

'Who's that?'

'The man you were... The man whose caravan you were in.'

She sat up in the bed, frowning. 'You mean Mike?'

'You know him as Mike, that's fine. We want to know what happened to you. That's it.'

She reached over for a cup of water and sipped at it. 'Why?'

'Because you're not the first he's done this to.'

She put the cup back on the nightstand and grimaced. 'It was my first time. And it hurt.'

'You poor thing.' Chantal sat by the bed and reached out a hand.

Elsa took it. 'Why did he do that?'

'He's not a nice man.'

'He seemed it.'

'They all do. Men like this Mike. Until they get what they want.'

'But he seemed so nice.'

'You want to tell us what happened? It's okay if you don't.'

'Right.' Elsa clenched her jaw. 'Mum works as a cleaner, clearing out people's caravans every week. I go along, do my homework while she works. Sometimes I help her. But he

started chatting to me when Mum was emptying her bucket.'
She shut her eyes. 'Am I going to get into trouble?'

'Why?'

'Because I was drinking.'

'No way.' Chantal held her gaze, each passing second
adding to the trust pile. 'His name is Derek Farrell. He has
raped five women that we know of. You're the sixth.'

'Oh my god.'

'Tell me about the drink.'

'He asked if I wanted some bev. That's what we call it.
Mum was still outside. I said, of course. He said to come
round later. Mum works in a pub in the village, leaves me on
my own. But I sneaked out, went to his caravan. He gave me
some vodka and coke. It was lovely. Then I don't remember
much. He was stroking my hair. Then he took my bra off.
And my pants. And...' She shut her eyes, her face twisted by
tears.

Footsteps thumped out in the corridor. 'Where is she?'
Then a ruddy face in the doorway, a fierce-looking woman
scowling at Chantal, then Hunter, then Elsa. 'Oh my god,
poppet. Are you okay?'

Hunter gave her space. Hard not to feel a world of anger
for letting her daughter get into this situation. But he also
empathised with her. Clearly a single mum, doing her best
to raise a girl on her own, working at least two jobs, struggling to hold her shit together, while the father was nowhere
to be seen.

Where had he seen that before?

HUNTER STOOD in the shelter outside the police station in Inverness, watching the rain lash through the darkness. Beginning to feel like a second home. A car hissed past, taking it slow.

The front door opened and Cullen came out, holding two mugs, the steam wafting out. He handed one over. 'Found a cafetière and some ground coffee that wasn't too dusty.'

'Cheers.' Hunter wrapped his hands around it and savoured the warmth. 'How's your plums?'

'Still sore, but I'll live.'

Hunter wanted to ask about Yvonne. The perfect opening. 'Any sign of the lawyer yet?'

'A criminal defence lawyer at this time on a Tuesday night in Inverness? Good one.'

'Robertson said one's on her way.'

'Well, I never.' Cullen took a sip and nodded approvingly at the coffee. 'The amount of gear we found in that caravan... And the small matter of Elsa McGinty lying in his bed, out of her skull. She's thirteen, Craig.'

It hit Hunter in the guts like the butt of an AK-47. He nodded. Didn't want to tempt fate with his words, so he took a sip of coffee, bitter but with a malty sweetness. 'Can't believe Robertson lost that big Russian guy and didn't get the plates.'

'What was he doing there?'

'I don't know. And I don't like not knowing. Could've been there to kill him. Could've been after some drugs. Could've been after that schoolgirl.'

'Why would he kill Farrell?'

'The brick of heroin Keith found on the rig was in his kitchen drawer. It all ties together.'

'Farrell was the reason you and Chantal got kicked over to Methven, right?'

'Right. He's a serial rapist who deals drugs. Working on that Sexual Offences Unit, you see some pretty evil people. Derek Farrell's right up at the top. Five rapes that we know of. Plus Elsa McGinty. I don't know how these pricks do it, but they get the women to keep quiet months and years after they have any influence over them.'

'Sucks, mate. At least with vanilla murders, you've got hard evidence.'

'This is different, though. She's thirteen. No consent. Plus forensics and none of the shame you get with adult victims. Much as I hate to see it, I've seen so many adult rape victims pull out of testifying because of the shame.'

'Such a shitty situation.'

Bain squelched over to the door. 'Swear someone's pissed in that pool.'

'Smells like it too.' Cullen smiled. 'It would've been worth it if you'd actually caught him.'

'Piss off, Sundance.'

'Piss off, sir, you mean?' Cullen ran a hand through his damp hair. 'Or piss off, boss. Don't mind either way, just remember who you report to.'

'Load of shite, this.' Bain barged between them, absolutely reeking. 'Remember when you were my DC... Christ.' He trudged inside, leaving a trail of pissy footsteps.

'Another paid-up member of the Scott Cullen fan club, eh?'

Cullen grinned. 'Says the official club president.'

'Touché. What's his beef with you?'

'Same as with everyone else.' Cullen stood up tall and winced. 'Same as with the whole world. He's a toxic little man. He's always been an arsehole. Now he's my arsehole.' Another drink of coffee, then he shook out the dregs into the rain. 'Ach, he's not that bad. Used to be, but he's better now. You know that Peter principle, where people are promoted to the point of incompetence? He's been demoted back to the point he's barely competent.'

'Be careful yourself.'

A flash of carefully trimmed eyebrows. 'Still a few more rungs to climb before I get there, mate.'

Hunter laughed. 'Jesus, you're impossible.'

'I'm serious. But we should think about getting you some stripes on your sleeve.'

'Don't even joke about it.'

'I'll joke about a lot of things, but not that.' Cullen gave him a hard stare. 'You're a good cop, Craig. Maybe need a psych evaluation before we put you through the sergeants' exam.'

'You're winding me up.'

'I'm deadly serious.' Cullen clapped his shoulder. 'You see the calibre of officer I've got here. Methven's asked me to rebuild the team after that shite last year, and I just can't see Elvis, Buxton, or Eva Law as sergeants.'

'You've got Chantal.'

'I do. And I've also got Bain. I might try and demote him again. I've been speaking to an old mate in Dundee, but I doubt she'll up sticks to Edinburgh just to deal with my rabble. Either way, I'd appreciate you as well. Someone I can trust to call me a dickhead when I'm being one.'

Hunter stared hard at him. 'You're still messing with me.'

'I swear I'm not.'

A hatchback pulled up over the road, hidden from streetlights.

Hunter squinted at it. 'Is that the lawyer?'

A passing car lit it up. An orange Ford Focus.

Cullen groaned.

DI Sharon McNeill got out of the driver's side and crossed the road, flanked by a couple of female officers as stony-faced as her. 'Scott.'

'Sharon.' Cullen gave a polite smile, hiding the dark feelings that had to be surging in his gut. 'You made good time getting up here.'

'I took the piss during the average-speed stretch, cleared a hundred all the way from Perth.' She joined them on the steps, frowning at Hunter as her acolytes headed inside. 'I've got priority on this case.'

Cullen laughed. 'No chance. This is mine. You're only here because I had the courtesy to phone you and you happened to be checking my sloppy seconds in Perth.'

'Come on, Scott, you're better than that.'

'I'm really not. But Craig and Chantal are on this case, they can cover for you.'

'They're no longer my officers.'

'But they were. They know how your mind works. I never did.'

Sharon squared up to him. Hunter felt like he was watching them in the bedroom when they were still a couple, a toxic mix of fighting and shagging. 'Lauren Reid called me, by the way. Local units picked up the caravan owner in Edinburgh. One Steven West. He was on a pub crawl with a load of idiot friends from his university days. Picked him up when he was gurning into a camera outside the Basement Bar on Broughton Street. Guys are in their forties but still drinking like teenagers.'

Cullen nodded, a mischievous grin flashing over his lips. 'I remember going for a drink with you in the Basement Bar a long time ago.'

Hunter cut between them, focusing on Sharon. 'What did the caravan owner say?'

She focused on him like she was looking at the underside of her running shoe after bombing through a field filled with cowpats. 'He said he has no idea who's staying in his caravan. Not been up for months. Got a call with a letting agency in Aviemore, could be it's all above board.'

'Or he could be squatting.' Hunter tried to assess it, based on their intel, but it all came up short. 'Seems unlikely he didn't know Farrell. Guy could've shown up at any point, right?'

'Well, Constable, you're welcome to head down to Edinburgh and find out.'

'Craig's got to interview someone with me, Sharon.'

'I told you, I want in on that.'

Cullen laughed. 'This is my case and you know it.'

'Scott, you're being immature.'

'No, this is my case.'

'He's raped five women.'

'Six. And the latest is an underage schoolgirl.'

Sharon puffed out her cheeks. 'Shite.'

'Murder trumps rape. Sorry. We'll get him for all of it. Don't worry.'

'I wish I could trust you.' She narrowed her eyes at him.

'Look, you and I can sit in the obs suite. Let Craig and Chantal speak to him. They've got previous with Farrell.'

'Works for me.'

HUNTER SAT in the obs suite, looking at Farrell on his own in the interview room. Sitting there, smirking and laughing at something. Sick little bastard. 'You all right?'

Chantal looked over at him. A black eye was forming around her left, but he knew not to even mention it. 'I just want to interview that piece of shit.'

'I want to smash him through a wall.'

'Where is that—'

A knock on the door and an Asian woman peered in. Her eyes widened when she got a look at Chantal. 'Oh.'

Chantal stood up tall. 'Can I help?'

'I'm here to represent Mr Farrell.' She held out a hand to Chantal. 'Anna Patel, working for MRPX Associates.'

'DS Chantal Jain.' She shook it with a broad grin. 'The new name for McLintock and Williams, right?'

Patel took her hand back with a shrug. Didn't seem to be in a hurry to offer it to Hunter. 'As was. We were all partners in the previous company and decided to rebrand following events of last year.'

'MRPX sounds like a high-speed Subaru mode.' Hunter smiled at her. 'You'll be the P and I know the M and the R. So who's the X?'

'That isn't important.' Patel kept her focus on Chantal. 'My client won't tell the full story unless there's some sort of deal on offer.'

'You're having a laugh.'

'No, I'm not. I'm deadly serious.' Patel smoothed down her hair. 'Sergeant, I completely understand your position. We can reach a compromise.'

'Really.' Chantal barked out a laugh. 'You want us to reach a compromise that lets your raping piece of shit get out and be able to do it again?'

'Listen to me. If you can get my client off with minor drug dealing, ideally a fine but less than a year served, then he'll talk.'

Chantal stared hard at her, that look that meant she was considering slicing her throat open. 'I don't think you understand the situation. We've got your client on possession for the intent to supply and whatever charges come from the child.'

Patel tilted her head to the side. 'So you don't want him to help you find your brother?'

30

Hunter stomped along the corridor, Chantal following a few steps behind. 'Seriously, we can't even think about letting that raping bastard get off with this.'

'That's way above our pay grade, Craig.' Chantal stopped, forcing him to turn to face her. 'Look, there are ways and means. You know that. We can use some sleight of hand to cover the deal, get what we want and'—her jaw clenched slightly—'let Sharon's team prosecute him for the rapes.'

Hunter pinched his nose. 'I hate this.'

'Craig, it's where we are. Okay?'

Hunter stared at her, eventually seeing the truth in it. Aside from the broiling emotions in his gut, there was a policing matter here. He saw that. No matter how much Farrell needed to go down, if he was offering up this drug-smuggling ring, then they had to take the bigger fish.

He thumped the wall. Didn't even dent it. 'Bloody hell.'

Chantal stroked his arm, slow and steady. 'How did your

brother get wrapped up in this?'

'He's a bloody idiot.'

'There's being a bloody idiot, and there's getting into this shit.'

'Right.' Hunter let the breath out slowly. 'I think he was in the wrong place at the wrong time. That urbexing shit... You're playing percentages. The more you do it, the more likely it is you'll come a cropper. And sometimes your luck runs out.' He opened the canteen door.

Cullen and Sharon stood in the middle of the empty room, their shouting cannoning off the bare steel surfaces.

'—never loved you!' Sharon jabbed a finger in Cullen's face. She spotted them and shut up. Cullen jerked his eyes over to the door. Sharon wheeled off into the corner of the room, arms folded but her rage still simmering away.

Cullen kept his gaze on her, but he was trying to smile through it. 'Well?'

Chantal went first. 'I thought you'd be wanting to speak to his lawyer rather than comparing each other's genitals.'

'Shut up!' Sharon stomped back over to them. 'What happened?'

'The lawyer wants a deal.'

'A deal?' Sharon shook her head. 'Jesus Christ.'

'She's happy to take a year served for the drugs.'

'I've not driven all this way to let that bastard get off with what he's done.'

'This isn't about you, Sharon.'

'Piss off.'

Chantal laughed out loud at that. One long breath and she looked at her new boss, ignoring the old one. 'Scott, he's offering juice on an international drugs ring.'

'This is bullshit.' Sharon started pacing, shaking her head. 'Complete bullshit.'

Hunter got in her way. 'Look, he's talking about getting a cell with a view, versus one where he's the mattress, pardon my French.'

That stopped Sharon. She looked over at Cullen, forehead twitching. 'Scott, you can't—'

'Young Elsa's at the hospital, doing a rape kit. The paramedics said there was semen in both—' Cullen cut off, visibly sickened. 'If we leave her out of the deal, would he still accept that?'

Hunter started thinking it through. 'Maybe.'

Chantal didn't look so positive. 'The bigger problem is you've got half the Edinburgh drugs squad going through his caravan and finding enough coke to supply the lowlands for a month. And they've not even searched under the floorboards or in the walls yet. He's looking at twenty years just for the drugs. And the rapes would be, say, thirty-five on top of that.'

Sharon stared up at the ceiling. 'We can stand around all day arguing about it, but really it all comes down to what he gives us.'

Cullen eyed her nervously. 'I'm not taking anything to Methven unless he brings this whole thing crashing down.' He focused on Chantal. 'But I don't want him getting off with it. Do you think we could get this past the lawyer?'

Chantal looked away.

'Jesus Christ.' Sharon clenched her fists. 'You mentioned Elsa to her! How could you be so—'

'Shut up!' Chantal got in Sharon's face. 'I worked that case for a year. Me.' She patted her chest. 'I interviewed those women. Me and Craig. We've got that raping bastard. Even though it's not my conviction any more, I'd hate to lose it over some drugs. And I didn't mention it. Jesus, you must think I'm stupid.'

Cullen switched his focus to Hunter. 'Craig, what do you think?'

'While he's a rapist, he's also a drug dealer. Standard operating procedure would be to get him to turn and give up his superiors, right?'

'This isn't a standard case. Anything but.' Cullen seemed to make a decision. 'Okay, if we can get him to give up what he knows on this drug-smuggling ring, and we can keep Elsa out of any deal, then we prosecute him for that. Sharon?'

Sharon scowled at them. Out of habit, as much as anything, she looked at Chantal for her opinion.

'I spoke to Elsa at the hospital. She wasn't in this realm of existence when he was... You catch my drift?'

'Sadly, I do.' Sharon ran a hand down her face. 'Fine, I'd settle for that prosecution. We just need to get him on tape, admitting to it.'

Cullen stood there, thinking it through. 'This is risky as hell. But let's do it.'

PATEL WAS SITTING BOLT UPRIGHT, like someone had given her a backbone. Her gaze brushed over Chantal, before settling on Hunter. 'So. Have we got a deal?'

'Depends.' Chantal splayed her hands on the table. 'What information does your client wish to provide?'

'I'm sitting right here.'

Patel raised a hand to shush him. 'We agreed terms on a deal. Do they still pertain?'

'If your client gives up useful information on this drug-smuggling ring leading to a conviction,' Chantal raised her finger, '*if*, then we'll charge him with possession of a class A. The highest sentence for that is one year. He'll likely serve that, given his priors.'

'I'm not doing any time!'

Patel grabbed hold of her client's arm. 'And the alleged rapes?'

Chantal's eyes narrowed and her lips twitched. 'We'll charge him with the current slate of investigations.'

'That's not going to wash.'

Hunter laughed. 'Listen to me, your client is going away for a very long time. The only way he'll get any nice treatment in there is if he plays ball. The only deal he's got is whether his coffee comes with or without spit.'

'That's unacceptable.'

Farrell sat in the interview room, listening to Patel like he was completing a mortgage application. His wrists were still red raw from where Hunter had cuffed him that little bit too tight on Friday night. Hunter stared hard at Farrell. He wanted to smash his head off the desk and keep hitting him until the little bastard stopped breathing. He was a serial rapist, a disgusting little snake who hadn't changed his ways. Instead he got worse, pulling Elsa into his lair. Torturing her, tormenting her. To feel control over someone.

Hunter's gut clenched again. He wouldn't have to formally interview Elsa, but someone else would. And he'd been in a room with her. No matter how little she remembered of what Farrell had done to her, she would remember something. And that something would follow her for the rest of her life. All because she wanted some 'bev' to escape teenage boredom.

'I've spent a lot of time taking statements from the women he's abused. Torn clothing, torn flesh. Pain, self-doubt, self-hatred. Suicide attempts. Descent into self-medication from drugs and alcohol. He's not getting out of here.'

Patel cleared her throat. 'My client would accept such a deal.'

Hunter felt a slight lurch of hope. The loophole was still open. He looked at Farrell and felt the rage burning away again. 'Let's hear it, then.'

'Get the feeling you don't like me, mate.'

'Do I have to?'

Farrell laughed. 'At least be honest with me.'

'I'd rather you served a hundred years inside for what you've done.' Hunter tried to keep his voice level. 'I'm not a fan of the death penalty, but you push my belief in that.'

Farrell put his hand on his heart, his lips pouting. 'That saddens me.'

'I'm not saying anything you haven't heard before, you stoat.'

'Stoat.' Farrell burst out laughing, head back and roaring. 'Haven't heard that in a while. Anyway, all my partners are over-age.'

'Bullshit.' That got a kick in the shins from Chantal. 'Okay, so who was this big Russian guy then?'

Just like that, Farrell lost all of his humour. 'You'll need to be more specific, friend.'

'Big lumbering guy.' Hunter leaned across the table,

elbows touching wood, and crunched his hands together. 'The one you either tried to escape with this evening or who was trying to kill you.'

And now it seemed Farrell couldn't make any eye contact with Hunter. 'I've no idea who you're talking about.'

'Well, this guy knows you. He drove up to your caravan. Looked like he meant business, too. And he's got previous. In assassination.'

Farrell's eyes bulged. His fingers were clasping and unclasping. A bead of sweat ran down his neck.

'People who you seem to know too. Keith Wilson. He was also scoping out Shug's cottage in Fortrose.'

'Christ.' Farrell put his head in his hands. 'Christ.'

'You're safe with us, Derek. Nobody can harm you in here.' Hunter let him squirm, holding the offer over his head like a sword ready to strike. 'Now why would someone want to kill you, Derek?'

Still nothing.

'Right now, I can see six good reasons someone would want to kill you. Probably a lot more victims than that who just haven't come forward.' All that got was a shake of the head. 'But this big guy?'

Farrell looked over at his lawyer and cleared his throat. He sat back and folded his arms, staring at the table top, clearly avoiding their gaze. 'He's called Admir.'

'Admir? Doesn't sound Russian to me.'

'That's because it's not.'

'So where is he from?'

Farrell kept quiet.

'Keep talking or I walk out of here and you're going to be inside for a long, long time.'

'I don't know his surname. But I do know he's Albanian.'

Hunter looked round at Chantal, saw his fears reflected in her eyes. Albanians were the worst news around. Big gangs running a lot of illegal business in the UK. And brutal with it, too. Then back at Farrell, whose eyebrows surely couldn't go any higher. 'Persuade me.'

'I know Admir. Or rather Big Neil does.'

'Who is he?'

'Big Neil. He's a friend. That's all you need to know. He's involved with these Albanians, or rather he'd like to be. It's his caravan I was staying in. He rents the caravan off someone. Could be Al Capone for all I know. Who cares?'

'I do.'

'Well, I can't help you, friend.'

'It's yourself you need to help. Probably worth you winding the clock back to before we found you in Edinburgh.'

'Right, I heard you were looking for me. I knew Big Neil had access to a caravan in Kingussie, a few miles from Cromarty.'

'A few miles? It's an hour's drive.'

'Is it?' Farrell shrugged. 'Well, I figured I'd stay there until the heat died down on the... on what you were investigating me for. But then he had to go to London for some Albanian shite and I was getting really bored. Went to Cromarty and got chatting to some guy off the boats, Shug. That guy put this couple on to me. Like this American couple who wanted a lot of gear. Had money to burn. Coke, E, special K, bit of speed. Pair of them were up and down more than my eight-incher.'

Patel elbowed his arm. 'Keep it civil.'

'But that was later, after I got back from Edinburgh. First was this guy Shug seemed to be mates with. Said he was a journalist or something. I thought I was in the shite, but turns out they had this block of pure heroin. Pure heroin. Not street stuff, uncut pharmaceutical-grade.'

Hunter's heart started racing. 'He give you his name?'

'Keith.' Farrell's eyes narrowed. The little shit knew he had something Hunter wanted. 'Asked him where he got it, but he wouldn't say. Got in touch with Big Neil, he told me to pay half up front, get the guy's details and they'd sort it out. Turns out his Albanian friends had lost some heroin. Had to drive down to Edinburgh to hand it over to them. Part of me was hoping to get in with them, maybe get some protection from them, but you don't mess with Albanians. And that's when you found me. Someone tipped you lot off about my presence back in Edinburgh and I had to scarper back to Kingussie.'

'A stupid arsehole selling pharmaceutical-grade heroin in Edinburgh is going to ruffle a few feathers.'

The insult bounced off Farrell. He focused on Hunter, his beady little eyes drilling into him. 'Got away, didn't I?'

'You know what happened to Keith?'

'Said he was going back home to Inverness when I bought the heroin off him.'

'We found his dead body in that flat.'

Farrell's throat bobbed up and down. He let out a gasp. 'What?'

'You know who killed him, don't you?'

'No, this—' He gasped and shut up.

'This what, Derek?'

'I can't...'

'The co-owner of Shug's boat was found murdered in Perth too.'

'Christ.' Derek shook his head. 'Look, when I got back from Edinburgh, this big guy came to my caravan, asking where the heroin was. I told him Keith had it.'

'Admir?'

'Right. He believed me, that Keith had it. Left me alone. This guy had killed people.'

The door opened and Cullen stepped in, eyes narrowed to slits, focused on Farrell. 'Admir believed you, just like that?'

'Not just like that.' Farrell pulled up his shirt to show his bald chest. His nipples and the surrounding flesh were dark purple, like someone had gone to town on him with electrodes and pliers. 'Big Neil told me after, Admir's a bit of a sadist, but I got to see it with my own eyes.' He pulled his top back down. 'Do you know how sore this was?'

'He got the truth out of you, though?'

'What he thought, anyway. If he'd have checked the cupboards, I'd have been in real trouble. Kept telling me I wasn't the first to be hurting after messing with his operation. He'd already caught some boy at his drop point and kept him for fun.'

Hunter leaned forward. 'He mention a name?'

'All he told me was Murray.'

Hunter stood up, but almost toppled over. Light-headed and weak. 'You know where I can find him?'

'Not exactly, but when I went to Kingussie, Big Neil advised me to steer well clear of the Oswald estate after dark.'

31

The car rumbled along the road, cutting through the early morning darkness. Hunter peered out of the passenger window into the pitch black as Cullen climbed a hill. To the south, light crawled out of Inverness like a yellow-and-white-neon spider, scuttling across the Moray Firth and up through the Black Isle, just a few isolated pockets with Cromarty over by the black ink of the sea.

Hunter's watch read midnight. Bang on, Hunter's step counter refreshed to zero. His heart rate was in the hundred-and-tens, like he'd been drinking hard. Cullen-level drinking.

'Wonder how we prove any of that.'

Hunter looked over at Cullen, then back out into the blackness, struggling to see anything. 'We get in there and see what's what.'

'You know I have a reputation of being a cowboy?'

Hunter rolled his eyes. 'Really, I hadn't heard.'

'We can't just raid the place based on the statement of one man.'

'We surely have enough to get a warrant.'

The tang of salt air blew through the cracked-open window.

'As far as I see, Scott, our only play here is to get in there and search for my brother. If anyone gets a wind of it, then...'

There's a low moaning, like there's a big monster in there. Has the monster got Grandpa? Has Grandpa turned into the monster? I take Murray's hand and squeeze it, trying to make him feel better. Then I sneak past him into the kitchen, taking it very, very slowly, like Prince Adam and not He-Man.

Ahead, the road led to Cromarty, cones of light illuminating the tarmac.

Cullen looked over, his face glowing in the red light. 'You think Lord Oswald's involved in this?'

'I've considered it. He was all full of shame and surprise and indignation. Meaning he's hiding something, but none of it made sense. Now, things are slotting into place. Farrell's story checks out with the video footage of boxes of heroin.'

'But smuggling heroin? Torturing your brother? That's a hell of a stretch.'

Good point, but it fitted together enough in Hunter's head to warrant serious investigation. 'Have you got a better plan?'

Cullen shrugged. 'I've spoken to the guy and you're right, he has the look of a man trying to hide something.'

They passed over the ridge and descended down towards the Oswald estate. Faint night-lights glowed red in the office building. Cullen slowed as they approached the front gate.

Beyond, the house was mostly dark, just a light on up in the belfry.

Hunter blinked through his tiredness, but still saw two or three of everything. Looked like the gatehouse was unmanned. He got out into the cold air and hauled the gate up, the screech howling in the night, just enough for Cullen to squeeze the car through. He hopped back in and Cullen trundled along a rough old road through mature woods, only lit up briefly by the headlights.

Hunter leaned between the seats. 'Kill the lights.'

With a deep sigh, Cullen cut them and his speed, easing the car through almost pitch darkness as the road wound round to the right, and the office surrounded by trees.

Cullen pulled up outside it and they got out. 'Right, let's see what we can find.' He led them slowly and carefully along the path around the structure. Halfway along, he clenched his fist. 'Stop.'

Hunter tasted bitter cigar smoke, harsh and rubbery. Up ahead, a man was lit up by a red dot glowing in front of him.

Hunter pulled Cullen into a thick leylandii hedge and put a finger to his lips.

The guard came over to their position, his smoke lingering in the air. He seemed to be looking right at them. Then his radio crackled, and some indecipherable words hissed out. He put it to his lips. 'I smell something.'

'Probably the chicken farm.'

'Smells man-made.' The guy was peering right at them. Surely he had to have seen them. The guard turned away, still holding up his radio. 'I don't like this.'

They were here to assess things. But this was a threat to the whole process. Cops should announce themselves. But if

Murray was inside? These guys looked like they meant business.

Then the guard was back, a pistol in his hand, prodding at the foliage near Cullen.

Hunter jumped out at him, smothering his mouth and taking him down, wrapping an arm around his throat. Within seconds, the guy was out like a light.

'Christ!' Cullen raised his hands. 'What are you playing at?'

'He was going to spot you, Scott.' Hunter picked up the guy's gun and checked it. Didn't recognise the make or model but it seemed to be working. He scanned the area. Looked like the rear entrance was a hulking steel door lit up from above. He found a ring of keys—about ten, identical. 'I'm going in there.'

Cullen stayed still. 'Be quick.'

Hunter set off, his feet squelching in the damp bark, pistol held in both hands like an FBI agent readying for a raid. He tried the door. Open. He looked round again. Cullen was staying hidden in the hedge, along with the sleeping guard. Hunter pocketed the keys and entered the building alone, into a long corridor. Craving silence, each footstep like a cannonball. Six doors on either side, another at the end. He tried the first on the left. Locked. Same story on the right. He kept going, getting yet more locked doors. He opened the end door. A metal staircase led down. He tried to match the layout with his memory of the outside, but all he remembered was a big single-storey box.

Nothing ventured...

Downstairs was a replica of the upstairs corridor, but it seemed at least twice as long, maybe three times. A fire door broke it up, probably directly beneath the office. Hunter set off down it, trying doors. Murray had to be behind one. But the keys didn't work. Christ, where was he? Then one worked, six along on the left.

Pistol drawn, Hunter nudged it open. A man sat behind a desk, facing away, punching the screen. 'No! No! No!' The desk was filled with screens showing rooms, each one looking set up for a different torture method. Waterboarding. A rack. A cage full of rats.

Hunter crept up on him, gun out, ready for anything.

The man turned round. Lord Oswald, eyes wide, mouth hanging open. 'Thank god.'

Not what Hunter expected to hear from him. Hunter pointed the gun at Oswald. 'Where is my brother?'

'Your what?'

'My brother. Don't be coy with me. You knew all about him this morning. Where is he?'

'I can't!'

'Why, will your henchman attack me?'

'My henchman?'

'Admir.'

'You've got this the wrong way round.'

'What?'

'He doesn't work for me. He's forcing me to work for him.' Oswald pleaded with his eyes. 'Listen to me. I'm not the big moustache-twirling villain here. I'm screwed. I don't want to be doing this, but the Albanians have me by the short and curlies.'

'Explain.'

'My business was failing, and I needed money, otherwise I'd lose everything. I'd been a bit cavalier with certain deals, meaning I couldn't go to the usual banks. A trick my father used. You bankrupt companies when you don't get deals you want. Trouble is, you do it too many times—'

'—and you stop getting credit.'

'Correct. So I found a business offering not-very-nice terms, but terms. Beggars can't be choosers and all that. But it turned out the company was a front for the Albanian mafia. Admir works for them. They were in the shit after an operation down south got closed down last year. Needed to get heroin into the country quick-smart, so they forced me to help.'

'Why not go to the police?'

'Because they've got kompromat on me. You don't run a business like this without doing things by other means. I've bribed people and they've got evidence of it.'

'I need you to help me find my brother. Or his body.'

'I can't. Don't you hear me? I'm ruined if I help you!'

'This is my brother we're talking about.'

'I'm terribly sorry but I'll lose everything. My home, my title, my *wife*. Christ, my children will never speak to me.'

'You're coming with me.' Hunter grabbed his arm and frog-marched him back to the corridor. He pushed him along, then opened the door to the stairwell.

A thud came from above.

Cullen?

Hunter led him up the stairs, gun drawn, and eased the door open. The corridor was empty.

Someone lay on the floor.

Hunter darted over. It was Oswald's guard, Callum. Hunter didn't even need to put a hand to his neck. Dead, shot in the same way as Keith Wilson and Wee Ally McCoull.

'My god.' Oswald's mouth hung open. 'Admir!'

'He's done this?'

'He was here. Locked me in one of his rooms.'

'What does that mean?'

'He tortures people in them. Anyone who steps out of line. You've got to understand! He'll kill me!'

Hunter pulled him close, got right in his face. 'You're going to tell me where my brother is. NOW!'

'He was here, but I know where Admir will have taken him.'

32

Cullen was still with the guard, just by the thick hedge.

Hunter led Oswald over. 'Did Admir come this way?'

'Your big friend?' Cullen shook his head. 'Not seen anyone. Heard a car but that was all.'

'Shite.' Hunter scowled at Oswald. 'He's got away.'

'Craig, Methven's just got a search warrant, so the team are on their way over.'

'I need to get out to the oil rigs. Admir's taken Murray there.'

'Are you serious?'

'He thinks so. And I believe him.'

Cullen grabbed Oswald and started marching him away towards his car. 'What's going on up on those rigs?'

'The Albanians smuggle heroin in from Venezuela. They take them to Osprey Alpha, winch the barrels up. Then we transport them to Osprey Bravo. There's a walkway between them, it extends out to connect them. His men roll the barrels over and they cut the heroin there, under the guise of the decommissioning work.'

'Why do you think he's taken Murray there?'

'One, for leverage against your friend here.' Oswald eyed Hunter. 'And two, he needs to cover his trail. I don't know where he's going, but he's been panicking for the last week since he found your brother. He wants to close off all loose ends.'

HUNTER STOOD on the harbour at Cromarty, looking out to sea. Hard to make out anything through the pissing rain and the darkness, just the muddy smudge of the oil rigs in the water, Osprey Alpha lurking among them. He brushed moisture out of his face. 'Any word?'

Phone to his ear, Cullen stood by his car, Oswald in the back seat. 'Coastguards are going to be an hour getting here.'

Hunter felt it like another punch in the guts. 'That's way too late.'

A car pulled up on the promenade. Jock's Passat. Chantal got onto the pavement, waving over at them. She opened the back door and helped Fiona out.

Fiona joined them by the harbour. 'Alright, bud? Bit late, isn't it?'

'This way.' Hunter led Fiona over to the harbour. 'How's she looking?'

She leaned down and took a look at *Dignity*, running her hand along the length of the boat. 'Good news is nobody's messed about with her.'

'And the bad?'

Fiona smirked. 'You'd have to be a idiot to even think about going out in this weather.'

Cullen groaned. 'You've got to be kidding me.'

'I'm heading out there, Scott. Christ knows what he could be up to.'

'Jesus Christ. Right, I'm coming with you.'

THE MOTOR WHINED as Fiona steered them over to the oil rigs. Lights flashed up on the platforms, just like the other day. Someone was up there. Admir? And did he have Murray?

Cullen swayed on the boat, rolling with the rocking motion. Sheep-shagging bastard grew up in the north-east with a rich old man, of course he had sea legs.

Hunter stood up, trying to control the nausea, watching the small jetty rush towards them. He jumped over and landed with a thud and dull ache in his ribs, then shot to the ladder and pushed himself up. His rhythm was tight and fast this time, and he made it to the halfway platform without falling off.

Back down the ladder, Cullen was taking it slow and steady. Fiona stayed in the boat.

Hunter raced up the second ladder, his fingers slipping more as he neared the top. As much as he hated it, he had to keep it slow. The last few rungs were tough, his hands like lead. Stop, gust of wind. Right hand, right foot. Another gust of wind. He pushed himself over the top onto the derelict platform. Rain and wind lashed his face. Osprey Bravo was much the same as its sister over the water, but had more superstructure still standing. A hulking great industrial block looked like a factory.

A flash of light over by the crew quarters. Two figures stood in the gloom, soaked through. The entrance was clear, though.

A hand touched Hunter's arm. Cullen. 'What do you think, Craig?'

'Fifty-fifty between those two.'

'I'd check that block. It's not guarded. Then we'll know.'

'Stay here.'

'I'm not staying here!'

'Scott, *please*.'

'As if we're not in enough shite. Fine.'

'Cheers.' Hunter set off, checking the gun was still in his coat pocket. He darted over to a barrel and hid behind it, the drone of machinery getting louder.

The guards were chatting, probably bored out of their minds. The tedium at the heart of an international drug-smuggling ring.

Hunter spotted his next move, a big crate, all packaged up and ready to go. He shot over and pushed to the left, rounding it slowly.

One of the guards lit a cigarette. The other laughed.

Hunter scanned the door now. A giant shed, with a hangar-like door, a smaller one cut into it. He checked his pocket for the keys he'd taken from the guard back at the office building. Hopefully one of these would fit. He eased his way this time, using the shadows to curve round in an arc towards the entrance. The light missed the side and he leaned flat against the door, reaching over to the try the keys. Got lucky on his third go.

A bark of laughter caught the wind. The guards were looking over.

Hunter froze, holding his breath and keeping as still as he could. He clocked Cullen, squatting in the shadows, shivering and soaked through.

They turned away and stamped their feet in time, trying to keep warm.

Hunter let his breath go and slipped inside the shed, nudging the door shut behind him. The hall probably used to be an oil storage room. A series of doors and vaults, open up to the roof. Hunter tried the first door with a key.

A click behind him and he turned.

Too late. Something hard hit his shoulder and pushed him forward. He stumbled to his knees, his gun spinning off across the floor plates.

He tried to shift round, but was pinned in place, face on the ground.

'My friend, you were on the rig when you shouldn't have been. Now you're again where you shouldn't be. It's over, my friend.' That accent.

'Admir?'

Something hard dug into Hunter's neck. 'How do you know my name?'

'He-Man always beats Skeletor.' I hold the two action figures in my hand. 'But it has to be difficult. Okay?'

Murray nods like he's paying attention, but he's much more of a Real Ghostbusters *kid than* Masters of the Universe. *He's got his little figures out, much smaller than my ones, but there's more of them and Grandpa bought him their van too. It's not fair. I* asked Mummy for Castle Grayskull for my birthday but she didn't get me it. Said if I was a good boy, maybe I'd get it for Christmas. I'm always a good boy and Murray's always horrible and he gets all the best things. It's not fair.

He-Man is getting beaten hard by Skeletor. I don't have Evil-Lyn but I can imagine she's there, helping Skeletor.

'Where's Grandpa?'

Murray's frowning. Worried. Staring at Grandpa's empty deckchair. Three tins of Tennent's Lager sit to the side. I hate it when Murray goes all quiet like that. Like Daddy just before he...

I cough. 'He said he's getting another beer.'

Murray nods, like that makes things better for him. 'Have you ever had a beer, Craig?'

'No, beer's disgusting.'

'You're disgusting.'

I punch Murray in the arm, harder than I meant to. It makes him cry. Murray tries hitting me back, but I'm too big and too strong for him. I do that thing he hates, where I grab his head and he's punching and punching but he can't hit me, so he cries even more.

I hold him there really long, his crying getting worse and worse, then I let him go, and he scurries off inside.

Crybaby, running to Grandpa.

So I follow him into the house, running to make sure he tells the truth and doesn't get me into trouble.

'STOP!' A big, meaty hand blocks me getting inside. It's Daddy and he's looking angry. Blinking at me, like he sees two of me. 'Craig, what are you up to?'

'I'm chasing Murray!'

'It's too early for this shi— hassle.' Daddy rubs his forehead. 'Isn't your grandfather looking after you?'

'He's gone to get a beer.'

'Bloody hell.' Daddy pinches his nose. 'Right, come on.'

But I slip past him and skip ahead of him into the house, through to the kitchen at the back.

But Murray's standing in the kitchen doorway, clinging to the handle.

'What's up?'

But he doesn't say anything.

There's a low moaning, like there's a big monster in there. Has the monster got Grandpa? Has Grandpa turned into the monster? I take Murray's hand and squeeze it, trying to make him feel better. Then I sneak past him into the kitchen, taking it very, very slowly, like Prince Adam and not He-Man.

Grandpa's lying on the floor, gasping, clutching his chest. His face is pale like Skeletor and he's staring right at me. 'Please, son! Get your father!'

A big hand pushes me to the side and I grab hold of Daddy's leg.

'Ah, Christ. Donald...' Daddy grabs my hand and pushes me out of the kitchen. 'Boys, get back outside. Ah, Christ.'

Hunter stared at the floor. Counted the number of doors. Listened to the painful machine drone. An open door at the end, a high-tech security console glowing under harsh lights.

Back in the here and now.

Admir planted a foot on his back and pushed him cheek-first to the ground. 'You filthy pig!'

'You should run. This place is surrounded. We've got twenty armed cops on their way here, right now.' He nodded towards the security room. 'Go see for yourself.'

Admir grabbed Hunter by the collar and hauled him up

to standing, then pushed him over to the room. Three screens showing outside, the infrared picking out the guards with AKs and—shite—Cullen. Admir swore in his native tongue. 'I will need to dispose of another pest.'

Hunter stepped to the side and lashed out with his hand, chopping through Admir's throat. The big man gasped and Hunter followed up with a knee to the groin and pushed through his shoulders, sending Admir sprawling over the security console. His gun rattled across the floor.

A red warning light started flashing, and a siren call burst out.

'Stupid pig!' Admir lashed out with a knife, swishing through the air.

The blade caught Hunter's wrist, but it didn't hurt. Not straight away. Then pain flashed, tearing up his arm. He dived low and grabbed Admir's spilled gun. No time to check the safety, and he fired blind.

Admir caught a slug in the shoulder, his knife clanking off the floor. He stumbled forward and landed on Hunter. Heavy fists pounded down. Hunter couldn't keep hold of the gun, but he managed to toss it away, under the console. Admir kneed Hunter in the side, winding him like he'd fallen from a helicopter again.

Footsteps raced away from him.

Hunter forced himself up. The siren was hurting his head. Blood dripped down his hand. Fresh pain stabbing his ribs. No time to get the gun, no idea where his own was. He picked up the knife and went back into the corridor. It'd have to do.

The door at the end hung open, the din louder than ever.

Admir was rounding some grinding machine, limping heavily.

Hunter tried sprinting, but the thickness in his head and the flaring pain in his arm and ribs slowed him down.

Into a giant hall filled with industrial machinery. The noise hurt worse than his injuries. A metal latticework floor.

Admir escaped through a door at the end, shutting it behind him.

Hunter stepped up the pace, but slipped in something, crashing to his knees. Blood.

The door behind him slammed. Trapped.

He got up and looked around. The machines seemed to be slowing, if anything.

Then Hunter caught sight of something he didn't expect.

Murray, chained up in a cage. Naked and ill-looking, fresh scars dotted with drying blood. 'Craig?'

33

Hunter inched towards the cage. His little brother. He tried the lock but it was shut. 'Hold on!' He fumbled his keys, dropping them to the floor.

'Craig? What the hell is going on? Where's Keith?'

'I'll get you out of here, Muz.' Hunter picked up the keys and tried the cage. 'Was this Admir?'

'Right. I uncovered stuff when we were urbexing at the other rig. Admir killing someone, it went up on YouTube. Deadman's switch. Why I'm still alive, probably. Where's Keith?'

Fourth key and Hunter was in. He tore open the cage door and reached in for Murray, grabbing him by the wrists and helping him up to standing. 'What's he done to you?'

Murray grinned through what looked like severe pain. 'Easier to say what he hasn't.' He coughed and blood dribbled down his chin. 'I've seen a power drill do things...' Another cough and blood flobbed out onto the floor.

'Come on, bro, let's get you out of here.'

Murray let Hunter undo his chains, then started towards the door. 'We need to get out of here. Admir's set off an alarm. This place will blow in five minutes.'

'What?'

'He's destroying the rig.' Murray was struggling to stay upright, let alone walk. 'He told me. This is all going to burn. I was going to roast alive. It might explode first.'

That sparked Hunter into action. 'Come on.' He grabbed Murray and lifted him in a fireman's carry, taking it slow and steady across the steel latticework floor. Deep breaths, like he was on a strongman challenge. The metal clanked and resonated with each step. Into the other room, quieter now. He had to rest and set Murray on the floor. He was breathing hard.

Murray pushed himself up to standing and opened the door. He peered out. Looked clear. But no sign of Cullen or the guards.

Murray tugged at Hunter's sleeve. 'This is going to blow up!' He sprawled forward, toppling out into the cold air.

Hunter crouched to help him up, putting an arm over his shoulder. Still no sign of Cullen.

An explosion rang out from behind them. The shockwave ripped through them, pushing them flat to the wet steel. Metal flew through the air, a chunk landing right next to Murray. The block started shaking, the nearest corner tumbling in.

'They're demolishing the place.' Murray pointed up as a second corner toppled in. A fire raged already.

Hunter picked him up again in a fireman's carry and tried to get distance between them and the collapsing structure.

Another explosion, but further away. Then another, and a fourth. The industrial block crumbled inwards, flattened. Then a fifth explosion, right in the middle. Flames started licking the air, the heat touching Hunter's face.

'Craig!' Cullen's voice was barely a whisper above the bedlam around them. 'What the hell is going on?'

'Controlled detonation.' Hunter breathed hard. 'Admir's burning the evidence. We need to get away.' He grabbed Murray and set off across the platform, heading for the ladder back down.

Through the noise, Hunter could make out a speedboat motor. No sign of Fiona now. Admir was clambering down another ladder to the jetty.

Hunter put a finger to his lips, getting a nod from Cullen, then sneaked over towards them.

Admir was on the middle platform, talking on a radio in his native tongue.

Hunter kept it slow as he climbed, listening for cues and watching for body language, anything to show him wrapping up his call, anything to show he was aware of Hunter.

Admir looked up when Hunter was five metres or so above him.

He let go and plummeted, landing on Admir.

Admir tried to elbow him but Hunter caught the move, shifting his weight to the side. Crack. Hunter kneed him in the kidneys. An open-palmed punch on the back and Admir sprawled forward, his head thunking off the floor. Hunter pinned him to the platform, pushing all his weight onto him.

'You sick bastard.' Hunter pulled him up to standing and started walking him to the ladder. 'You bring drugs into this country and ruin people's lives. Including my brother's. Why shouldn't I just throw you off the side?'

'You should kill me now. I will get away.'

'No, you won't.' Hunter stopped him by the rungs. 'You'll be in prison for a very long time.'

Admir elbowed him in the ribs, and a million sharp teeth bit into Hunter's chest. Admir made a break for the ladder and Hunter threw himself at Admir, sending him flying. Hunter landed on his back and grabbed hold of him by the throat.

A fresh explosion rung out and the whole oil rig rocked to the side.

Admir slipped out of his grip and Hunter slid across the platform. He caught the ladder, now at a strange angle, and held it tight. Admir was rolling and Hunter reached for him. He grabbed a hand and held on.

Another explosion rocked them. Hunter struggled to keep his grip on the ladder and Admir's hand slipped. The Albanian fell into the sea, arms and legs windmilling as he flew, like King Kong plunging to his death.

Hunter held on to the ladder, his fingers ice cold and struggling. He looked around. No sign of Cullen or Murray. Shite! Another explosion. A deep moaning sound tore out. The rig was going to tip over.

Down in the water, Admir's floating corpse was caught in the lights, his face red raw. Very dead. Then he dipped below the surface.

Hunter had one move here. Get into the water, stabilise his breathing, then swim far enough away from the rig. Or try for Osprey Alpha. He took it slow going down, his fingers slithering around the slimy metal. The wind lashed at him. His fingers slipped and he dropped.

He plunged under the water with a cold blast. He surfaced, breathing stuttering out like a machine gun. Panicking. Heart racing. Shivering. Shaking.

Then a hand grabbed him, pulling him back. Up and over. 'Come on, big guy.' Cullen.

Hunter's teeth were chattering, his whole body felt like melting ice.

Murray was sitting next to him.

34

'Is she safe?'

Three o'clock in the interview room in Inverness, and Hunter was held together by rancid machine coffee. 'Who?'

Oswald rolled his eyes. 'My wife. Is she safe?'

'She is, aye, but you should be more concerned for yourself. You're going to prison for a long time.'

'Be very careful.'

'Excuse me?'

'You heard me.'

'Are you threatening me?'

Oswald just looked at his lawyer, Anna Patel. She seemed to have cornered all the players in this drug ring. Neither said anything.

'You think that, as a lord, you're above the law. That it?'

'After the assistance I gave you? Finding your brother?'

'You were dealing in pure heroin. Helping an Albanian gang to transport it into the country on boats to one of your oil rig platforms, cutting it on a second before you brought it ashore.'

'Okay...'

'You're admitting it?'

Oswald sat back, arms crossed, lips pursed.

'You held my brother captive, tortured him.'

'You should consider writing this down, I'm sure James Patterson would publish it under his own name.'

'Wait, you're denying all of this?'

'Of course I am. You've trespassed on my property, twice. The first time, I could forgive. But the second, you were responsible for the destruction of the Osprey Beta. I don't know how you did it, but we were in the process of decommissioning it.'

'It looked very much like a heroin factory to me.'

'Well, I'm sure you'll have experts in trying to prove some spurious connection, but that was a standard industrial operation.'

Hunter looked at Cullen and got a nod. 'Iain Oswald, I'm arresting you for—'

THE CUSTODY SERGEANT led Oswald away by the arm.

Cullen patted Hunter's shoulder. 'Good work there, Craig.'

'Really? Can't help but think he'll get away with this.'

'You've got your brother back and we've bust apart a drug-smuggling ring. We've solved two murders. I think. Might be three. I'm so tired, I can't even remember. Either way, that's decent work, by anyone's book.'

Hunter let his breath out. 'Feels like Oswald's getting away with it.'

'Well, there's nobody left that can or will testify against him. His wife won't. That Admir guy's been fished out of the sea.'

'I can't figure out if he was lying and he's behind it all.'

'I don't know, mate. That's for the PF to progress. Way above our pay grade.'

'And yours is way above mine.'

'Speaking of which, you want to take me up on that offer?'

'You really think I'm a sergeant?'

Cullen grinned. 'You telling me you're not?'

'Fine, Scott, I'll take it.' Hunter let out a weary groan. 'Look, I'll be counting the costs for a while, though. Murray's—'

'Alive, Craig. Your brother's alive.'

'True.'

The far door opened and Chantal walked through. 'Get off my case!'

Yvonne appeared next, holding out some paperwork. 'You need to get this signed off and...' They headed away, cutting off their voices.

Hunter shook his head at Cullen. 'You should've told me about Yvonne, you dickhead.'

'See, this is exactly why I didn't. You can be a right twat at times.' Cullen grinned, but it faded to a frown. 'Are you upset?'

'No, it's just...' Hunter fought hard against a yawn. The worst way to undermine your anger was to look like you needed a couple of days' sleep. 'Okay, I am. You ruined a perfectly good relationship. You shagged her behind my back.'

'So did she.'

'When the dick is hard, the mind is soft.' Hunter scowled at him. 'That's not a good excuse. In fact, it makes you seem like a total prick.'

'Craig, I'm sorry I upset you. Maybe one day you'll get over it. You've got Chantal now and you seem happy for the first time since I've known you. You and Yvonne were never suited to each other.'

'And you and her are?'

'I think so. I mean, you were arguing all the time. At home, at work. You were miserable.'

Hunter locked eyes with him and saw the truth, right there. He was miserable with Yvonne. Depressed. All those raging arguments, shouting matches going on into the middle of the night, screaming at each other, until neither could remember what it was even about. He was right, they weren't suited. Too much alike, or too different. Either way, it wasn't what he needed at the time, and it clearly wasn't what she did. He smiled at Cullen. 'I just wish you'd stop being such a twat.'

'Never going to happen, and you know it.' Cullen clapped him on the back. 'Maybe one day we'll remember what happened and you'll feel better about it.'

35

H unter got out of the car and yawned. 'Jesus, I
need my bed.'

'You're just up.' Chantal looked across the car
roof at him. 'Maybe you need longer than three hours'
sleep?'

'Right.' Another yawn, felt like he was going to split his
lips at the side. He shook his head violently and set off
through the morning rain, half asleep.

Jock stood in the hospital entranceway, fiddling with his
mobile phone.

Hunter stopped dead. 'Oh god.'

'You okay?'

'Not really.' Hunter glanced at Chantal. 'My PTSD's been
bad. I forgot to take my meds and the flashbacks were back
with a vengeance.'

'*Craig.*'

'I had this one I'd completely forgotten about. When my
grandpa died, and Jock was hungover as hell. That wasn't

long before he left for good. Well, left for the first time. Mum went to pieces, her old man dying like that. Heart attack. I didn't remember it until now. It's all coming back to me. And it's also tough being with the old bastard, you know? He's my dad, but he's a total dick.'

She rubbed his arm. 'You don't have to have anything to do with him, you know that?'

'I know. I just wish he'd say sorry, you know? For messing me up. For messing Murray up.'

'That's the last thing he'll do.'

Jock looked up and seemed to groan. 'Craig.'

'How you doing?'

Jock's turn to yawn. Maybe he'd caught it from his son. 'I'm okay, I suppose. Can't believe the state of my boy, though.'

'Me neither.' Hunter rubbed his forehead. 'We'll get Oswald for this.'

'Sure about that?'

Hunter could only offer a shrug. 'They fished the body of the gang leader out of the firth this morning. Admir.'

'Son, I'm sorry about being such a dick about him being...' Jock sighed. 'About his sexuality. I'm fine with it.' He rubbed a nascent tear from his eye. 'I accept my boy for who he is.'

'That's brave of you.'

'Aye. It's a sair fecht, son.' Jock grinned. 'Maybe you'll give me grandchildren, though.'

'What?' Chantal looked like she was going to lamp him one.

Hunter held her back. 'That's a horrible thing to say and, besides, you're giving yourself your own grandchildren.'

'What the hell's that supposed to—'

'Jock!' A shrill voice from behind them. Then clacking footsteps, followed by a young woman throwing herself at Jock, landing with him holding her in a straddle. Red velour tracksuit, shiny dark ponytail, orange tan, giant hoop earrings and shiny white trainers. She snogged him, hard. 'My god, it's good to see you.'

'And you.' Jock kissed her back, then held her straddling him, holding her there. 'Craig, this is Kirsten.'

He got a look of her face now. She looked like a schoolgirl, all soft features, but with the built muscle of a mature lapdancer. And clearly in love with his father. In a deeply creepy way. Hunter had seen daddy issues before but this was something else. 'Nice to meet you.'

'And you.' She hugged Jock tight, then got down to standing and looked up into his eyes from at least a foot below. 'I need to speak to you.'

'Okay.' Jock winked at Hunter then set off through the car park.

'How the hell...' Hunter didn't care. Couldn't care anymore. 'Come on.' He entered the hospital and clocked the sign for intensive care. Not too far. Thankfully the Inverness hospital wasn't on the scale of one in the lowlands, even Stirling or Dundee.

'How do you feel about your new mum?'

Hunter turned to scowl at Chantal as they walked. 'She's not my mum. Christ.'

'I'm just winding you up.'

'Aye, no shit you are. Still, it's not funny.'

'She's crazy about him.'

'Then she's crazy.' Hunter turned the corner into another

long corridor. 'I mean, he's made his bed but he's messed up two kids. Me and Murray. I don't want to know what...' A bitter taste filled his mouth as he reached the nurse's station. 'I mean, she's pregnant with his kid. That's messed up.'

'Completely.' Chantal grinned at the nurse. 'Here to see Murray Hunter.'

'Right.' She checked her computer. 'Room six. Limit of three at a time, though.'

'How many in just now?'

'One.'

'Thanks.' Chantal led Hunter over to the room.

Murray lay on the bed, hooked up to more machines than a Transformer. His eye bags had puffed up, along with his face. Still had a dazed expression, but at least he recognised his brother. 'Hey, Craig. Chantal.'

'Muz.' Hunter sat on the chair and beckoned for Chantal to join him in the other. 'How you doing?'

'Banjaxed, bro.' He sighed. 'I heard about Keith.'

Hunter nodded. 'I'm sorry, Muz. I found his body. It was...' He shook his head. 'I'm sorry this happened to you.'

Murray smiled at Chantal. 'We'd been going out longer than you two. I loved him.'

'I'm so sorry. Really.'

'Thanks.' Murray stared up at the ceiling. 'We were just dicking about. How... How could it come to this?'

Hunter didn't point out the dead man's switch email contained a warning about the dangers of urbexing. He just held Murray's hand.

'I've been seeing a therapist for a bit. We've been talking about my need for adventure, to explore things, to rush in. He thinks it's so I can make Grandpa come back to life.'

'Grandpa?'

'You remember?'

'I do. I've been… I remember us finding Grandpa's body.'

'Still freaks me out. They should've given us counselling, Craig!'

'Jock just gave us a hot toddy. I was seven. You were four.'

'And I let that arsehole look after my hens. Not like I had a choice. They're not even mine. They're my ex's but he moved to Glasgow. I barely get any eggs out of them, but I can't just let them go. I'm going to have to let Keith go.' Murray cried into his hands.

It broke Hunter's heart to see him like that. He could get hammered with him, save him from fights, but he couldn't fix him. 'I'll help you get better, bro.'

AFTERWORD

I hope you enjoyed that...

I didn't!

It was supposed to be something short and punchy, but in the end it took me about three or four times as long as anything else I've done recently. Ugh. But I got there in the end, and I'm pleased with the result if not the process to get there.

The idea for this was to take my rubbish vampire book (the vampires weren't rubbish, the books were, and actually it's maybe more the sales that were bad than the writing) and turn it into a police thriller so I didn't think about it anymore. Well, that didn't exactly work. The location is vaguely similar, though the far north is desolate compared to the lush surroundings of the Black Isle just north of Inverness, an area I've come to know and love over the last few years. I highly recommend a trip there, just don't buy any drugs in pubs.

Thanks for dev editing help go to Russel D McLean,

Allan Guthrie, John Rickards and, as always, Kitty. Thanks to John Rickards for the copy edit and Eleanor Abraham for the proof read.

One final note, if you could find time to leave a review where you bought this, I'd really appreciate it — reviews really help indie authors like myself.

-- Ed James
Scottish Borders, October 2019

NEXT BOOK

The next Police Scotland book is out now!

"THE COLD TRUTH"
Starring Cullen, Hunter and... Bain

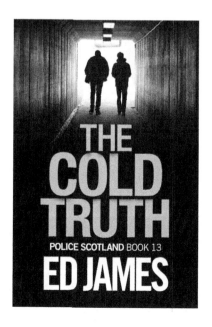

Get it now!

If you would like to be kept up to date with new releases from Ed James and access free novellas, please join the Ed James Readers' Club.

ABOUT THE AUTHOR

Ed James is the author of the bestselling DI Simon Fenchurch novels, Seattle-based FBI thrillers starring Max Carter, and the self-published Detective Scott Cullen series and its Craig Hunter spin-off books.

During his time in IT project management, Ed spent every moment he could writing and has now traded in his weekly commute to London in order to write full-time. He lives in the Scottish Borders with far too many rescued animals.

If you would like to be kept up to date with new releases from Ed James, please join the Ed James Readers Club.

Connect with Ed online:

Amazon Author page

Website

OTHER BOOKS BY ED JAMES

DI ROB MARSHALL

Ed's first new police procedural series in six years, focusing on DI Rob Marshall, a criminal profiler turned detective. London-based, an old case brings him back home to the Scottish Borders and the dark past he fled as a teenager.

1. THE TURNING OF OUR BONES
2. WHERE THE BODIES LIE (May 2023)

Also available is FALSE START, a prequel novella starring DS Rakesh Siyal, is available for **free** to subscribers of Ed's newsletter or on Amazon. Sign up at https://geni.us/EJLCFS

POLICE SCOTLAND

Precinct novels featuring detectives covering Edinburgh and its surrounding counties, and further across Scotland: Scott Cullen, eager to climb the career ladder; Craig Hunter, an ex-squaddie struggling with PTSD; Brian Bain, the centre of his own universe and everyone else's. Previously published as SCOTT CULLEN MYSTERIES, CRAIG HUNTER POLICE THRILLERS and CULLEN & BAIN SERIES.

1. DEAD IN THE WATER
2. GHOST IN THE MACHINE
3. DEVIL IN THE DETAIL
4. FIRE IN THE BLOOD

5. STAB IN THE DARK
6. COPS & ROBBERS
7. LIARS & THIEVES
8. COWBOYS & INDIANS
9. THE MISSING
10. THE HUNTED
11. HEROES & VILLAINS
12. THE BLACK ISLE
13. THE COLD TRUTH
14. THE DEAD END

DS VICKY DODDS

Gritty crime novels set in Dundee and Tayside, featuring a DS juggling being a cop and a single mother.

1. BLOOD & GUTS
2. TOOTH & CLAW
3. FLESH & BLOOD
4. SKIN & BONE
5. GUILT TRIP

DI SIMON FENCHURCH

Set in East London, will Fenchurch ever find what happened to his daughter, missing for the last ten years?

1. THE HOPE THAT KILLS
2. WORTH KILLING FOR
3. WHAT DOESN'T KILL YOU
4. IN FOR THE KILL

Other Books

Other crime novels, with Lost Cause set in Scotland and Senseless set in southern England, and the other three set in Seattle, Washington.

THE COLD TRUTH
PROLOGUE

I hit the button and step away from the bin lorry. The metal jaws crunch the cardboard and swallow it all down. Good work!

'Let's go!' Big Jim pulls himself up to the hand hold and thumps the side of the lorry. His belly hangs out the bottom of his Celtic home shirt, the green-and-white hoops smeared with all sorts of muck.

An audiobook blares out of the speakers in the cabin, some ridiculous post-apocalyptic crap about Nazis and zombies, or something, but Billy the driver seems to hear the signal, as the lorry rumbles off down the street.

Big Jim hangs there, scratching his nose with his gloved wrist. 'Keep up, you big South African bastard!'

'Nothing wrong with South Africa, mate.' I grab the handle and haul myself up with the kind of grace Big Jim can only ever dream of. I'm topless, just like every other day, and my abs look awesome in this light. The definition is perfect. 'Like to see you in Jo'burg. Wouldn't survive five minutes.'

'Ah grew up here in Glasgow, pal. Handle that, can handle anything.'

'You didn't grow up, mate.' I hang on as the lorry trundles along the dark street. In the distance, the sun pops up over the horizon, giving a flash of light against the tower blocks in the distance and the old tower in the graveyard just over the road behind the factories. 'Beautiful sky, eh?'

'No' as beautiful as *that*, I tell you.' Big Jim waves at the pavement.

Two schoolgirls trudge along in the darkness, passing between cones of light, tapping at their phones, oblivious to the middle-aged pervert ogling them. Short skirts, black tights, school ties barely done up in their low blouses. Maybe fourteen. *Maybe.*

Sick, sick bastard.

I shoot Jim a scowl, raising my eyebrows to show how harshly I'm judging the seedy creep. 'Mate, they're really young.'

'Aye, well.' Big Jim gives me a leery grin, his tongue hanging loose. 'Grass on the pitch, eh?'

'Sick bastard.'

It's my turn to slap the side of the lorry and I hop off before Billy pulls it to a stop. I gave him the thumbs up, not that Billy tears himself away from his gripping audiobook. I kind of want to tell him about Big Jim, but he's never interested in all that banter.

Sod him.

I sidle off up the lane, but my trousers slip lower with each step. Christ, I need some new strides.

Next up—just like every bloody week—are three bins that the hipster bastards in the microbrewery haven't wheeled out to the road. They're sitting in the factory car park, one flickering light catching them.

Usually a two-man job to shift each one, but I always like to try to move them on my own.

Could leave them, but we got a shitload of hassle from the boss last time we didn't take them out. Some bastard in the factories must've phoned in to complain.

Big Jim raises a gloved hand in front of my face. 'Dinnae mention that to the boys at the depot, right?'

'What, that you're a paedo?'

'I'm no' a *paedo*.' Jim's scowling at me, but I can't tell if it's one of anger or confusion. 'Those were lassies, no' boys!'

Confusion, then.

'Mate, it's not about their gender, it's about their *age*.'

Big Jim seems flummoxed by that. 'Nothing wrong with admiring the female form.' His chin dimples as he snarls. 'You're the one who's a poof. Now *that's* unnatural.'

'I'm not having this chat again.' I set off up the lane towards the dumpsters. 'I'll do these myself.'

Big Jim doesn't disagree. He tears off a glove and leans back against the lorry, phone out already. Hate to think what that sick bastard is watching on that thing, or who he's contacting and about what.

Maybe the prick's getting ahead of me, calling up the boss and pre-emptively defending against any shit coming his way.

I'll get the prick if he does.

I stop and grab the first dumpster's handle, flexing my biceps and pectorals.

And there she is. Same as every week, the woman in the flat above is looking down. Damp hair scraped back in a towel, her dressing gown open wide enough to show her cleavage.

I give her a saucy wink, even though she's about eight inches short of being my type. Nice to be admired, eh? Then she's gone, her curtains shut.

And this bastard dumpster isn't moving. I grab the handle again, but it feels way too heavy to shift on my own. Another sharp tug and it still doesn't budge.

I'm all out of moves here. Much as I hate it, I need Big Jim.

He's marching up the lane, so at least that saves a trip, but he grabs my arm. 'Rich, that was—'

'Get off me, man!' I swivel round and get into the basic stance, ready to fight, ready to win. 'Those gloves are disgusting!'

'Chill oot, you radge bastard.' Big Jim holds his mobile in an ungloved hand. His Celtic shirt is covered over by an acid-yellow high-viz jacket. 'Davie says to make sure you've got your top on.'

'I keep telling him, I don't wear a top. This temperature is perfect for fat burning.'

'Anyone ever tell you that you're a weird bastard?' Big Jim reaches for the handle. 'Here, let us help.'

Course I know what Big Jim's up to here. Trying to get in my good favours so I don't mention the under-age perving to the other lads. 'I've got this.'

'Doesn't look that way to me. This is a two-man bin, and if there's one thing I know it's—' Big Jim screws up his face, nostrils twitching. 'What's that smell?'

'Can't smell anything.'

'It's *minging*.' Big Jim grabs the lever and pulls it, popping the lid. 'Have a deek inside, bud. I'll hold it for you.'

'If it'll shut you up.' I vault up and hold myself there, peering into the bin.

The rubbish is piled up along the side, stacked-up cardboard boxes and loose wrapping plastic. That explains the weird camber when I pulled it, but what's on the other side makes it impossible to shift.

A man lies in a puddle of bleach, naked except for a nappy. Eyes wide open and very, very dead.

THE COLD TRUTH is out now. You can get a copy at Amazon.

If you would like to be kept up to date with new releases from Ed James, please join the Ed James Readers Club.